Blood
Flowers

Mary Judith Ress

Santiago, Chile

2010

iUniverse, Inc.
New York   Bloomington

Blood Flowers

Copyright © 2010 by Mary Judith Ress

iUniverse books may be ordered through booksellers or by contacting:

iUniverse
1663 Liberty Drive
Bloomington, IN 47403
www.iuniverse.com
1-800-Authors (1-800-288-4677)

Because of the dynamic nature of the Internet, any Web addresses or links contained in this book may have changed since publication and may no longer be valid. This is a work of fiction. All of the characters, names, incidents, organizations, and dialogue in this novel are either the products of the author's imagination or are used fictitiously.

ISBN: 978-1-4401-9458-0 (pbk)
ISBN: 978-1-4401-9459-7 (ebk)
ISBN: 978-1-4401-9460-3 (hbk)

Printed in the United States of America

iUniverse rev. date: 02/12/2010

Blood
Flowers

Chapter 1

October 1, 1975

Meg glanced at her watch, then settled wearily back in her seat and lit a cigarette. 2:15 p.m. Another hour before the plane landed.

On the tray table, her leather notebook with the letter she'd started glared back at her.

> *Dear Aunt Kay,*
>
> *Once again, thanks for your generous contribution for buying yet another "pagan baby" and saving it from the jaws of hell.*

Dear Kay, her fat, exotic Japanese aunt from New York. Meg must have written dozens of these bread-and-butter letters from Chile during the last five years to thank her for the checks she sent to "save the pagan babies."

When had that joke about the pagan babies started? Oh yes, Meg remembered, taking a long drag on her cigarette. It was the summer she and Theo traveled to New York for a last fling before the two nuns left for Latin America—Meg to Chile and Theo to El Salvador. Meg had done her mother's bidding and paid what was to be a perfunctory visit to this black sheep relative.

It was coming back now: the surreal apartment with its profuse assortment of antiques and erotic nudes jumping off the walls, Sumio quietly floating in and out to fill the sake cups. Meg never figured out if he was Kay's servant, her spiritual son, or her lover. Kay herself in a bright orange pants suit, bejeweled to the nines, layers of fat rippling all over her body. Not sexy, yet somehow sensuous.

Meg had been about five when her Uncle Joe moved his Japanese war bride and their little son, Chuckie, from her grandparents' farm outside Pittsburgh to out-of-visiting-range Syracuse. She suspected he made the move because the family never accepted Kay's "foreign ways." Joe died ten years later and Kay moved to New York and set up a boutique—no one was quite sure what it was she sold, but family gossip had it that her aunt was doing more than just getting by.

Meg squirmed in her seat recalling that visit. She had dragged Theo along and was slightly annoyed that her friend seemed nonplused by what Meg felt were her aunt's exhibitionist ways. Yet Kay had drawn them both out—and how she probed! Why had they decided to become nuns? How did one endure being celibate when the union of male and female was ordained by God himself? Why did they want to be missionaries in Latin America? Meg had been caught off guard by the frank questions, by Kay's black pin-point eyes gazing knowingly into her soul.

"I'll write you," Kay promised as she hugged her niece good-bye. "And every once in a while I'll include some money so you can save a pagan baby or a pagan adult from the jaws of hell."

I gave your last check to a young mother of four whose husband had been picked up by Chile's secret police several months ago and has not been seen since. He was a factory worker and I guess the dictatorship thought he was a subversive.

Mario. Factory worker, fantastic guitarist, community organizer. One of the latest in a string of friends who had disappeared under the Pinochet regime.

Meg crushed out her cigarette in the ashtray on the arm of her seat and snapped shut the metal top. That's the last one, she promised herself. No smoking in El Salvador.

With six years of experience in Chile under her belt, she was now heading for another country under military rule. From what she'd read, El Salvador had been headed by one general or another for the last hundred years. *Even so, it can't be as bad as Chile*, she thought. Meg glanced at her dull, scuffed reflection in the plane's window. She could make out some gray in her sandy blond hair, some lines around the eyes—they seemed a darker blue then the last time she looked in a mirror. How long ago was that? She couldn't remember. She tried out the old winning smile she knew was her best asset. It still worked if she tried hard enough, she thought, sighing with relief. Just a bit out of practice. Funny how her mouth felt as if it had tightened over the years. Well, no one, not even Alfredo, ever praised her for her voluptuous mouth.

Meg appraised the rest of her and decided she was still

relatively attractive. Five feet four and 120 pounds with the map of Ireland printed on her face, as her Da used to say. Back in the Novitiate, Molly had convinced her that she was Aphrodite incarnate. "You prove all my relatives wrong, Meggins," Molly was fond of telling her. "My Uncle Micky thinks the convent is a stomping ground for the world's plainest women. Uncle Charlie bets that most nuns have been jilted by their fiancées. And my cousin Bridie believes we're all closet lesbians."

Because she was beginning a new mission, Meg had donned her lightweight gray rayon suit, complete with the mission cross on her lapel, and her sensible black pumps, the prescribed dress for a Sister of Charity. But she felt like a cutout that no longer fit. She wondered if she could go back to her hippy nun look of jeans and a sweat shirt once she'd rolled up her sleeves and got to work in El Salvador.

She leaned back and closed her eyes. Meg had to admit that she was burnt out. She was certainly no longer the young nun who'd set out so enthusiastically in 1969 to bring God's word to the Chilean people. Mother Ursula was probably right to reassign her. Besides, she knew that every move she made was closely watched by the secret police. She didn't mind them stalking her, but she didn't want to endanger *Madre* Rosa and Molly and her friends back in La Bandera, the shantytown on Santiago's south side where she had worked these past six years.

She reached for another cigarette, then remembered her resolution and restlessly folded her hands in her lap. Here she was, a thirty-four-year-old nun, a supposed expert in bringing Christ's love to Latin America's poor. That's what being a Catholic missionary was all about, wasn't it? God knows that message had no edge these days.

Good Lord, was she actually praying? Meg opened her eyes and sat up. How long had it been since she'd really prayed? How long since she'd felt God's presence, felt him breathing down her back? She fleetingly remembered a line from her Novitiate journal: "I want to act on a Big Stage, be part of a mythic epic where good conquers evil. I want to slay dragons, battle demons, and forge common pale flesh into sainthood. I want to get inside God!"

She absently twirled the silver ring on her left hand, a symbol of the religious consecration she made so solemnly on that July day in 1969. Who in the hell was she wedded to now? God? The Sisters of Charity? The Chilean people? The memory of her martyred Alfredo?

Meg glanced down at her weather-beaten notebook with the breastplate of St. Patrick engraved on the cover. A gift from her mother on Profession Day. She pulled out the photos she kept tucked inside the jacket. Despite her melancholy mood, she smiled as she cupped the first one in her hands for a moment, as if to warm it. The Three Musketeers! There they were—two versions of them—encased in a yellowing plastic badge embroidered with Theo's fine needlework. On one side, a photo of the three of them together on their Mission Sending Day. The date scrawled underneath was August 15, 1969. In dark suits, white blouses, and their newly placed mission crosses around their necks, they stared into the camera wide eyed, apprehensive about where their adventures in Latin America might take them. Although it was a black-and-white mug shot, Molly's hair was still a wild mass of unmanageable curls, her freckles black upon what should have been her always blushing face. Meg in the middle, a younger, happier likeness of the plane window's reflection. And Theo, the darkest of the three—and the most serious—her hair parted severely down the middle and tucked behind her ears. From behind her rimless glasses, Theo looked back at the viewer with her own peculiar mixture of curiosity and kindness.

Meg turned the badge over. There they were again, on the day they were clothed in the habit, three pairs of sparkling eyes squared off by newly starched coifs, grinning back at the camera as they held up their long gray skirts to reveal their handmade garters embroidered with "Jesus loves me." Meg chuckled softly as she remembered how, during the seven-day retreat leading up to their Clothing Day, she and Molly had crocheted the garters. Molly made one for Theo as well, who put it on laughingly as they slid into their new habits. When all three of them had gathered with their families in the Motherhouse courtyard after the ceremony and everyone began taking snapshots of the new novices, the Three Musketeers had gone public with their garters by hoisting up their skirts and striking an "oo-la-la" pose. Afterward, Sister Bernadette, their novice mistress, had royally chastised them for their show of exhibitionism and "scandalous behavior" on that most solemn of days in the congregation's life. They were duly reprimanded by having to scrub the refectory floor on their hands and knees for weeks. But the photo was salvaged and treasured.

The three of them had pledged to carry this badge of their friendship wherever they went. Meg's was crocheted in purple, her favorite color. Molly's in red, to match her hair. Theo's in olive green.

Meg sighed as she slid the badge back into the notebook's jacket. How long ago those happy-go-lucky days at the Motherhouse now seemed, when all they had to do was meditate on the meaning of the vows, learn to sing Gregorian chant without a "Blowin' in the Wind" beat, and debate keeping or ditching the traditional habit and veil of the Sisters of Charity.

Next she pulled out the only other photo—a snapshot of her team in La Bandera before the military coup. How thin and solemn they all looked. But then, they were all determined church workers set upon making Chile into a socialist state where the kingdom of God could get a good start ahead of most of the world. She and Molly now wore jeans and ponchos. Alfredo, with his black-as-coal beard and his pipe, looked for all the world like Che Guevara. José, also bearded, was a carbon copy Alfredo, only younger. *Madre* Rosa was a tiny, frail figure in her gray veil and green sweater. All except Rosa had their fists raised and their mouths in an open smile, because they were shouting *presente* for the photographer, who had come down from *Newsweek* to write about the election of their new socialist president, Salvador Allende.

The seatbelt sign flashed on as the pilot announced their final approach to the Ilopango airport in San Salvador. She put this last photo away and hurriedly finished her letter to Kay.

> *I've been reassigned to El Salvador. I guess the community thinks I need a change. But it's so hard to leave after everything that's happened. I'm weary unto death of all the killings and the violence.*
>
> *Must close now. The plane's about to land. Will write more later. Whether they are the Buddhist or Catholic variety, just keep the candles burning in earnest for me and for my dear Chile.*
>
> *Love,*
>
> *Meg*

Meg pushed her tray table into the seat in front of her and buckled up. The solution for it all this, of course, was to pitch her tent in another country, to lock horns with another repressive government.

At least she'd be with Theo again, her best pal from Novitiate days, her other self. Theo was a much better nun than Meg would ever be—or ever wanted to be. She was genuinely holy, the result of her bottomless acceptance of people. It was probably because she grew up dirt poor, even though she didn't realize it until she went to nursing school in Columbus. After all, she had two dresses—one with yellow daisies and the other with red tulips—both lovingly sewn from scratch by her mother. And she had a fine pair of sturdy brown oxfords, which she polished every night. All she needed.

To hear Theo tell it, she was raised as a free spirit in the Appalachia foothills of southern Ohio and allowed to roam the hollers to her heart's content with her dog Shadow, then one or another of Shadow's offspring. Theo said they were "farming folk" for as long as anyone could remember. She was the oldest of twelve kids. The whole family worked on their long-suffering piece of land outside Steubenville.

Her dad never did any other kind of work except farming, hunting, and fishing, and they only saw cash when he sold some rabbit skins or helped a neighbor seed his field. Only once did he get roaring mad, Theo said, and that was when somebody passing through the general store had called him "white trash." So what if they didn't have a car or a TV or a washer? So what if their toilet was outside? They had a fine radio in a mahogany case. They had a piano and every year it was tuned. The Katzes were Polish and held firmly to the belief that there had been a great musician among their ancestors. It was a good guess, because during their

Novitiate days, Theo could easily hit all the high notes and was their class's top soprano.

Theo told Meg she always knew she would become a nurse. She'd learned about herbs and seeds from her mother, a shy, seemingly frail woman. But once Meg got to know Mrs. Katz, she understood where Theo's keen sense of observation of both people and the natural world came from, as well as her straightforward, no nonsense determination. Her friend told her she was happiest looking after her sisters—all twelve of the Katz kids were girls—but she was also in her glory when she could help the cows calf, or accompany Old Nelly when she birthed her foul. She didn't drop out of school like most of her sisters. No, she was "the smart one," Theo's dad confided to Meg on Clothing Day. He wasn't the least bit surprised that his daughter won a full scholarship to Ohio State. "Come back, Theo-y. Come back and be our nurse, pa-leeze?" But Theo couldn't. At least not before she'd try giving her life to God as a Sister of Charity. "It just seems to me the world should be a better place… and I gotta move it along that direction," Theo told Meg on the first day they entered the convent.

Meg loved her friend dearly, even if Theo was terribly unsophisticated about political theory or even theology. Meg winced as she tried to picture her in Chile's urbane political circles with her spontaneous openness, her tactless questions. No doubt about it, she'd be an embarrassment. Thank heavens she had been assigned to Chile with Molly, the class intellectual and literary genius.

It would be fascinating to see how El Salvador had changed Theo. Would she still find herself drawn to her, despite her lack of sophistication and her gawkiness? She smiled when she remembered that her class had nicknamed Theo "Tweetie," because she was always flitting around helping everyone. There was something about Theo that centered her. What was it exactly? Some kind of plodding resignation to life as it unfolded? Would Theo still try to mother her? Did she want Theo to mother her? Probably. The Chilean experience was too raw not to want to cry on Theo's shoulder.

Besides Theo, there would be Sister Bernadette, their former novice mistress, Scripture scholar, and expert in the ins-and-outs of monasticism. After launching their class on the path of religious life, she'd decided at the age of sixty that she too was called to be a missionary and joined Theo in El Salvador. How would she be adopting to the rigors of mission life? Meg couldn't imagine this short, round nun, so proper in her bearing, now dressed in jeans and teaching Thomas Aquinas' proofs for the existence of God to Salvadoran peasants. But then Mum always surprised them with her versatility. During her twenty years as novice mistress, she managed to get inside each of her charges to find out exactly what it would take to turn that particular neophyte into a finely honed Sister of Charity.

Meg remembered with a nagging discomfort how "Queen Mum" could always read her heart. The long, deep look under shaded lids discretely observing you. Mum's face was ageless, and although she'd tried over the years, Meg couldn't imagine her as a young, frolicking girl. Good thing she was scheduled to return to the Motherhouse soon, and to a well-deserved retirement.

Back in the Novitiate, Mum would patiently listen to her unwind. Then, asking a question or two, she'd press Meg to find the answers for herself—whether the topic happened to be the nature of grace or the Blessed Virgin Mary as a manifestation of the Great Goddess of Neolithic times or her objection to the symbol of the Holy Spirit as a bird. Yes, Queen Mum had helped

Meg over some rough spots. If she was honest with herself, it was always the same "rough spot"—the infamous vow of chastity. One day she burst into the Novice Mistress's office and blurted out that she was lusting after the seminarian who cut the grass on the Motherhouse grounds, proof that she was called to be an airline stewardess instead of a nun.

"I think I am supposed to fly physically, not spiritually," she'd quipped.

Thankfully, Mum had seen the pain behind her outburst. "Chastity is much, much more than being celibate, Sister. Chastity is about bonding with others, loving others deeply and passionately, but with a pure heart, without manipulating the other. Do you have the greatness of spirit for that kind of love, Meg Carney? I think you do!" Then she was given permission to take a two-hour swim at the convent pool "to cool down."

Meg would be joining Theo and Mum in pastoral work at the parish of Aguilares, a sugar cane region about thirty miles north of the capital city of San Salvador. The parish was run by the Jesuits. Meg had always liked the Jesuits; they sported an intellectual vigor and curiosity she'd come to count on. Mother Ursula had written that the team was doing some innovating work among the peasants, forming small grassroots Christian communities, and that Meg could be a real asset with her catechetical skills. Maybe. Now she wasn't so sure.

The plane touched down on the runway and the pilot began braking immediately, forcing them to a jerky stop. "Not much of a runway," Meg complained to no one in particular as she unbuckled her seat belt and gathered her duffel bag from under her seat. She fell in line behind her few fellow passengers and walked toward what the stewardess pointed out as the terminal—a low, dimly lit concrete building back up the runway.

"Hot here," she said to the swarthy man walking by her side. Perspiration was running down Meg's back and her hair felt like a wet mop plastered to her scalp.

"You get used to it," he answered curtly.

"I suppose so." The man was wearing a three-piece suit and a tie and didn't seem wilted in the least.

"Do you live here?" Meg asked as they lined up to go through customs.

"Yes."

"My mother sent me a recent article from the *New York Times* about your country. Things seem somewhat unsettled here," Meg ventured, hoping she came across as a bright-eyed, inquisitive American tourist.

The man shot her a dark look as he moved aside to let her present her passport to the immigration officer. "If you lived here, you'd realize that is a subject no one cares to talk about—especially to strangers," he said in a low voice.

The official raised his eyebrows when he saw the Chilean visa stamped in her passport.

"How long were you in Chile, *Madre?*"

"Almost six years."

"What were you doing there?"

"I mostly worked with children, *señor.* Preparation for the sacraments. First Communion, Confession, Confirmation."

The man continued to thumb through her documents.

"A brave soldier now rules that country. But he's had his

hands full trying to weed out so many Communists."

Meg forced a smile but said nothing as the official stamped her passport.

"While you are here in El Salvador, stick to teaching children about what it means to make their First Communion, *Madre*."

"Thank you for the advice, sir." Meg hurriedly grabbed her bag as he waved her on.

Now she was soaked to the skin. She wondered how the Salvadorans stood this heat. All she wanted to do was to strip off her suit and jump into the nearest body of water. She claimed her two suitcases and hauled them over to be inspected. The man in the suit was beside her again at the baggage pickup.

"Take that official's warning to heart, *Madre*," he said in a kinder tone. "Be careful here. This country is much, much different than Chile. Here, take this," he said, thrusting a card into her hand. "Call me if you ever need me."

Meg glanced down at the card as the man hurried away.

"Hmm, a doctor." She slipped the card into the back of her passport.

While two customs officers went through her luggage item by item, Meg fished a mashed Kleenex out of her skirt pocket and mopped her forehead. She glanced around, looking for the exit. There, through the glass doors, she suddenly spied two light-colored heads among the sea of black ones. Theo and Queen Mum, both clad in white blouses and blue skirts, were waving madly. Heaving a sigh of relief, Meg waved back in earnest. She could feel the lines around her mouth relaxing into a wide grin.

There she was. Theo. Those same big, soft brown eyes that always comforted behind her glasses; that wide, crooked smile that seemed too large for her long, narrow face. That lanky frame towering over Queen Mum, who looked thinner than Meg remembered. Oh, it was good to see them both again! She suddenly felt lighter, as if some huge weight had just slid off her shoulders.

The luggage inspection ended once Meg opened the safety catch on her Lady Schick to show the inspectors what it was. She zipped up her bags, waved off a young man who offered to help her carry them with a "not heavy, not heavy," and plowed through the glass doors into Mum's arms and a kiss on both cheeks from Theo.

"Mum, Theo, how long it's been?" Meg laughed, tears clouding her vision as she hugged each one tightly. "This is the nearest thing to homecoming I've had in a long time."

"Welcome to El Salvador, Meggie." Theo's eyes were also wet. "I know you've left your heart in Chile, but this place has a way of growing on you." She bent down to pick up one of Meg's suitcases, then stopped and faced her friend again.

"You look a little worse for wear, Sister," she said, sliding her arm through Meg's.

"Mother Ursula said you've been through some pretty tough times in Chile. We were all so shocked to hear that the priest you worked with had been killed."

"Alfredo. And yes, some real tough times, Theo. A far cry from picking apples back at the Motherhouse in Ohio." She gave a short laugh.

Just then the doctor passed the three women and gave a brief nod.

"Stuffy old goat," Meg said.

"Why, that's Dr. Gomez," Queen Mum said, returning the nod with a friendly wave. "Didn't recognize him in his fancy clothes. He's no old goat, Meg. He's one of the few medical people who'll go out of his way to treat the poor. And they say he's a very devout Catholic."

Theo picked up Meg's bag again and guided her toward the Toyota jeep, parked a short distance away. "Well I guess you know that you certainly haven't come to the land of milk and honey."

"Whatever happens, Theo, it won't be as bad as Chile—or as wonderful," Meg retorted. Her voice trembled slightly.

"Now, now, Meg. You've served the poor Chileans long and well. We know that and thank God for your generous spirit." Queen Mum took Meg's free arm and gave it a motherly pat. "But remember, dear, none of us has a corner on courage or sacrifice. We do what we can with our gifts wherever we are. Recall what Paul, the greatest missionary of them all, said: 'Paul plants, Apollo waters, but it is God who giveth the increase.'"

The affection shining from Mum's sunken but still piercing blue eyes and the warmth beaming from her round, wrinkled face caught Meg off guard.

"Oh Mum, you'll never stop being my conscience, will you?" Meg was trying to laugh, but her mouth was twitching strangely. *Paul plants, Apollo waters, but it is God who giveth the increase*— the mantra her novice mistress had drilled into her charges' hearts year after year.

"Not until you become the Sister of Charity you are meant to be," the older woman said softly.

"Come on now, you two," Theo said a little impatiently.

"No one ever promised us a rose garden, as the song goes. Who knows, Meg, maybe you'll find a mustard seed or two here that you can coax toward growth. But let's get going now, shall we? You've got a lot to learn about this country."

Chapter 2

October 15, 1975

El Jícaro

Meg wiggled around until she was more or less comfortable in the hammock. These things were great for daydreaming or reading a book, but they were impossible to sleep in, unless she could think of her back as a curved banana.

The two hammocks, a small plastic table covered with a faded green piece of oilcloth, and a bed pan seemed to be recent additions to the sacks of corn and sorghum piled up to the ceiling along the hut's walls. The Sisters had been offered hospitality in this storehouse, owned by one of the community's leaders.

Meg and Theo had arrived late yesterday afternoon in El Jícaro, a *canton* of about two hundred people a half hour's jeep ride from Aguilares, her new home. They were to stay in El Jícaro for the next two days and give a boost to the Christian community. She would be preparing the smaller children for their First Communion, and the teenagers for Confirmation. Teaching the sacraments would give her a chance to check out their levels of literacy and their overall family situations. Theo had already set up her mobile clinic to minister to the long line of people cued up to seek her help.

She tried to enjoy the quiet of siesta time. Alone for an hour or so, she was free to doze and to dream.

Hammocks, storehouses, bumpy jeep rides over roads that felt more like horse paths—all part of the adjustments Meg had been forced to make in her first two weeks in El Salvador—the land of "the Savior." The ancient Nahuatls called this mountainous land with its verdant valleys Cuscatlán, "the jewel by the sea." If she didn't know better, she might have thought she'd landed in the Garden of Eden itself, where every fruit and flower flourished, where it was summer all year round, and where the sea was as warm as a baby's bath. But this breathless tropical beauty was literally only skin deep. Below its thin layer of topsoil lay volcanic rock. This was a country of massive seismic activity—volcanic eruptions and earthquakes were *pan de cada día*. How much did these great shifts in the earth itself affect the psyche of these people of the Savior? She would need to find out.

Within a day after her arrival, she learned that Aguilares was controlled by a handful of wealthy landowners who grew and processed sugarcane for export. The region's *campesinos*— an estimated thirty thousand of them—struggled to survive on their *milpas*. These minute plots of rocky, barren soil clung to the surrounding mountains and miraculously sprouted corn, beans, and a smattering of vegetables.

She supposed she was getting used to the steady diet of tortillas and beans but figured she'd become as chunky as Queen

Mum in a couple of months, unless she could squirrel away enough oranges and mangos to go on a crash diet.

She longed to sink her teeth into one of Chile's red-ripe peaches and feel the juice roll down her chin again, or pick a handful of grapes from the arbor behind *Madre* Rosa's ramshackle house-turned-clinic. She'd eat so many she'd have diarrhea for a week, but it would be worth it.

She turned in the hammock and tried not to think of Chilean grapes. It was cool here in the storehouse as long as she lay still. The tropical heat made her lethargic. She wished she could spend the whole day with her head under a spigot—or imitate the kids. At first she was startled to see them running around naked—or "barefoot all the way up," as Mum more delicately put it—but now she was used to it and even envied them. Thank heavens for the afternoon siesta to get through the hottest part of the day.

Despite her sense of herself as a seasoned missionary, Meg had to admit that she was appalled by the terrible poverty all around her. She'd thought the Chilean working class was bad off, and they were, but *this* poverty was devastating: no running water, no sewage, no electricity, no gas or kerosene to cook with—it felt as if the clock had been turned back to her great grandparents' time in rural Ireland. Poverty was poverty, Meg knew, whether it got you in Harlem or in Donegal or in a shantytown in Santiago or in a village in El Salvador. Nevertheless, she was reeling from the shock of the differences between Chile and this new country. Was this more the "real thing"?

In Chile, at least, the down-and-outers had managed to elect an Allende and to try out their own homegrown brand of socialism as a way of altering the imbalances between rich and poor, even if the military coup had crushed the effort in the bud.

But here, she didn't pick up any revolutionary rumblings in the air. So far she just saw cowed, submissive people and misery: the dull look in so many kids' eyes, the result of perpetually empty stomachs, no doubt; the tired faces of the women she had met in Aguilares. Doña Luisa, only twenty-seven, pregnant with her seventh, "four of whom are still alive, *gracias a Dios.*" Luisa seemed so worn out, so meek. What would make that woman come alive? A lively *peña* with some gusty singing? That would work in La Bandera.

Then there were the men. Such servile ways they had, taking off their hats and bowing. If you told them, "The moon flew away to another galaxy yesterday," they'd probably still answer, *Sí, Madre.* But pump a little cane alcohol into them and they changed into real macho types, swinging their machetes, ready to slash anything that took their fancy. Some of the parish's veteran catechists bore the horrid marks of their purported binges: Leonardo missing an ear, Domingo half a leg, Pancho with a huge scar that began below his right eye and ended somewhere under his always clean, always pressed blue shirt. Maybe if they had a revolution to keep them busy they wouldn't vent all their frustration by slicing up one another!

She noted that her new teammates managed to take it all in stride. Meg had to admire their enthusiasm. Besides the Sisters, there were four Jesuit seminarians more or less on permanent loan to the parish. All of them worked for—and apparently adored—Father Rutilio Grande, the pastor.

She smiled sadly as she thought of the seminarians. They reminded her of José, the seminarian on her team back in La Bandera.

Carlos, Ricardo, Pablo, Ervi. They were all in their mid or late twenties and were so terribly serious about their pastoral work, especially in the formation of small Christian communities in each village that fell under the jurisdiction of the Aguilares parish. She knew she would eventually see the uniqueness of each, but right now these young men seemed to be Rutilio clones.

Meg felt the cramp in her shoulders and sat up. Cautiously, trying not to rock the hammock too much, she threw her legs over the edge so that her feet reached the ground. Her rump suddenly scraped the mud floor, and her knees popped up in front of her. The hammock was definitely too low for a woman her size, but if she tied it up higher, would it hold? All she needed was to break her back sleeping in a hammock! She sighed and settled into a squat position, letting her mind drift back to her meeting with Rutilio.

"*Madre* Margarita, welcome to El Salvador and to our humble parish," he had said in English as he shook her hand when they met in the rectory the day after she arrived. "We have received a most enthusiastic endorsement of your skills in pastoral work from your superior, Mother Ursula. It is a great pleasure to have you with us in our mission of serving the poor."

"Thank you. I'm honored to be here," she said as she shook his hand. "But please, speak in Spanish. I've been with *chilenos* for the past six years, and I think the kids taught me every cuss word in the book."

She had meant to be funny, to cut through the formality of the situation, but the priest only cleared his throat, embarrassed, and launched into a ten-minute lecture on the history and development of the pastoral work in Aguilares without ever once pausing to ask her opinion.

She guessed that Rutilio must be in his early forties. Brown skinned, stocky, just about her height. Nothing remarkable about his features, just very Salvadoran looking—as if he could be on the national soccer team, but if you didn't know he was number thirteen, you couldn't tell him apart from the other players. Very formal. Very polite. It wasn't hard to pick up that he wasn't really a people person; he certainly was not much at ease with women. She felt he patronized her, which was very Jesuit of him.

From the few meetings she'd sat in on with him, Meg grudgingly admitted Rutilio *had* found a powerful method of gathering *campesinos* together to reflect on their faith in light of their day-to-day experiences. And he was also forming leaders who were organizing their *barrios* and villages in everything from healthcare to literacy classes to agricultural improvement and cooperatives.

But even with that record, Meg found him stuffy, too cautious and methodical for her liking. Maybe she'd appreciate Rutilio as time went on. She'd observed that he was more relaxed with Theo, but then her friend had always been a good listener. And his admiration for Queen Mum seemed boundless. Was this another one of those spiritual mother-son relationships, like the one that she'd witnessed between *Madre* Rosa and Alfredo? Mum and Rosa were remarkably similar in their ability to size up people and counsel them, even though Mum had to have been Rosa's senior by a good ten years and double her size. But Rutilio and Alfredo were nothing alike. Not in the least.

She sighed then carefully leaned back into her hammock, first lowering her head and torso, then her feet. The banana effect again.

This Salvador stint was just an interlude, wasn't it? If she stuck it out for a couple of years, surely Mother Ursula would honor her request to return to Chile. That was where she really belonged, plugging away with Madre Rosa and Molly. Even without Alfredo there, even if she was watched, she could manage somehow…

The reed matting that served as a door was suddenly shoved aside and Theo came in carrying two bottles of Coke. She handed one to Meg. "Sorry it's warm. No ice cubes in this part of the world."

Kicking off her loafers, she flung herself expertly into the other hammock. She took a swig of her Coke, then placed the bottle carefully on the mud floor beside her. She lay back with a groan of tired pleasure and stretched her long frame to fill the hammock's limits.

"Would you believe that just about every kid in this whole village has scabies," she sighed. "Scabies and worms."

"Well, you're Cherry Ames, mountaineer nurse. Can't you pull something out of that black bag of yours to cure them?" Meg was gulping down her Coke. "Tastes a lot more sugary without ice."

"Just another thing to get used to, old girl." Theo grinned. "Yeah. I can give them some relief, but it won't last long. You know the old saying about not giving a man a fish, but teaching him how to fish. Well, in this case, it's a matter of changing the course of the whole stream."

"Tut, tut, Theo. You sound like a radical. That's subversive talk where I come from."

"It's subversive talk here, too. Chile doesn't have a corner on repression, you know," Theo said as she put one leg on the floor and languidly rocked the hammock.

"Granted, I'm a newcomer, but there doesn't seem to be the political organization or the socialist vision here as there was in Chile. It was that vision and that organization that brought Salvador Allende to power—"

"I'm not so sure of that," Theo interrupted. "Scratch a little deeper. There's organization, and the core of it is in the Christian communities like this one. We studied this, remember? When we were in Cuernavaca at the Mission Institute. "

She looked over at Meg and caught her eye. "El Salvador is becoming a sort of test case. As they study the Scriptures in the light of what is happening in their own lives, these *campesinos* discover that there are *structures of evil* engulfing this country that are responsible for their oppression. Surely you, of all people, can see that."

Theo sat up in the hammock and continued passionately. "I've seen the light go on in so many *campesinos'* eyes. They begin to discard their fatalistic worldview—that they are poor because it is somehow God's will for them."

Behind her glasses, Theo's soft brown eyes sparkled with energy. She tucked her lank hair impatiently behind her ears and shot her companion a crooked smile. "These downtrodden men and women gradually become convinced that they have to change this horribly unjust situation because that's what God wants of them. They realize they live in such poverty because a few powerful men have cornered all the land and that they, the people who actually make the land produce, are letting them get away with it. Now it's time to right this wrong."

"And as for the vision, that's there too, but I'd say it's more biblical than political. In Chile you called it socialism; here we call it building God's Kingdom on earth."

Meg took a long, slow swallow of Coke, swung her legs out of the hammock, and sank to a squatting position. "Sounds awfully utopian, Sister." She shrugged as she clutched her knees into her chest. "Theocracies don't work in the twentieth century, from what I've seen."

Theo gave her friend a puzzled look, then shook her head. "Hey, Meg, what's with all this cynicism?" she said, hurt showing in her voice. "You were always the great idealist back in the Novitiate, the one who was involved in the civil rights movement, the grape boycott, getting the nuns out to the anti-Vietnam protests. Where's all your passion gone? All you've managed to do these past two weeks is to sit on your high horse and look down your nose at us. Oh, I know, I know. You suffered some rough times in Chile. But that doesn't give you the right to pontificate on people who might be forging a more just society by a slightly different route. So how about canning it?"

Meg blushed furiously and turned her face away from Theo's searching gaze. She recalled how, back in the Novitiate, she would always melt on those rare occasions when her friend rebuked her.

"I-I'm sorry. I'm really not down on your country—you're doing some really impressive work. It's just that, well, with all that happened in Chile, I'm just not quite myself yet."

Theo sighed, swung herself out of her hammock, and walked over to where Meg sat. She placed her hands on the woman's shoulders and said softly, "You're really wiped out, aren't you, Meggins? Just the other day, Queen Mum remarked that you seem so troubled, so… well… negative about everything. Come on, now," Theo said, dragging Meg out of the hammock. "We have a few hours before the evening session with the villagers.

25

Let's take a walk and do some talking."

The nuns emerged into the bright November sun and began walking toward the edge of the village. As they wound their way through the well-worn dirt paths, a rag-tag group of mostly naked children followed them and giggled when they heard the two *Madres* talking in English. Theo turned laughingly and introducing them, tussling in turn each child's hair. "Meg, this is Alonso, Paco, Juancito, and Justo. And this little girl's name is Margarita—that's the new *Madre's* name," she beamed, pulling her braids. "Shall we call you Meguita too?' The little girl blushed and smiled shyly, burying herself in the folds of Theo's skirt.

"Ah, Theo, you are the proverbial pied piper when it comes to kids," Meg said in English as she took in the children's worshiping, upturned faces as they hung on their giant *gringa's* every word.

"Run along now, kids. We're going to take a little walk so you won't hear the new song we're going to teach you tonight." She swooshed them away like a mother hen.

"Still doin your Tweetie-bird act," Meg teased.

Theo threw her head back and guffawed. "Lordy, lordy. Nobody's called me that in years!"

"Cause nobody here knows it, except Queen Mum—and she's not gonna squeal."

"Don't you either, okay? The seminarians would never let me live it down, let alone all the kids I try to mend. Imagine being named after a silly bird from a cartoon."

"It always fit back in the Novitiate, hon. If you weren't tying an old nunnie-bunnie's shoelaces, or scrubbing someone down with Epsom salts, you were out in the woods hunting for

Queen Anne's lace or dandelions to brew up another one of your concoctions to heal warts or stop an earache, remember?"

"Sure I do, sure I do." Theo continued to chuckle softly to herself. "A whole lifetime ago…"

The two women walked along silently together, each lost in her own thoughts, until they found a clearing on the outskirts of El Jícaro.

"What a magnificent view," cried Meg as she sank down into the tall, sweet-smelling grass. From this vantage point they could look down on the whole valley, shining in the afternoon sun below them. On the one side of the valley, the earth divided and divided again into tiny plots of furrowed land inching up the mountainside. Meg could make out people—women and children mostly—turning the soil. On the other side of the valley lay acre upon acre of earth swaying with thick, bright cotton balls. If it wasn't for the heat, Meg could almost believe she was taking in the winter's first snowfall.

"In another month, the cotton will be ready to pick," said Theo. "Then every able-bodied man, woman, and child in El Jícaro will work picking cotton for the *patron*. If they're lucky, families will earn enough to pay the rent for their *milpas* there on the other side of the valley."

Theo stretched her six-foot frame out on the grass, put her hands behind her head, and looked intently at Meg.

"Tell me about Alfredo."

Meg's blue eyes darkened. "What about him?" she whispered almost inaudibly.

"Last night you cried out 'Alfredo, Alfredo' at least half a dozen times as you tossed in your hammock."

Meg didn't respond, so Theo filled in. "I know he was the priest you worked with—and admired so very much, and of course that he was killed."

Meg gazed silently across the cotton fields below. A minute passed, then another. Finally, she raised her head. "I think I need to share him with you, Theo, or I'll go crazy. But I wonder what you'll think of me once you know the whole story."

"Try me."

"I fell in love with him," Meg blurted out. "I fell in love with Alfredo and would have married him if he hadn't been murdered." She gave Theo a defiant look, but her lip started to quiver and she quickly looked away.

Theo's face stiffened. She sat up from her spot in the grass, tucked her skirt between her legs, and sank into her familiar lotus position. "Oh, Meggins," she said sorrowfully. "What trouble have you brought upon yourself this time?"

"This was not some girlish infatuation," Meg said crossly. "I struggled long and hard with my vow of chastity. I'm sure Alfredo did too. But our love was so great..." Her eyes were glistening. "Oh, Theo, if only you could have known him! His passion for justice, his love and gentleness with the poor, his wit, his clear vision."

She smiled as she remembered how Alfredo had kept her up until dawn that first day in La Bandera, trying to show her every corner of the parish and tell her all there was to know about the country.

"Perhaps I would have fallen in love with him too," Theo said cynically, her face clouding into a frown.

Meg shot her companion a baffled look, then gave a short

laugh. "Yeah. You would have, come to think of it. You love everybody. You'd have loved Alfredo like you love Rutilio. Like a brother."

She lowered her voice. "But this was different."

Theo heaved a sigh and abandoned her lotus stance. She rolled over onto her stomach in the grass, her hands propped under her chin.

"Okay, Sister. Let's start at the beginning. You need to tell it—and I need to hear it. All of it, or we'll keep on marching to different drummers like we've been doing these past couple of weeks. And that won't do for best friends.

"Let's see, you and Molly arrived in Chile in early 1970, the same time I arrived here. We'd just finished our six-month stint studying Spanish in Cuernavaca, where you also managed to fall in love with Father Pete from Dublin, remember? Thank heavens he was assigned to Nicaragua."

Meg shivered slightly despite the heat. She hadn't thought about Pete in years and wondered what ever happened to him. She'd enjoyed flirting with the wild, hairy Irishman with the brogue. But everyone was flirting in those days—a last fling before hitting their assignments in the trenches of Latin America. They were all scared silly about what might be awaiting them. One of their professors, a crusty Mexican monk in charge of their course on acculturation, was fond of saying that while the American church was pouring thousands of dollars into training missionaries to 're-evangelize the poor of Latin America,' no one was giving any money to help train the communities that had to receive these well-intentioned but naive *gringos*.

"Cuernavaca seems like a lifetime ago, doesn't it?"

Theo nodded but said nothing.

Meg took a deep breath then plunged into her story with a zest she hadn't felt in months.

"Molly and I arrived in time for the presidential campaign that Salvador Allende won in 1970. Chile had just democratically elected the first socialist president—a real milestone! Can you imagine the thrill, Theo? I felt I was *inside* history, helping it happen—"

"Something like what a midwife experiences, I bet."

"Right. Midwifing a non-violent revolution. A great metaphor, kiddo! That year, Molly and I were assigned to work in La Bandera, a lively *población* on Santiago's south side. You know all this from my letters."

"True enough, but remind me anyway."

"From the horse's mouth, so to speak," Meg grinned and felt her body relax.

She could finally blurt it all out. How she and Molly were to work with this very popular priest, well known for his commitment to the poor. Padre Alfredo Ahumada.

She could still remember the first night they arrived in La Bandera and how Alfredo went on and on enthusiastically describing the community-organized food co-ops, the health brigades, the nutrition campaigns, the new spirit of openness and debate at the university—and how a college education was now available to even the poorest worker's son or daughter. He also talked about the new sense of Christianity that was developing. Christians for Socialism. Only later would she learn that he was one of its leading lights.

Meg stretched out on the grass and smiled dreamily. She

let herself remember the electricity she felt as she fell under this man's spell. For Alfredo, there was a wonderful sense of building a new Chile from the bottom up.

Alfredo had quickly drawn Molly and herself into his pastoral and political work—the two were inseparable in his mind. He was La Bandera's only priest and therefore pastor to its sixty thousand people.

"By El Salvador standards, La Bandera would be considered quite prosperous," she said apologetically. "But this barrio was one of Santiago's poorest, a sprawling mass of makeshift shacks sown together by a ring of dirt roads and an eventual string of light bulbs. In its ten-year history, its people had managed to pressure for water and sanitation facilities, a local grade school, and a clinic, which *Madre* Rosa ran."

Meg gazed into the distance. A slight breeze wheezed through the cotton fields below and they shimmered yellow-white in the fading sunlight. How fast those first almost fairytale years in Chile had gone. Then after the military coup, time seemed to come to a standstill.

But before that fateful September day in 1973 she had been so busy—mostly just appreciating, now that she thought about it. She'd be the first to be allowed to hear the music group's latest composition. The kids were all determined to be the rock stars of a New Era. Folksinger Victor Jara became Chile's Simon and Garfunkel:

> *The words of the prophets*
> *are written on the subway walls and tenement halls*
> *and whispered in the sounds of silence*

undergirded

Levántate y mírate las manos,
para crecer estréchala a tu hermano
Juntos iremos unidos en la sangre;
hoy es el tiempo que puede ser mañana.

Both were prayers of hope.

In her role of all-purpose cheerleader, Meg would be called upon to oh-h and ah-h over the new babies' robust health and to congratulate their mothers on in their commitment to *la leche* movement and to their baby clothes exchanges. She'd hurrah over the clean-up campaigns and the cooperative housing project as it inched along, nail by nail. She helped organize bazaars and raffles and dances to raise money to send this *compañero* to Peru or that *compañera* to Europe to 'tell the story of Chile's new experiment in socialism.'

She had loved every minute of it and felt wonderfully alive and happy. It was and always would be the Golden Age of Meg Carney, and she dearly hoped that it had also been the Age of Song for Alfredo Juan José Ahumada Montero.

Theo broke into Meg's reverie. "Weren't there others on your parish team besides you and Molly and Alfredo?"

"Of course," Meg said. "Besides Molly and me, Alfredo had recruited a young seminarian, José. He'd taken a year off from his studies to do pastoral work among the poor—basically the same thing Rutilio has done by recruiting the Jesuit seminarians to help at the Aguilares parish. And Theo, you wouldn't have believed the resemblance between the two of them! Jose looked enough like Alfredo that they could have passed for brothers. Both thin, intense, beards like Che Guevara, forever smoking.

I've got a picture of the team back at the parish, so you can see for yourself."

But unlike Alfredo, José was shy and not much of a leader. His admiration for Alfredo was, she recalled, almost obsessive. He tried excruciatingly hard to copy his mentor's every step, his every mannerism. With hindsight, she thought he really did violence to himself in the process. People saw that and were gentle with José. She remembered that Molly and she often wondered what would happen to José if Alfredo ever fell off his pedestal.

"Hmm, we might have a similar situation with Carlos and Rutilio. All that kid wants to do is to become a Jesuit like *el gran Padre.*"

"We'll keep an eye on Carlos, you and I." Meg gave Theo a wink. It felt good to care for someone together again, to help a protégé grow. She continued, "The other member of the team— although she had recruited *Alfredo*—was Sister Rosa, known only as *La Madre.*"

"Strong voo-man?" Theo inquired, using the intonation they had invented in the Novitiate to describe the "Amazon woman" personality type.

"Oh my, yes. A true-blue, one-breasted Amazon lady. If not in body, certainly in spirit." Meg laughed.

Rosa was a story all by herself. She was born of French parents who had migrated to Argentina, and at an early age joined a community of teaching nuns. She was sent to Chile to teach in one of Santiago's exclusive girl's schools. Over the years, she became more and more disillusioned with teaching the wealthy, and she finally asked her congregation to transfer her to one of the poor schools in a Santiago slum. The congregation refused, so Rosa left religious life and came to live in La Bandera in the early 1960s.

"That took guts."

"Yes, it did," Meg agreed.

She told Theo how Rosa taught at a state-run school and in the evenings went back to school herself to learn health skills because she was so appalled at the sickness and malnourishment of so many of the shantytown's inhabitants, especially the kids. She eventually became a nurse and set up shop in her little shack, which still served as La Bandera's round-the-clock clinic. Rosa must have been about fifty when Meg first met her. She had taken private vows, including a fourth, one of eternal service to the poor.

"She's a great woman, Theo. You might be like her one day." She grinned shyly at her friend lying next to her in the grass.

"I like her already; she sounds more down to earth than either Alfredo or José. More like the salt-of-the-earth variety."

"Yeah. Come to think of it, you and Rosa would have been great friends. She's become a pillar of the La Bandera community in her ragged green sweater and her gray cotton veil. Just like you, she's an expert on everything from infant diarrhea to alcoholism to frigidity in marriage."

Meg knew that Rosa was undoubtedly a saint, although God knows *La Madre* laid down the law to more than one of her spiritual sons and daughters who in her view were getting out of line.

"*La Madre* jokes abound in La Bandera, like how she always manages to appear out of nowhere just when a couple is about to go all the way. She supposedly taps them on the shoulder and asks them to help her take out the garbage!"

"Better just give them a condom," Theo chuckled. "Despite the church's outmoded teachings, it's the only effective way to cut down on unwanted pregnancies. But get on with your story."

Meg explained that in her opinion, Alfredo and Rosa had developed a mother-son relationship. Never was he meeker than when he was in *La Madre's* presence. She'd question him sharply on what she considered his extremist political positions. So although Alfredo was the pastor and Molly and she were supposedly pastoral coordinators and José the trusted foot soldier, Rosa was really in charge—if not by clarity of leadership, then by longevity and by her total commitment to the people. There was no doubt about it: *La Madre* reigned as the undisputed leader of the community.

"She's still there, having outlasted us all, binding up the wounds of life's cruelty, laying the dead to rest, birthing La Bandera's squirming future."

"One would have thought," Theo interrupted, "that such a wise woman would have immediately seen the relationship developing between Alfredo and you and sent you packing."

The question caught Meg up short. "I don't know why that didn't happen," she answered slowly.

"You don't suppose it was because she'd seen Alfredo fall in love before?"

Meg blushed angrily. "I know what you're thinking. We've both met enough Latin American clerics who are big flirts and play at being Mr. Available. But Alfredo was no Don Juan. Believe me. I *know.*"

"Okay, okay, Meggie. I believe you. Just doing some reality checking. You can be somewhat of a flirt yourself. Remember poor Pete?"

"Oh come on, Sister, I resent that. Pete was out for a good time in language school. So was I. This was entirely different."

"Tell me, why would I have liked Alfredo?"

"Why? Because he was so *transparent,* Theo," Meg exclaimed joyfully. "Transparent and humble, maybe even somewhat naive. And you would have enjoyed talking to him about theology and politics; after all, he was a minor light in both church and political circles."

She hugged her knees to her chest. She'd thought a lot about what made this priest so attractive, not just to herself but to everyone who knew him. She believed that Alfredo grew in experience and wisdom and class consciousness as the people of La Bandera did; one mirrored the other. The eternal struggles against the cold, cruel winters, when there was never enough kerosene for the stoves; the leaky roofs, the hungry eyes of the kids, the deaths of too many infants struck down by dysentery or whooping cough, too many teens forced to leave school in search of work, too many mothers aborting their unborn because they couldn't face the thought of having yet another hungry child crying to be fed, too many alcoholics, too many men working their asses off for a pittance. As the people of La Bandera raged against their lot and dreamed of a better day, so did Alfredo. As they joined political parties, as they discovered Marxist categories for explaining their situation of oppression, so did Alfredo. As they organized, protested, went out on strike, marched in the streets, wrote songs about their plight, and shouted *el pueblo unido jamas sera vencido*, there Alfredo was in their midst, being converted to this flesh and blood extension of himself.

"He sounds like Christ incarnate, m'dear," Theo murmured,

with only the faintest hit of irony. "Maybe *you* should write the songs, the poems—"

Meg continued her eulogy as if she hadn't heard her friend. "La Bandera found its hope, its best self, its possibilities as a community reflected in Alfredo. In the end it was the people of La Bandera themselves who made Alfredo into an incessant fighter for socialism as well as a sensitive priest."

She knew that his joy sprang from these people—his laughter, his immense love for life. And his anger also rose from their experience of impotence, from their perpetual situation of being screwed by their bosses, by *los high*.

"Well then, why in God's name didn't you affirm him in his priesthood as you should have done as a vowed religious woman, Margaret Carney?" Theo demanded hotly.

Meg felt as if she had just been punched in the stomach. She stared back at her friend, suddenly short of breath.

"Why did you let him fall in love with you?"

Meg felt hot tears stinging her eyes. Yes, that was the crucial question. "Because I began to love him more than I loved myself," she said fiercely. "More than I loved my community or my God or even you, Theo. I felt so much *more* than just Meg Carney from Pittsburgh, Pennsylvania, when I was with him."

Meg met Theo's gaze and saw both reproach and pity reflected back. The two women sat silently together for some moments.

Then Theo asked, "Where was Molly in all this? What did she think of your falling in love? You and she are so much alike that I know she could have sniffed out what was happening to you almost before it started."

Meg shifted uncomfortably in the grass. "Sure. Molly knew.

I-I think she too had... ah... fallen somewhat in love with Alfredo, and perhaps was—I don't know—maybe a bit jealous of me. Molly and I—our lives became so full of people and activities—well, we sort of drifted apart during those first years in La Bandera. Only after the military took over did we reconnect. But by then, it was too late."

Theo pressed on, "But did your commitments mean nothing to any of you? Could you really toss over priesthood and religious consecration so lightly? Especially since your vocations were so tied to serving the poor of La Bandera?"

"You sound like *Madre* Rosa," Meg said bitterly. "But in the end, she would have given Alfredo and me her blessing."

Theo raised her eyebrows. "Really?"

"It's not as if we just nonchalantly threw our vows of celibacy out the window, for God's sake!" Meg was almost shouting now. "We would have continued to work with the poor; we would have continued to live in Latin America—Peru, if we couldn't have stayed in Chile—and we would have continued to try and serve God and build his kingdom, for Christ's sake." She was crying now. "But then it doesn't matter what we would have done, does it? He's dead. Dead, dead, dead," she sobbed, rocking back and forth on the ground.

Theo sat up quickly and moved over to Meg's side. Heaving a long sigh, she took the distraught woman into her arms and tried to sooth her. "Have a good cry, Meggie. Have a good cry. You deserve it."

After a minute or two, Meg's sobs subsided. She gently released herself from Theo's arms but held onto her hand. "Theo-y," she said softly, using the way her friend's family addressed her. "Don't ask me those questions now. Later, maybe, but right now I can't take them in. I'm still trying to absorb his awful death."

"Do you want to tell me how he was killed?"

Meg nodded. She had to tell her friend the circumstances of Alfredo's death or she'd crack up.

"I don't know why we didn't see the coup coming. Lord knows, there were enough signs around." She recalled the CIA destabilization campaign, the international credit blockade against Chile spearheaded by the Nixon administration, the growing discontent within the armed forces. But somehow, being wrapped up as they were in the daily struggles of La Bandera and being reassured by Alfredo's fatally-flawed trust in the Allende government's strength, the coup caught them all off guard.

"For those of us outside Chile, it was evident that Allende couldn't last too much longer. The country was too divided. Chile itself didn't seem to know what to do with its 'experiment in socialism.' There was so much hording, so much distrust."

"Yeah, Allende wasn't exactly Jesus," Meg grunted. "In hindsight, his government made lots of mistakes. People were afraid, and there were wild rumors about how the poor were going to violently take over the houses of *los high*, rape their daughters and carry off their sons to the Soviet Union to be brainwashed—"

"The rumor mill working overtime."

"Doesn't it always?" Meg took a deep breath and went on, her eyes fixed on the whitened fields below. "Somehow I remember thinking to myself on September 11 of that year, which dawned a bright, sunny day, 'Oh, another spring's almost here. Time to wash the curtains, air out the mattress, put a fresh coat of paint on the front of the *casita*.'"

But as the day marched on to mark the black events of history, she remembered how the sky clouded over and in the late afternoon it began to rain. It seemed to her that even nature itself was crying out at the atrocities committed in seeming effrontery to another winter's end.

"The truth was there was no spring in Chile that year," she said. "Everything remained gray and shriveled. Santiago was wrapped in shadows, peopled with ghosts and specters."

On the morning of the coup, she'd gone downtown with some of La Bandera's women to pick up provisions for their local food co-op from a central government distribution center. There, the workers nervously informed them that one of the army regiments had risen up against Allende. They thought the rebellion might only be an internal army squabble, but they weren't sure and warned them to stay off the streets.

As the women were piling back into their pickup truck, they heard planes overhead. Meg remembered looking up and seeing that the planes were flying so low that she could clearly make out the *Fuerza Aerea de Chile* emblazoned on their sides. Then, right before her eyes, the planes swooped down over La Moneda and began dropping bombs on the presidential palace. Not a soul was in the streets. The women were terrified—they didn't know if they should run back inside the distribution center or try to make it back to La Bandera. They decided to risk the twenty-minute dash to home; the women wanted to make sure their children were inside and Meg wanted, well, to be where she now belonged.

They made it back to the *barrio* in record time and Meg had headed straight for *La Madre's* house-clinic where she found Rosa, José, and Alfredo gathered grimly around the radio. They were listening to Allende talking to the nation from La Moneda.

"'But… but they're bombing La Moneda! If Allende is in there…'" she remembered shouting, but no one reacted. José came over and put his arm around her; he was visibly trembling, and she found herself trying to calm him down. Everyone continued to listen to the besieged president's voice until it gradually faded out. Then the radio began to broadcast a military march.

She recalled that toward late afternoon, the announcement came that Allende had committed suicide and that the rest of his cabinet had surrendered to the military. The government had been taken over by the commanders of the Armed Forces. General Pinochet and his generals intended to "save Chile from the jaws of Marxist-Leninism," as they announced later that day. A state of siege was declared, and all constitutional liberties were indefinitely suspended. A curfew from eight at night until eight in the morning was in effect and anyone seen out on the streets would be summarily shot.

Meg paused a moment and looked over at Theo. "Do you know all this? Am I boring you?"

"No you're not boring me," Theo answered quietly. "But yes, believe it or not, most of us know the story of Allende's overthrow, although maybe not in such detail. Chile's experiment in socialism has been a major topic in our pastoral reflection meetings these past few years."

"Oh, I didn't realize that," Meg said, surprised.

Then she went on to tell Theo the hardest part: how she had awakened the next morning to Alfredo's quiet tapping on her window. He was clenching the morning paper tightly in his hands. It held the first *bandos*—arrest warrants. The list included all high officials of the Allende administration and all national opposition party leaders.

"'In a few days, you know my name will appear on one of these lists,' he told me. 'I'll have to go underground until I see what all this means.' We held each other then, Theo-y, in that cold gray dawn. That was the last time I saw him."

She stopped speaking for a moment and concentrated on breathing deeply. She clasped her friend's hand tighter and went on in a strained voice.

"The next months were, without exaggerating, a living hell. The sirens, the raids, the nightly shouts of 'No, no, *por Dios*, don't take him, he's only a boy' or 'Please, please, he's old and sick, can't you see?' On and on it went, the searches, the chilling knock on the door, and then yet another friend dragged off for questioning."

"Yes," Theo said sadly. "We heard how Santiago's National Stadium became a giant coliseum where dissenters were thrown to the lions over and over again."

"You knew all that?" Meg shook her head incredulously.

"Yeah, kiddo, we did. In those days, everyone followed what was happening in Chile. We all wondered how it would affect our own governments."

"It gives me goose bumps to hear that. I had no idea there was so much concern…"

In a bitter voice, Meg told Theo about how only the lucky ones survived to face expulsion from the country. Most of the poor were simply given what became 'the usual'—torture followed by imprisonment without charges. Sometimes they were released, sometimes they were executed; mostly they just disappeared. She told of how *La Madre* became La Bandera's unsung heroine.

How she hid those on the run and squirreled them away often only minutes before her house was searched yet again. She went with mothers and wives to the police stations, the stadium and to the fledgling new human rights groups to petition for the whereabouts of so many of her spiritual sons and daughters. The frail figure in the gray veil and ragged green sweater was suddenly everywhere at once.

Meg was ordered to be Rosa's handmaid, accompanying her wherever she went, because the police weren't going to touch a *gringa* nun. Molly was dispatched to the archdiocesan office, where she became part of the social service staff at the church's newly set up Vicariate of Solidarity.

"If Rosa knew that I was torn apart with worry over Alfredo, she never showed it. And I knew that she too was worried sick about him. She worked herself to the bone and me along with her."

Then, toward late October, Alfredo's name did appear on the list of those wanted for questioning. But Alfredo had evaporated. The secret police let it be known that things would go easier on La Bandera if they'd "cough up the commie priest." One after another, the community's coordinating team was picked up and interrogated. Those who were eventually released reported that the first question they were asked was about Alfredo's whereabouts. If they knew, one or another of Alfredo's leaders would have given him away. One had to be an extraordinary human being to withstand the electric shocks, the near drowning, the stretching on the rack, the gang rape.

In the late months of that awful year, it hit even closer to home. *La Madre* was picked up and questioned. But she wasn't tortured. But José, poor, weak José! They were sure that "if he just thought a little harder," he could come up with some ideas about where Alfredo was hiding. Again and again they shot him through with electricity, then the drowning in the tub of water until he lost consciousness, then came the dogs and the rats…

Meg took another deep breath and went on. José had stood it for two weeks and then he broke. Not that he knew anything about Alfredo's whereabouts, but he knew many of Alfredo's friends—members of his political cell and where they might be. They released him then, suddenly a very old little boy, his body broken, his spirit crushed.

Meg was suddenly back in Rosa's tiny house. "We tried to tell José that *anyone would break under that kind of torture.* Over and over again, we repeated it, 'Anyone, José, anyone.' *La Madre* even slapped him once and shouted at him, 'You're stupidly proud and *machista.* Get back to work and bind worse wounds than your own, for heaven's sake!' But all our cajoling was useless. I think he was so ashamed and so afraid Alfredo would find out and never forgive him. On Christmas Eve, our José hanged himself from a tree overlooking La Bandera's garbage dump."

"Oh, that poor kid!" Theo cried, shaken. "How utterly tragic! Oh, Meggie, I didn't know about José. I'm so, so sorry. May he rest in peace at last."

"Yes," Meg said wearily. "He was so haunted by how he thought he'd failed us. May he finally be at peace."

The two remained silent, their heads bowed in prayer for a long moment. Meg could feel Jose's presence there beside them. "*Sí, José, que descances en paz.*"

Then she went on to describe the summer of 1974. Even with the repression, Chileans were Chileans. Santiago shut down as usual during the month of February, and everyone went either to the beach or home to visit relatives in the south. She and Rosa took a group of Bandera kids to the archdiocese's summer camp at Punto de Tralca for a week of sun and rest. And it was there, during one of their last days at the beach, that Meg told Rosa of her love for Alfredo.

"No, Theo, she didn't approve. But she loved Alfredo. Maybe she thought it would pass. Maybe she sensed that deep happiness would be his if he married and had children."

"From the way you describe her, I can't believe that she wasn't harder on you than that," Theo interjected gently but firmly.

"Perhaps it was the time we were living in," Meg said, heaviness creeping into her voice. "It seemed somehow almost surreal to be talking about love or even a future that summer of 1974. Maybe she didn't want to begrudge me a few happy moments. She simply said, '*Las cosas que pasan, las cosas que pasan,* only God knows why. His ways are not ours.'"

It was dusk now in the little clearing where Meg and Theo sat. Meg paused in her narrative and, out of habit, twirled her ring around on her finger as she watched the sun sink over the horizon. Somehow, not even her best friend understood the depths of her love for her Fredito. Theo couldn't comprehend how a vow could be broken, no matter how sacred. And the terrible irony of it all was that it didn't matter anyway.

"We'll never know what we would have done in the end, of course," she began again in the same bitter tone. "Other events got in the way. That conversation between me and Rosa took place February 27. On March 2, the two of us were back in Santiago, renewed from our time at the beach and ready to take on the dictatorship's stepped-up network of terror. But two days later, on the night of March 5, we were called down to the central police station to identify Alfredo's body."

Meg's voice began to break. She seemed to have momentarily forgotten Theo's presence. "Was it really him, this bloated and bruised mass of human flesh?" she whispered, staring blindly out into the growing darkness.

"They told us they had found the corpse floating down the Mapocho River. How did they know to call us? Why were they so certain it was Alfredo? The body was decapitated and beginning to decay. The fingertips had been cut off. The arms and legs were disjointed. '*Oh my love, my dove, my beautiful one, why have they done this to you?*'" she prayed from the Canticle of Canticles.

She remembered her friend again on the grass beside her. "He was so mangled, Theo!" she moaned. "That's what haunts me so. I can't help dwelling on what they must have done to him to make him so, so mangled."

Again Meg paused as she tried to steady her voice. She felt Theo's arm around her again. "Just let me finish. Let me finish," she pleaded.

"Okay, finish. Yes, finish. Once and for all. I'm right here."

"We took him home to La Bandera," she went on in a barely audible voice.

She described how the men made him a wooden casket, how the women covered it with garlands of flowers, how they waked him for a night and a day, then buried him the following evening in a niche next to José in Santiago's general cemetery. It was a strained burial, with enough police around to make the liturgy tense, almost perfunctory. The military government wanted to make sure that La Bandera residents didn't make a political event out of those last rites.

"Afterwards, we straggled back to Rosa's. That night she served the best of Chilean wines in honor of Alfredo. I allowed myself to get royally drunk." She looked up at Theo and gave her a sheepish look. "You know how I can't hold my booze."

Theo smiled sadly and nodded but said nothing.

"When morning came, I went to bed and stayed there for a week. Finally, Rosa literally dumped me out of bed and threw me in the shower. 'Yes, you must grieve, but you must go on living. *Por dios,* be brave, Meguita!' she shouted.

"I did get up then, but I wanted to be alone, alone, alone. I shut out all intimacy with my friends from La Bandera, although I still went on helping them as best I could. I shut out Molly. And I even shut out Rosa, to my everlasting shame. In my own self-centered pain of loss, I forgot how much they too were torn apart by Alfredo's awful death."

She took a deep breath. Now she just wanted to finish. She told of how Alfredo's murder had far-reaching repercussions. How it even moved the archbishop of Santiago to speak out against the regime. Alfredo became a *cause célèbre.* His picture appeared on posters, songs were written about him, a pamphlet on his life that contained some of his writings appeared as well.

"He would have groaned to see it all." Meg gave a short laugh through her tears. "I can almost hear him moaning, 'Just what I always wanted—to be immortalized on holy cards.'"

Alfredo had thought his absence would stop the military surveillance of La Bandera, but he had been badly mistaken. The dictatorship was convinced that the *barrio* was a veritable beehive of subversives and that its inhabitants were plotting to overthrow the military through armed struggle. Persecution of the people became more acute.

"So, for the last year and a half, I've just tried to do what I could to protect the people with my *gringa* presence. But I had no energy for it. And last year, when Mother Ursula came down for her annual visit, she must have sensed how washed out I was. Molly also probably told her how tough the situation was in La Bandera.

"Mother wanted me to go back to the States and rest for a while, but I couldn't think of giving up on La Bandera, Theo! My guess is that sometime during the visit, Rosa talked to her about me because after that Mother looked at me in a different way—you know that piercing gaze she has."

"I sure do. That's why she's our Mother Superior."

"Yeah, she's psychic or something," Meg agreed.

"So a month later, I received the letter inviting me to join you and Mum here. Rosa told me she thought it would be wise to go."

She remembered Rosa's parting words: "Go. Go to a new land, *mi querida Meguita*. Perhaps there you will find the Lord's face again and then, when you do, you'll be able to come back and share that beauty with us."

Meg looked over at her friend's bowed head and was comforted by the arm still resting on her shoulder.

"Now you know everything, Theo. I've broken my vows by falling in love with a consecrated person like myself, a priest. And I have lost him to death. I feel angry at God," she said through clenched teeth. "And… and sometimes guilty. Yes, I admit it. Isn't that what you wanted to hear? But most days I wish I were dead too. I've lost all zest for living."

She lowered her head and wept in earnest.

Theo took the weeping woman's head in her large, calloused hands and held her gaze. Meg saw pain and compassion and the slightest flicker of reproach reflected in her friend's golden-flecked eyes.

Then Theo was hugging her. "Meg, Meggie. Oh, hon, I had no idea what you went through, all the atrocities around his death. Honestly I didn't," she whispered as she held her tightly. "Go ahead. Hold onto this old friend who loves you so much and believes that, despite it all, you'll find a reason to go on living."

The next minute, she was on her feet, pulling Meg up with her. "And a couple of those reasons are right here in this village waiting for a song from us. One of them is your namesake, and you're going to sing her a special Chilean song your music group in La Bandera composed."

"Oh, Theo, I can't." Meg pleaded, half horrified and half pleased at the suggestion.

"Yes you can, even if you've no heart for it right now. I think we'd both do well to trust your friend, *Madre* Rosa. She believes you'll find the Lord's face in this new land, among these people—and so do I. So come on now, let's get to it."

And with that, she took Meg's hand and began to pull her back up the path toward El Jícaro.

Chapter 3

Christmas 1975

Bay of Tamarindo

Meg dove under water one more time. Down, down she went, to the coolest part of the sea. How good it felt to have the bracing sea water rush through her hair, flow over her body, refreshing every inch of her. Finally out of breath, she surfaced, stood up, and began wading back to shore.

"I could be a mermaid," she laughingly shouted ahead to Theo, who was sitting in the sand, her nose stuck in her new Agatha Christie mystery, a Christmas gift from her family.

Meg flopped down beside the other woman. "I can't believe we're actually swimming in the Pacific Ocean on Christmas Day," she sighed. "We never did this in Chile."

But here she was, along with the whole Aguilares pastoral team, taking over the Jesuit Retreat House on the Bay of Tamarindo for a few days of R and R.

"We deserve it, don't you think?" Theo said, looking up from her book.

"No doubt in my mind at all, Sister."

The team had been run ragged by the demanding schedule of accompanying the *campesino* communities in their Yuletide celebrations. Meg had been paired with Carlos and the two of them must have traveled some sixty miles by jeep yesterday to participate in the Christmas celebrations in three different villages: first in El Jícaro, then in El Paisnal, and finally in Aguas Escondidas. She'd enjoyed working with Carlos. He wasn't at all like José, and although he resembled Rutilio slightly, he had none of his mentor's dogged seriousness of purpose. They had discovered they were both fanatics of Chilean songwriter Victor Jara and Meg had lent him her treasured collection of Jara albums.

Carlos enjoyed life and a good laugh. "Hey, if we're gonna be martyrs, let's do it big time and get nailed to a cross and go out singing the Blues," he joked to Meg as they bounced along in the rickety parish Land Rover. "The best Jesuits are usually dead Jesuits, did you know that, *Madre*?" He gave her a sideways wink. "Too bad you can't be a Jesuit. Too bad we don't take women. Hey, can I call you Meguita?"

She and Carlos had arrived back in Aguilares just in time for Midnight Mass, which was celebrated by Rutilio. He gave a sermon Meg would never forget. He began by reminding those huddled together in the crowded church that Jesus had been born among a people who were at that time dominated by Rome, the greatest power on earth. Then, instead of concentrating on the birth itself, Rutilio turned to the account of the Holy Innocents.

"The birth of a child on the outskirts of a small city worried King Herod; the smell of the stable filtered up to the king's palace and the fear the newborn savior evoked in the king led him to slaughter many innocent children. Unjust and untimely death became intertwined with the life that had just begun. Tragedy surrounded the joy of birth…"

Rutilio appeared much more alive in the pulpit than he was in person, Meg thought as she watched the ordinarily shy man preach to his captive audience.

"The searing cry of Rachel who wept for her children continues to be heard in our country," Rutilio said to his hushed listeners. "It is in the cry of our mothers who see one out of every five of their children die in their first year of life. The blood of innocent children continues to drench the history of El Salvador. It is the price we are expected to pay because we came out on the short end when the world's goods were divided up. But this situation, these early deaths, are unacceptable to those of us who believe that this small, insignificant baby was God's son. And it is the celebration of Christmas that reminds us of God's promise that life will overcome death. The 'peace on earth' proclaimed to the shepherds is what is demanded of us if we are to build a just world, a world, Jesus tells us, where peace will only come when there is justice for all."

Rutilio sounded like an Old Testament prophet that night as he preached those words in the Aguilares plain white-washed chapel, splendidly decked out with the red poinsettias Salvadorans called "blood flowers."

Remembering the way the people seemed to hang on the priest's every word, Meg shivered slightly as she sat toasting herself in the sand next to Theo.

Her friend noticed and again looked up from her book. "You can't be cold in this heat."

"I can't get over how alive the Scriptures are to these people. Like the clock has been turned back and I've been plopped into the times of the early Christian church. I sometimes have the sensation that I'm literally walking through the pages of the Bible."

"That's odd, coming from someone who's worked with the poor in Chile."

"The people of La Bandera were poor and Christian too. But they didn't have the same vivid sense of the Gospel stories. Chileans are more politically astute. Even the poorest cobbler or domestic servant is familiar enough with Marxist theory to explain why they're poor and who's exploiting them."

"Don't kid yourself," Theo laughed. "Salvadorans also know who's screwing them and why."

"Sure. But it seems that the only analytical tool they're being given to understand the structural roots of their exploitation is the Bible. Highly laudable and very touching, but a bit quaint, even dangerous, don't you think?" She was warming to the topic and enjoyed distracting Theo from Agatha.

"How in the hell can you expect *campesinos* to organize and take on the landowners unless they have some categories to analyze their situation? Some history of how other revolutions have been brought about? I know my skepticism bothers you, but honestly, it seems like you all are working here to bring back the Garden of Eden instead of a workable socialism."

Theo heaved a sigh, closed her book, and flopped over on her towel. "Well, I'm not the philosopher that you are, but I think that Marxism and Christianity share the ideal of a utopian society where 'there shall be no more weeping or gnashing of teeth,' right?"

"Right"

"Look at it this way, then. In Chile, Marxists are called subversives. In El Salvador, the Christian communities and those of us who work with them are called Communists. I think that, in the last analysis, both are making the powers that be very uncomfortable."

"But the first group was building its project for a new society on a solid foundation, while the second group is mucking around in sentimental quicksand trying to build the Kingdom of God ahead of the appointed time."

Theo gave her friend a sharp look. "That, Meg Carney, is a very snobbish thing to say."

She rolled back over and picked up her book again. "I'm truly amazed at what a self-proclaimed expert on political theory you've become," she grumbled under her breath. "I suppose that's really your lovely Alfredo talking."

Meg couldn't miss the sarcasm. "Theo, it's just plain fuzzy thinking to believe that Christian communities are going to bring about a revolution here. Why, you don't even—"

"Let's just drop it, okay? Get a little more experience in this country. Then we'll have this discussion," Theo snapped.

Meg sat up and took hold of Theo's shoulders, pulling her around so she could see her face. Theo's wide brown eyes avoided hers. "No, let's not drop the subject. I want to know just what you mean by that crack about Alfredo."

"I'm sorry, Meg. I didn't mean it," she said in an exasperated tone, again turning her face away.

"Hey, but you did mean it!" Meg firmly took her friend's chin in her hands and gazed directly into her eyes.

There was a look of hurt in Theo's eyes. She sighed and gently removed Meg's hands from her face. "Look, Meg. I really am sorry. I want to be supportive and sensitive, honest. You've been through some excruciatingly painful times, and your wounds are still raw. Yet," she said, looking down at her own brown hands, "I was so overjoyed to think that we'd be together again, that we would be as close as we were in the Novitiate, and, well, I just wasn't prepared for how changed you are."

"But Theo, underneath I'm still the same old Meg!"

"Are you?"

"Of course—and hopefully a much better person because of Alfredo."

"But that's just it, Meggie," Theo said softly, looking out toward the sea.

The two women were silent for a minute as they watched the white caps rolling in toward the shore.

Meg finally spoke. "If I didn't know better, I'd say you somehow resent Alfredo."

Theo stiffened, but she kept her gaze fixed on the waves breaking a few yards from where they lay. "I'm sure he was as wonderful as you say he was," she said, picking her words carefully. "Rutilio even knew him and we prayed for him when we heard of his murder. No, I don't resent him. But I-I don't know what I feel about you. You fell in love with him... well, I suppose that could have been predicted. If you remember, in the old days you would get a mad crush on just about any good-looking male who walked through the Novitiate doors. But you were a novice then; now you're a religious Sister with the vow of chastity. Yet you lead me to believe you broke that vow. It seems to me that you're somehow flaunting that infidelity, somehow asking for my approval at the same time that you ask for my sympathy and sorrow for your loss."

She glanced over at her friend and took in Meg's reddening face, then turned abruptly to gaze at the sea again. "I don't mean to be unkind, Meggie, but I've thought it over a good bit since you told me about Alfredo in El Jícaro last month. It strikes me that you've perhaps overindulged yourself in bemoaning this great love of yours who has been so brutally killed."

She continued rapidly, in a firmer voice. "It seems to me you don't think enough about what his death meant for the people of La Bandera or to the Chilean church. And even more worrisome to me, you don't seem concerned about the infidelity involved here. Those traditional attitudes of contrition such as acknowledging sin, asking forgiveness, doing penance, resolving not to sin again. Instead, you pine away for Alfredo with admirable sentimentality and deliver political ultimatums on revolution and socialism."

Meg could feel the tears of anger pricking her eyes. How could this woman who had rocked her in her arms after she heard her tragic story, how could her best friend be so cruel?

"If there was one person I wanted to talk to about Alfredo, it was you. If there was one person I wanted Alfredo to meet, it was you," Meg cried shrilly. She knew she was pleading. "Over and over again I imagined the day when I could say, 'Alfredo, dearest, this is my very best, my dearest friend, Theo. Theo, dear, meet my lovely Alfredo. Even if it was breaking my vow, I thought you'd be so happy because I had experienced this great love in my life."

"Why would you ever think that?" Theo said angrily. "You're supposed to already have a great love in your life. You're vowed to Christ, remember?" Compassion then returned to her voice. "Ah, Meggie, it's the same old dilemma. I stand for the Sisters of Charity, remember? I'm your family, your community—and you sometimes so easily forget that you're wedded to this family. I can understand what happened in Chile, and I can offer you a shoulder to cry on when the memories become too raw, but I simply can't rejoice in your relationship with Alfredo. In the name of all your Sisters, I must call on you to again be faithful to your religious vows. Come back to us, Meggie," she said gently, searching her companion's eyes.

Meg looked incredulously at Theo. "Are you sure you're not just pain jealous, Sister?" Meg asked in a low, quivering voice.

Theo winced at the question, but remained silent for a long moment. "Perhaps I am, Meggins. Perhaps I am," she finally responded. "Jealous for myself, jealous for the Sisters of Charity, jealous for the people of El Salvador. We want you for ourselves, Meg. We want the wonderful you we commissioned six years ago to serve the poor in Latin America. We want your vision, your enthusiasm, your creativity, your undivided heart."

Now it was Meg who stared out at the sea as it rolled in closer and closer to where the two nuns lay in the sand. It was so much easier to love a flesh-and-blood man than an absent God, she thought bitterly. She had to admit that she'd pushed the transgression of her vow of chastity to the back of her mind and let herself bask in the wonder of being loved by so great a man as Alfredo. Maybe they would have wrestled more intensely with their commitments to celibacy if the times hadn't been so crazy, if Alfredo hadn't gone into hiding and then been killed. Maybe after a while, their passion would have subsided. But as it was, she'd never know. And now, here was Theo, calling her back to the roots of her commitment. Calling her to a remorse she was reluctant to own. And why was that? Because it had felt so good to be loved—and to be able to boast about it, especially to Theo?

A familiar voice interrupted her thoughts.

"Hey, you two beach bums, time for Christmas dinner!"

It was Mum. She was bouncing down the beach toward them, decked out in her bright red kimono and her broad-rimmed straw hat—her Queen Mother look. "Come on now," she huffed as she reached the spot where the two nuns were sunning themselves. "Get out of those swimming togs and put on something a little more proper so you don't scandalize the Fathers. We have a veritable banquet awaiting us."

The old nun took in the strained look on the younger women's faces. "Hmm, it seems I'm interrupting something?"

"No, no, Mum. Just a bit of reminiscing," Meg grumbled as she reluctantly stood up. "A bit of stock-taking."

"Well, that's not such a bad exercise at the end of another year—a year that's been especially full for you, Meg," she said as she searched her young companion's eyes.

"Not a bad exercise at all," Meg agreed, looking at Theo who had stood up and was folding her towel.

"Just think about what I've said," Theo told Meg in a low voice. "I hope I haven't been too hard on you, but it needed to be aired." Then, in a louder voice, she said, "Come on, now, I'll race you back to the house. Let's see if I can still leave you in the dust, like I could back at the Novitiate. Here, Mum, take my book and my glasses and hold our towels." And the two women set off at a clip down the beach, leaving their elderly companion to walk back alone weighed down with towels and Agatha Christie.

***

Two hours later, the Aguilares team sat lazily on the retreat house veranda watching the sun slowly sink down over the bay. By El Salvador standards, the meal had been a banquet—the chicken such a treat after so many meals of beans and rice. And Queen Mum had outdone herself with that apple pie. Not exactly what her mother and brothers would be eating back in Pennsylvania, but it would do, it would certainly do.

Ervi had produced his guitar and began leading them in some of Salvador's favorite Christmas carols.

She was getting to know the seminarians—and to genuinely like and admire them. They were no longer just carbon copies of their mentor. Ervi was dreamy, soft, and pliable. He was the parish's self-appointed sacristan and loved to lay out the Mass vestments for Rutilio, or change the altar cloths according to the seasons—purple for Advent and Lent, gold for Christmas and Easter, green for the long Pentecost season. He seemed to live inside the parish church. He was also the organist, and he conducted the church choir, which was achieving some well-deserved acclaim around the capital.

"Oh, sure, I like to play the guitar, and the guitar's the instrument of tent people like us," Ervi told her. "But the organ—ah-h, now, her music becomes the voice of God!"

He was best friends with Pablo, who could pass for a slimmer version of a Japanese sumo wrestler. Dark and intense, he would expound to anyone within earshot about the history of labor law in El Salvador and the importance of the rural cooperative movement. Meg suspected that his political passion kept his sexual passion in check.

Ervi and Pablo balanced each other out. If the culture wasn't so homophobic, they might one day discover they were gay—and that they were in love.

Ricardo. The team's scribe. He was taller than most Salvadorans—tall and wiry and nearsighted. With a last name like Cortés, he had to have a Spanish ancestor floating around in his gene pool. Now there would be a record of whatever happened to Rutilio and the pastoral efforts of the Aguilares parish. Ricardo was faithfully tracking and recording the growing roster of human right abuse—and taking photos. Molly could give him some pointers, after working as the documentalist at the Chilean church's human rights office for these past two years. She made a mental note to give him Molly's address.

Carlos had become her favorite. Maybe it was because he had curly hair and wasn't so in awe of the *compañera* from Chile as the rest of them were. Hyperkinetic, he was everywhere at once. He was the parish youth director and pied piper to Aguilares' street kids. He could coax a sullen boy or a timid girl into just about anything—a folk-singing group, a play for Mother's Day, an outing to visit rural neighbors, or raffles for Walter, who needed a wheelchair because of his paralysis, or for Beti, who needed a notebook for school. This exuberant, large-hearted, laughing seminarian would one day be a bishop, Meg would bet on that.

"Meg, a special song by Victor Jara for you and for all the Chilean *compañeros*," Ervi called out. He then launched into Jara's well-known love song, "Te acuerdo, Amanda." The seminarian sang the plaintive song well. Yet how strange to hear it sung in Salvadoran Spanish, instead of the familiar Chilean lilt. How moving that the love song between two factory workers had such universal appeal—especially to these young seminarians, would-be revolutionaries that they were. As Meg listened again to the tragic tale of Amanda and her lost lover, the faces of Alfredo, *Madre* Rosa, José, Molly, and so many of the others from La Bandera floated before her eyes. She was still smarting from Theo's sermon down on the beach. Well, one thing Theo was dead wrong about was her lack of concern and love for the folks back in La Bandera. She wondered how the community had celebrated this Christmas, how they were coping with the constant vigilance, who else had been dragged out of their homes and taken off by the secret police for questioning.

Again she wondered if she had made the right decision in coming to El Salvador.

She was so deep in her own thoughts she didn't realize that Ervi had stopped singing. She looked up to see them all staring at her. Mum heaved herself up from the chaise lounge she'd been stretched out on and walked over to Meg. She put her arm around her and handed her a Kleenex.

"That song brings back lots of memories, doesn't it, dear?"

Meg looked down at the Kleenex and realized she was crying. "Oh, I'm sorry," she mumbled, blushing. ""It's just that, well, that particular song was such a favorite of ours. And… and I guess you know, we can't sing it anymore. All songs by Victor Jara have been banned." She returned Mum's sympathetic smile and then looked around at Rutilio, Theo, and the seminarians sitting on the veranda. There was an awkward silence.

Finally, Rutilio got up from his chair and stretched. "Uff,

I'm stuffed. How about a walk along the beach, Meg? Come on, it will be good for your digestion." He took the somewhat reluctant woman by the arm and led her down the veranda steps toward the sea. They strolled along the beach in silence. The water was rougher now. It was high tide, and the bay was covered with whitecaps skipping their way toward shore. Above, the sky was rolling from lighter to darker shades of gray blue on its journey toward blackness. All was still, except for the sea's gentle, rhythmic groaning.

"I met Alfredo Ahumada many years ago, when I was taking a course in pastoral theology at Riobamba, Ecuador," Rutilio said quietly. "We spent a lively weekend sharing pastoral insights. He was a remarkable man, so full of enthusiasm and zeal for what might be possible in Chile." Rutilio paused a moment, then went on. "I know he was a dear friend of yours, Meg. Theo's told me you worked in his parish in Santiago—and that you were very close to him. I share your sense of loss at his brutal death. He joins the growing river of Latin America's martyrs."

Meg slowed her pace and turned toward Rutilio. "Yes," she murmured softly. "He was my dear, dear friend."

She could have kicked Theo for telling the priest about Alfredo. She knew she'd never share what Alfredo had meant to her with Rutilio. He was too much the cleric, too much the plodding pastor to be able to understand Alfredo's political commitment—and his love for the Dark Lady in his life.

"But of course I hope we will also become good friends," she said as lightly as she could. "I'm very impressed by what you and your team have done in forming such solid Christian communities among the *campesinos*. What's your secret? How do you have such a knack with these rural people?" Meg knew the priest was a top-notch theologian and had studied in Europe. Before becoming pastor of Aguilares, he had been the rector of the Jesuit university in San Salvador.

Rutilio threw back his head and laughed. "Because, in spite of all my theology degrees, I'm from pure Salvadoran peasant stock."

Taking in Meg's look of disbelief, Rutilio warmed to his story. "Didn't you know that I was born in Paisnal, where you and Carlos went yesterday to celebrate the Christmas liturgy? The chapel was probably crawling with all my cousins, aunts, and uncles. And I would be there still, working in the sugarcane fields, if it hadn't been for one of those legendary Jesuit missionaries who periodically came through the village. Well, this poor missionary—he's dead now, God rest his soul—was followed around from dawn to dusk by an eager ragamuffin of a boy who begged the priest to take him with him to be his permanent altar boy." He chuckled softly to himself. "I guess that old Jesuit must have seen something in the little ragamuffin, because he eventually arranged for the boy to go to the capital and study in the minor seminary there. Needless to say, that ragged kid stands before you right now."

"Well, I'll be darned," Meg whistled, astonished. "We used to hear stories like yours from the missionaries who preached at Sunday Mass once a year back in Pennsylvania!"

"I went into the seminary at the age of thirteen. I'm forty-seven now. Over thirty years in the Jesuits has certainly left its mark. But I hope I still understand my people and never become so much of a theologian that I forget where I come from."

They had reached that point on the bay where the sand gradually ebbs into the rocks that extend into the sea. It was dark now, except for the first faint stars glowing on the horizon. They turned and began retracing their steps toward the faint light that signaled the retreat house in the distance.

"And what about you, Meg? How did you end up a nun and a Latin American missionary?"

"Oh, the nun story is typical of hundreds of Catholic girls who grew up in good, solid Irish-American families in the Midwest during the 1950s. I probably couldn't help but become a nun. My dad used to gather the family around the kitchen table for the rosary every night. At the end of the last decade, he would always ask the Blessed Mother to bless our family with a vocation to the priesthood—I have two brothers, you see."

"Possible Jesuits? Even in the Midwest?"

"I'm afraid not. Dad died when I was fourteen and Micky and Tommy were twelve and eleven. My mother still managed to send us to Catholic schools. Even though my brothers were taught by none other than the Jesuits, Rutilio, it didn't seem to take." Meg cuffed her companion playfully on the arm, but he didn't seem to get the joke. Meg sighed. Maybe she hadn't put it right in Spanish. But on second guess, perhaps Rutilio just didn't have much of a sense of humor.

"On the other hand," she continued, "I was really taken by the nuns who taught me. The Sisters of Charity. One Sister— sometimes Mum reminds me of Sister Kathleen—became sort of my spiritual director and guided me toward the convent doors. She probably saw in me what that Jesuit missionary saw in you. Sister Katie just watered something that was already there."

"And what was that?" Rutilio asked.

The question caught Meg up short. Why had she entered

the convent in the first place? It had been a long time since she'd even thought about her initial motivation.

"Ah, well, to serve God more fully, I guess. Back in those days, girls of my background usually went to college for a few years, and then got married. And that was the end of their lives—or so it seemed to me at the tender age of twenty-two. A Sister, on the other hand, seemed to lead a much more adventurous life. They had each other, and from what I observed they enjoyed one another very much. Later of course, after my Novitiate years, I deepened my understanding of my vocation as a unique opportunity to know God and to dedicate myself exclusively to him through the vows."

Meg felt she hadn't done the question justice. She'd responded with the answer found in her novice manual. Mechanical. Rote. How to convey her original passion to "put on the mind of Christ" as her response to the Hound of Heaven's invitation: *Ah, fondest, blindest weakest, I am He whom thou seekest! Thou dravest love from thee, who dravest me*—one of the more poignant lines from Gerard Manley Hopkins's haunting poem. Or, *I am your reed, sweet shepherd, glad to be … breathe out your joy in me and make bright song … fill me with the soft moan of your love …* once her own love song to the Bridegroom, thanks to poets like Caryll Houselander.

It would take some more wrestling to come up with an answer that would satisfy her nowadays, give meaning to why she still stayed in religious life—even though deep down she knew she still belonged. The panic that rose in her gut at the thought of leaving convinced her of that.

A long-ago memory of Molly, Theo, and herself floated before her. The "three Musketeers" were strolling though the apple orchard at the Motherhouse one last time. The next morning they would board the plane for language studies in Cuernavaca, Mexico, and commence their new life as missionaries. She remembered how they had each solemnly promised to be faithful to their vocation in their own way. Theo pledged to "always tell each other the truth, no matter how painful." Molly promised that she would "come to know the mind of God." And what had she promised? Ah yes, she'd sworn "to live fiercely a life of desire." When Molly asked her where such a pledge came from, she told her friends that she had had a strange dream the night before: She was at the end of her life, old and wizened, and was strolling through a garden, where she met Christ, who was also old and wizened. "Did you find what you wanted?" he asked.

"Yes, I have found myself to be one of the earth's beloved."

"And how did you find this out?"

"Through desiring—always." Strange that she remembered that dream now, walking with this man she hardly knew.

Rutilio was waiting for her to continue. "As far as the second question, why did I become a missionary to Latin America," she hurried on. "Well, you know recent church history better than I do. Maybe it had something to do with Pope John XXIII's call to American religious communities to go to Latin America and 're-evangelize' the continent."

"Ah, of course, the famous invasion of foreign priests and Sisters to the slums of Latin America." She could feel Rutilio smiling.

"Right, well, our community jumped on the bandwagon very early on in the sixties and began sending Sisters to what became known as our 'Sister continent.' Out of our class, Molly Ryan and myself were sent to Chile, and of course Theo was sent to El Salvador—all in response to Pope John's initiative."

"I know from Theo and Sister Bernadette that you really had to leave Chile because of the growing repression there, but why did you decide to come to El Salvador?"

"That's easy," Meg blurted. "Because Theo's here." She blushed. Hell, that wasn't the answer she should be giving to the head of the team to which she now belonged. "And… and because I thought I could be of service to the people of El Salvador, maybe even use some of the organizing and analytical skills I learned in Chile with the grassroots Christian communities here," she added. Meg quickened her pace with a "My heavens, I think it's getting pretty late." She never liked giving her curriculum vitae; it made her uncomfortable. But Rutilio wasn't letting her off the hook just yet.

"Was your father's death unexpected?"

Again, the priest's question caught her off guard.

"Yes, very. His truck jackknifed across the Pennsylvania turnpike in a terrible blizzard in the winter of 1955—twenty years ago last month."

It had been a long time since she'd revisited her family's trauma. Only her mother and she knew that her father had been drinking heavily before the accident. The autopsy reports couldn't hide the high alcohol levels present in his bloodstream. They'd managed to keep it out of the papers, but there was no denying that her father had died of the Irish curse.

"My mother was a real trooper, though. She went back to teaching and sent us three kids through school. In fact, she's still teaching back in Pittsburgh, even though she's almost seventy. She's turned into a crusty old schoolmarm."

Her mother, her brothers. Had she been running away from them all these years, refusing to shoulder the realities of her family and the ordinary life of small town Middle America? Refusing to take her father's place, or deal with the family's alcoholic gene? Did her brothers drink? She didn't even know; they'd grown up without their sister around. And how to deal with her mother's remorsefulness, her resentment? Her mother's Christmas letter once again asked if she had failed her daughter in some way.

Her mom had failed herself somehow, Meg mused as she walked along beside Rutilio. She'd settled for less. It was written in the way she stood with her shoulders hunched in—to protect what? Her bosom? Her heart? She never remarried, but always remained the long-suffering widow. Why did her mother resent Meg, her only daughter? Maybe it was she who should have become a nun!

These thoughts haunted her more than she would like to admit, especially to the man walking silently beside her. Determined to change the subject, Meg asked, "Are your parents still living, Rutilio?"

"No. They've been dead for many years now. My mother died in childbirth after my youngest sister, Leticia, was born. My father died about the time your dad did. His lungs just gave out. I think he probably had advanced tuberculosis."

"Both your parents died of sicknesses related to poverty, then. That would make a radical out of anyone."

Rutilio slowed down. "I know I have a reputation for being a radical priest, Meg. The landowners in Aguilares are constantly telling the archbishop that I'm igniting subversive sentiment among the *campesinos* and encouraging them to join the peasant union. But no matter what they say to the contrary, I'm not preaching political messages—only the Gospel. The problem is that the landowners have never understood the Gospel's radicalism."

The priest caught his breath and continued with a vehemence that startled Meg. "You don't know our history, Sister. The landowners of this country are ruthless. The original sin that combines deep despair and apathy on the part the *campesinos* with the vengeful hatred of El Salvador's ruling class forestalls any *rapprochement*. This goes all the way back to the Spanish conquest of a land populated with the Nahuatl, or the Pilpils, as we call our original people. Only in light of that history does the cruelty, the greed, the lawlessness, the racism, and the disregard for human life of our ruling class make sense. They have such an entrenched contempt for the majority of us, descendants of our native population, that they consider us inferior human beings. We exist only to work for them, to serve them."

Rutilio's dark complexion had turned the color of molten earth. He was breathing heavily.

"I-I sense you have suffered very much *en tu propio cuerpo*, all this distain."

"Si, Madre, si." He stopped walking and turned toward her. He put his hand on his heart and took several deep breaths. In a few moments he was calmer, more himself.

"I surprise myself by such an outpouring," he said almost sheepishly. "You've shared something of your story. Would you like to hear some of mine?"

"You know I would—and you also know that, like Theo, I would hold that story in my heart."

"It is so different from yours—so, so different—but with

Theo and Sister Bernadette, I have learned to trust you *gringa* Sisters."

Meg said nothing. They had stopped walking and were standing together looking out at the darkening sea.

"Let's sit down on the sand a moment," he said as he pulled her down next to him. His gaze never left the horizon.

"I need to go back to my *abuelo*, my father's father, to begin. What we call *La Matanza* was written in his bones. You've read about this—the *campesino* uprising in 1932 led by our revolutionary hero, Farabundo Marti. We wanted our land back. But the uprising was brutally crushed. Thirty thousand of us were killed. Also killed was our spirit, our culture, our Nahuatl language, our songs, our traditional dress. *El abuelo* lost all seven of his brothers during *La Matanza*. And he didn't want to lose anyone else. He joined the mass of defeated, subservient peasants and taught his children to be that way too. My father grew up as a *peon* on the large sugar plantation belonging to the Alaya dynasty. Don Fermín was not only his *patron*, but a righteous god who must be obeyed in all matters. When I ponder my father's life with hindsight, I see he could not have been other than who he was—a man traumatized by the fear that if he did not obey, he would be slaughtered just like his uncles. My father would complain *con un chorro de quejas* against Fermin Alaya. At home, around our modest table, all he did was complain! But he never did anything about anything. He was—how do you say it—a milquetoast, a coward. And I-I was ashamed of him." Rutilio rested his head on his knees for a moment. Meg thought he might be trying to hold back his tears. But then he went on.

"My mother worked for Doña Elena, Fermin's *señora*. That must have been hard for him, to see his wife as a servant to this dynasty. And we know that any servant is also sexual fair game for the *patron*. My father never said anything, but I suppose that was also part of the humiliation he suffered. His wife, with whom he had six children, had been used by Fernín as so much chaff.

"I grew up playing with Don Fermin's children by Doña Elena. Ernesto and Lucho, his legitimate sons. They used to taunt me—*tu papá es un maricon*—your dad has no balls! And I would fight them until all three of us would end up crying in my mother's arms. '*Basta, ya, muchachos, basta*,' she would scold.

"Yet a strange thing happened. Ernesto and Lucho, my playmates, became my friends. Ernesto and I were always in a contest for one-upmanship: who could jump the farthest across the river, who could prove to be the best *adelantero* in our soccer games, who could get the better grades at the sugar plantation school owned by Don Fermín. I started to think we were best friends. Lucho, on the other hand, was always a bit slow. When he was a small child, he fell off a tractor while riding with his father. He must have fallen on his head, because Lucho is somewhat odd. And he has a bad limp from the fall. I hate to admit it, but I sort of used Lucho to ingratiate myself to Ernesto, who was somehow grateful I still liked him even though he had a retarded brother. And I really did feel sorry for Luchito and used to take him toy animals my own father whittled for me. These small gifts created a strange bond between us. I think Lucho has become rather famous for his whittling now.

"One day, 'out of the blue,' as you say, Doña Elena discovered that Ernesto thought of me as his best friend. This could not be. This crossed defined class lines. She must have talked with Don Fermín and together they devised a plan to humiliate me. *Querida Madre Meg*, I am not going to tell you what they did to me, what acts I had to perform to show that I was a servant, a mere *peon*—

never a friend to Ernesto. They are too raw to recount. Worst of all, Ernesto also began treating me like *un indio de mierda*. But instead of terrorizing me like they did my grandfather and father before me, the Alayas made me angry. That righteous anger is the motivation for my current pastoral work."

Meg took a deep breath and locked her arm through Rutilio's. He was shaking.

"*Calmáte, calmáte, amigo*. Raw memories, these."

"Yes. More than the theological arguments for what we are trying to do with the communities of Aguijares, there are the psychological ones—a kind of retribution."

Meg continued to hold Rutilio's arm. She was at a loss for words.

Both of them carried deep wounds from the past.

They continued to listen to the waves beat in upon the shore, carrying a balm and a strength they hadn't known they needed.

"We'd better be getting back," Meg said reluctantly.

Rutilio shook his head vigorously as if to shed a cloud of memory dust.

"Yes. Let's go. And let's leave the past to rest in peace and get on with our own lives, our own commitments."

They got up slowly and began walking back toward the retreat house. As they walked toward the Colman lamp that swayed like a tenuous beacon in the distance, Meg could feel Rutilio's silhouette through the darkness. She was aware that they had crossed a threshold into friendship.

They were nearing the Retreat Center. The singing floated out from the veranda to where they were standing. The music was a good deal livelier than when they had started out on their walk. "I've a hunch they've cracked out the rum and Coke," Meg said. "Let's get going or we'll miss our share of Christmas cheer."

Rutilio held back. They hovered for a moment in the flickering shadow cast by the lamp swaying back and forth on the veranda.

"I want to tell you something," he said somewhat formally. He took a surprised Meg by the shoulders and looked her squarely in the face. "I know you would rather be in Chile. But I'm glad you're here with us now. Your presence makes the days sweeter somehow—more hopeful. And I... just want to thank you, in the name of my people, for being here with us."

He gave Meg a little cuff on the chin. "Merry Christmas, *compañera.*"

Then he bounded up the veranda steps and helped himself to a tall glass of whatever was in the pitcher Queen Mum was just setting down on the table.

Chapter 4

February 1976

Aguilares, El Salvador

Dear Aunt Kay,

So you've decided to take on all the "pagan babies" in El Salvador too! I gave the money to the new farm workers' union starting up here in Aguilares. The leaders were overjoyed that even the Japanese are supporting their efforts to push for land reform!

I've been here for four months now. The country is terribly impoverished compared to Chile. Most of the land is in the hands of fourteen wealthy families who own El Salvador's coffee and cotton plantations. When they are not working for the wealthy growers, the campesinos must pay exorbitant prices to rent a small piece of land to grow the corn and beans they need to feed their families. It's so unfair!

Compared to the folks back in La Bandera, the

Salvadorans seem to me to be almost childlike, so innocent. All their energy goes into surviving from one day to the next, leaving little time to organize. And when they do organize or stage a land takeover, they are massacred by a group of thugs belonging to ORDEN, a paramilitary outfit many say is orchestrated by the military government. Oh, Aunt Kay, what have I gotten myself into this time? I've been absolutely appalled at the ruthlessness of the political violence here. In some ways it seems worse than in Chile. There it is selective; here it seems simply part of the air we breathe.

But if political organization is far from reaching the levels I witnessed among my Chileans, another way of organizing is taking place that is quite amazing. There are these so-called comunidades de base, or grassroots Christian communities springing up in every town and village throughout this tiny country. I'm still a bit skeptical about this phenomenon, because it seems so utopian to me. But the truth of it is—and I've been to their meetings and witnessed it with my own eyes—these illiterate campesinos, by reflecting on the Scriptures, find in God's word the strength they need to strategize about how to bring about God's kingdom on earth, which includes a more just system of land distribution.

The good news is that I am again living and working with two old friends who are also Sisters of Charity. You'll remember my classmate Theo, I'm sure. She was the nun who came with me when we visited you in New York back in 1969. You two really seemed to hit it off. She sends you greetings. My other coworker is Sister Bernadette, whom we affectionately call "Queen Mum." She was Theo's and my novice mistress and is a veritable reader of souls. But she's older now and about to retire to the Motherhouse in a year or so.

In your letter you say you can't understand why I didn't come home after Chile. How can I explain, Aunt Kay? Home gradually became all the people I worked with in La Bandera. Hopefully home will one day be this podunk town of Aguilares. I can't face the thought of returning to the United States, where everything runs so smoothly, but where there's no real life. Everything seems so plastic up there. Here, you see, even though there is so much oppression and poverty and violence, I feel so alive, so much a part of something bigger than simply Meg Carney from Pennsylvania.

So, no, I don't miss the snow or the Christmas lights or snuggling up in a comfy chair with a good book and a glass of wine before a warm fire. On second thought, that's not entirely true. I would have liked to celebrate the holidays with Mom and the boys—it has been so long since I've been with them. Sometimes I feel like I've run away from home. Like Uncle Joe, I couldn't take the smugness of the Midwest. Too provincial for would-be heroes like Joe and me—or maybe, in my case, it is easier to make them proud of me than letting them get to know me.

Hey, congratulations on becoming a grandmother again. Somehow though, I just can't see you being very grandmotherly—you are too exotic! And yet you must be very touched that Chuckie named both boys after their grandfathers.

I found your reflections on the links between generations thought provoking. Yes, somehow we are part of a continuum, joined through the years. We must hang onto the tails of the very young and the very old in order to understand our own centrality in the chain—and our rootedness in history. Very Japanese, that.

And of course only the Japanese aunt of a Catholic nun

would prod her niece on how she feels about not having children! Queen Mum would expect me to respond that, as a religious, we are called to be spiritual mothers to all the children and young people we work with. I'm not so sure I pull that off. I've been more like a big sister to the kids here and in Chile. I just plain enjoy their friendship, enjoy challenging them, calling forth their better selves. That gives me tremendous satisfaction—even though no direct link in your generational bonding chain. What do you Japanese do with celibates?

That's not giving you a very straightforward answer, is it? Well, if I'm honest with myself, I suppose I find my vow of chastity a burden at times. More often than I'd like to admit, I find myself daydreaming about what it would be like to be married, to have children. I am aware that I'm thirty-five, and almost through my childbearing years. I often think of Kazantzakis' **Last Temptation of Christ**—*how all Jesus wanted was to be ordinary. To marry Magdalene, have lots of children and become a fine carpenter.*

Deep down, I just want to be faithful, Aunt Kay. I'm not sure why—perhaps it has something to do with the freedom to be available. Freedom to go off to faraway places like Chile or El Salvador, freedom from anything or anyone who would hamper me from doing what I feel I need to do. I couldn't manage that if I were married and had a bunch of kids to raise, could I?

Must get to bed now. Tomorrow I'm going with Father Rutilio, the pastor of our parish here in Aguilares, to visit San Jacinto, the most remote of our little villages. It is supposed to be quite well-organized, thanks to local leadership.

Thanks again for your long letter. I so appreciate your honesty, concern, and love which comes shining through every page.

Love,

Meg

Rutilio and Meg started out before sunrise on the five-hour jeep ride to San Jacinto.

The village lay deep in the mountains. Beyond stretched the vast, sparsely populated department of Chalatenango, where, Meg had heard, the *campesinos* were even more impoverished than their Aguilares compatriots.

For the past three hours, they had been inching their way up the gutted-out road. At times, the landscape was so lush with vegetation that Meg thought she had been transported to the Amazon. But with closer observation, she saw that the soil was a hard clay and probably not very fertile. Scratch a little in most of El Salvador's earth, and you hit volcanic rock.

Finally Rutilio pulled over to eat their picnic lunch. Meg crawled out of the jeep and stretched her cramped legs.

"It's a miracle anyone ever goes to San Jacinto. It feels as if we were going to the end of the world," she said as she accepted a sandwich from Rutilio. "This road must be impossible in the rainy season."

Rutilio didn't appear to be tired from driving. His white shirt and black pants were dusty, but he appeared relaxed as he attacked his sandwich with gusto. "Oh, it's really not that far in actual kilometers. It's the condition of the road," Rutilio explained. "Only recently has it been widened for vehicles. I usually go by horseback—it takes a whole day."

"Too bad I've missed my chance to be the cowgirl I always dreamed of being," Meg laughed.

"You'll have your chance yet," Rutilio assured her. "I make this trip about four times a year, and I always try to bring along our newest team member. I'll enjoy watching how you adapt to the rugged life of the *campesinos*."

There it was again. That damn paternalistic streak that grated on her so. "Don't waste any energy worrying about me, *Padre*," Meg snapped. "I didn't exactly lead the life of Mary Poppins in Chile, you know."

Rutilio was halfway into wolfing down his second chicken sandwich. "I'm sorry if I've offended you, Margarita. Believe me, I know you're one of those committed religious Sisters who stood beside many poor Chileans in their hour of darkness. No one is questioning your dedication. It's just that life in these outlying villages is pretty raw."

"I think I can take it."

Rutilio continued as if he hadn't heard her. "San Jacinto is very much in the forefront of the growing farmworkers' movement. They've organized a peasant co-op and are negotiating with the government to buy land and seeds on credit so they can farm together. That way they won't have to rent individual plots from the landowners or leave the village each year to work as hired hands on the sugar plantations down in Aguilares."

The priest allowed himself a satisfied smile. "You have to admire their guts." His face then clouded over. "The landowners aren't exactly overjoyed at this turn of events and there have been some ugly incidents."

"Like what?" Rutilio had Meg's full attention now.

Last month some men from ORDEN came at night. They set many homes on fire. One of them raped a young girl, and those who tried to help her were badly beaten. Only when we got the news and rode out to the village did we learn that they had also dragged away three of the remaining young men. They were probably forced to join the army. That is what often happens."

Meg shuddered. "Who are these thugs? Where do they come from?"

"They're *campesinos*, just like those they terrorize. Unemployed peasants who've been given a horse and a gun and a cause. They've been brainwashed into believing that all efforts at organizing are subversive, unpatriotic and instigated by the Soviet Union."

"Maybe we should also be working with them; maybe they need to see what is really happening to their fellow *campesinos*. Sometimes people can be so blind."

"Ervi and Pablo would go along with you. They don't want their country to disintegrate into civil war. They argue that the ORDEN guys are only misguided henchmen in the pay of the wealthy who need to be challenged with the Gospel imperative to 'love one another as thyself.' Carlos, Ricardo, and I think they are naive. As you might imagine, we have some lively debates among ourselves around the rectory lunch table."

"Oh you Jesuits, always arguing about how many angels could fit on the head of a pin."

"No, *Madre*, that would be the Dominicans' theological question," he laughed. "We Jesuits are much more practical. St Ignatius was a soldier, remember? So we too go into battle to save souls—and bodies too."

Meg was suddenly enjoying herself. Nothing like a good

theological discussion. She could feel her companion relaxing; all he seemed to need was the confidence to speak his piece, as both a Jesuit and a *campesino*. She'd learned that lesson from their walk on the beach on Christmas night.

"Agreed," she said. "What I learned from my Christians for Socialism friends in Chile is that one has to take sides. There's no getting around it. Even though we still must love our enemies, it's foolish to think that there are no enemies. So we have to save the bodies and souls of the oppressed—they have to come first."

"That's why I am making this trip. The *campesinos* in San Jacinto want me to help them forge stronger ties to the national peasants' federation."

"Good for them," Meg said energetically

"What I must do first is clarify the situation. I can't directly help them in this matter of the federation," Rutilio responded, shielding his eyes from his companion.

"What?"

Meg couldn't believe her ears.

"Are you telling me that you, of all people, their hero, their prophet, the one who taught them how to read God's word as the two-edged sword that would show them the path for confronting their problems—that Rutilio Grande is not going to help them join the union?"

"Wait a minute before you call me a coward," Rutilio snapped. Beads of perspiration appeared on his forehead and his jaw began to tremble slightly.

"You don't understand. You haven't lived here long enough! The church and the union cannot be seen as linked in the eyes of the country at this time. The federation is considered subversive by both the government and the landowners—and even by some of the Catholic bishops. If they hear that Rutilio Grande is directly helping *campesinos* to join the federation, I'll be seen as being a pawn of some foreign group like the Cubans or the Sandinistas in Nicaragua and sent packing across the Honduran border. Try to understand, *Madre* Margarita! I believe in the federation—it's the *campesinos'* best hope at this time. But I'll fight to my last breath to put distance between it and the church to preserve the specific role of each. Don't you see?" He was pleading, his eyes bright filled with—could it be?—tears.

The priest had spoken with a passion that caught Meg off guard, although she was beginning to realize his veneer of formal correctness hid a heart full of emotion. She guessed he wanted some sort of confirmation for his stance. Well, she was not about to give it to him.

"No, I'm not sure I see at all, Rutilio," she said. "I see a man who is a great preacher. A man who can make poor people see that God does not sanction the oppression they are enduring. That's all well and good. You are preaching only what the popes and the Fathers of the church have proclaimed through the ages. But I also see a man who appears overly cautious, who shows the people the way, but then doesn't walk with them on their journey.

"And why is that?" she went on relentlessly. "Is it because you don't want to do anything that will compromise your standing in the church? After all, you've been rector of the seminary, so maybe after this stint at a poor parish you will have earned your points. Then maybe there's a bishop's miter awaiting you down the line if you mind your Ps and Qs. And, of course," she added sarcastically, "it wouldn't do to be labeled a 'communist' like so many of the leaders of the Christian communities are labeled, because that would certainly blemish your pedigree."

Rutilio's skin turned the color of *chicha morada*. He looked as if Meg had slapped him in the face. "You totally misunderstand me if you think I am a coward or that I fear being ostracized by the church, *Madre*," he said in a shocked voice. "Surely you cannot think that I would act from such motives!"

"Oh, I really don't think you're a climber, Rutilio," Meg said, pity creeping into her voice as she realized how stunned her companion had been by her words. "It's just that at times you seem so damn sanctimonious."

"I am, after all, merely a *campesino* from Paisnal, remember," he said coldly. "I am not Padre Alfredo Ahumada, renown Chilean theologian noted for trying to do to for Marx what Thomas Aquinas did for Aristotle. I am a humble, plodding Salvadoran, but like my race, I am also wily and stubborn. I will not hunt a jackrabbit with a machete, but I will prepare a trap for him. And I will not let the church be an instrument of the federation—that is not what she is called to do—but I will be there when my people need me. You will see. I will continue walking with them, as a man and as a priest.

"Come," he said, as he clumsily shoved the leftovers from their lunch back into the basket. "We've wasted enough time with this senseless debate. Maybe we'll pick it up after you know El Salvador better, but now we must get to San Jacinto before sunset." He jumped in the jeep and started the motor.

Even if she'd wanted to continue their conversation, it would have been impossible to be heard over the roar of the jeep. And Meg wasn't sure if she was up to this debate—she certainly had struck a chord in the priest. She guessed she'd wounded his Latin pride. She hadn't meant to hurt his feelings, but he seemed overly fussy about keeping the church and the federation apart, at least theoretically. She yawned as she made herself as comfortable as she could in the bouncing jeep as they climbed deeper and deeper into the mountains.

When they arrived at San Jacinto two hours later, the entire village came out to the plaza to welcome their guests. Don Chepe, the village leader, embraced Rutilio heartily.

Meg guessed he was about fifty. She liked the look on his lined face, weathered like the bark from an old tree.

"Welcome, Father." He took off his Cleveland Indians baseball cap and bowed, formally addressing the priest. "In the name of all the residents of San Jacinto, we thank you for coming in person in answer to our petition to help us join the federation."

"Ah, Chepe, we must talk about this matter before tomorrow's meeting," Rutilio responded as he hugged his old friend in return. Meg felt a twinge of envy as she observed the deep warmth the two men had for each other. Would she ever develop such profound friendship among these people?

Theo had told her about Don Chepe, a veritable legend among the parish team. He was considered one of their star leaders. Short and stocky with dancing black eyes, Chepe evidently could be counted on for a joke or a cock-and-bull story to keep any meeting from becoming too ethereal. At the same time, he was one of the parish's most intelligent and dynamic leaders. He couldn't get enough of the training courses the parish offered and was the first to sign up for yet another course in cooperative farming, first aid, or literacy skills.

One by one, Rutilio introduced Meg to the villagers who had formed a circle around the visitors in the plaza's dimming light. Meg guessed there must be about thirty families in all—some two hundred people, most of them children. And despite the picturesque location, Meg took in the fact that the village was just as shabby as those nearer the coast. The villagers lived in the same one-room lean-to shacks with mud floors and thatched roofing. Most were barefoot and the majority of the adults were toothless.

"Come *Padre*, come *Madre*. My wife is preparing supper for you. Then, before we retire for the night, perhaps you and I can talk, Father," Chepe said as he led his guests toward his hut on the plaza's edge.

After a heaping plate of beans, rice, and tortillas and a glass of *chicha*—apparently made especially to celebrate the pastoral team's arrival—Chepe's wife, Doña Antonia, shyly pointed out a hammock hanging in the hut's corner that Meg was to use for the night. As she groped her way back from a bathroom stop in the nearby woods, Meg was struck at how black the night was. Rutilio and Chepe had gone off somewhere for their talk, and now the village lay silent, except for the occasional whimper of a child and the faint, rhythmical snores that wrapped the night in a gentle purr.

Meg yawned, inched her way to the corner where she guessed her hammock hung, kicked off her sandals, and as quietly as she could nuzzled down into its folds, fully clothed. She fell asleep almost at once, aware that her bed smelled of corn and fresh hay and that she was getting used to sleeping in hammocks.

The next day began early in San Jacinto. Meg was half aware that Doña Antonia had risen and was scurrying quietly around during what seemed to be the middle of the night. The smell of frying cooking oil floated through the still-dark hut—there would be tortillas for breakfast.

It was the solemn round face of Olguita, Chepe and Antonia's ten-year-old daughter, peering down at her in the hammock that finally forced Meg to realize that it was time to get up.

"So are you the one on bugle call this morning?" She grinned sleepily up at her small visitor.

"My mother says breakfast is almost ready but that you're to sleep as long as you want. She says that you must be tired from yesterday's long trip."

Meg took Olguita's hand in her own. How thin the child was, noting the light-brown scars on her arm—probably the result of scabies. She looked down at the hand she held; the little girl's fingernails were cracked and the palm was as rough as any grown peasant woman's. Of course it would be. Kids as young as seven or eight spent their childhood in the fields picking cotton.

The girl was now stroking Meg's arm. "How fat and hairy you are!" Olguita said as she passed her hand gently up and down Meg's arm.

"Out of the mouths of babes… " she hooted as she swung herself out of the hammock and hugged the child. "Yes, I'm a big, fat *gringa* from the United States, but you, my little friend, are the future of El Salvador, *la tierra del Salvador*. You should be so proud of your mama and papa and your village here. They are doing brave things to make this country of yours a better place for little girls like you to live in." Her best pep talk.

Olguita, barefoot all the way up, gave Meg a wide-eyed look and nodded gravely. "Yes, I know. We all have to struggle to bring about justice and peace in our land because that's what Jesus taught, isn't that right, *Madre*?"

"Yes, *mi niña*, that's exactly what Jesus taught," Meg said softly. And she let the girl lead her to where the others had gathered for breakfast outside the hut.

Rutilio was already up, sitting on the household's one rickety chair at the end of a low wooden table that leaned up against the outer wall of the hut. He was gustily shoveling down the fried beans and bananas Dona Antonia served him, but he looked up with a gruff *buenos días* as Meg and Olguita joined him on the bench beside the chair. The priest's hair was tousled and his pants and shirt were wrinkled; Meg couldn't help seeing that, for all his Jesuit training, Rutilio did indeed come from the same stock as Chepe.

Meg dived into her own portion of beans and bananas while Don Chepe and the children hovered close by.

His breakfast finished, Rutilio told Meg what he and Chepe had decided about the day's schedule. "I'll say Mass for the community this morning and some of the children whom Chepe has prepared will make their First Communion. Then we'll reconvene in the school about four in the afternoon to talk about the federation," Rutilio informed her.

He cleared his throat and spoke in a low voice so the others couldn't hear. "Chepe and I had a long discussion about what we had talked about yesterday along the road. He understands and respects my point of view," he said without looking at Meg.

Without waiting for a response, Rutilio got up from the table and went with Chepe to get ready for Mass.

"Another cup of coffee, *Madre?*"

Doña Antonia smiled shyly at Meg.

"Yes, I would love one. Won't you sit down and join me?"

The bright morning sun flooded this corner of Chepe and Antonia's yard. In a few hours, the air would be stifling. But at this early hour it was cool and pleasant. Antonia refilled Meg's white tin cup. Then, bringing over her own cup brimming with coffee, she sank down with a heavy sigh next to the nun.

"Are you getting to like El Salvador, *Madre*?

Always the first question. Always the eagerness to know what outsiders thought of them.

"The heat takes some getting used to," Meg said, laughing. "But in general, people have been very welcoming."

"That's because you are a *Madre,* and so our people trust you."

"Your trust in us is a great honor and a great responsibility." She studied Antonia's face as the two women sipped their coffee. The wide cheekbones, the dark skin puckering around the eyes, lines crisscrossing into a patchwork of premature wrinkles.

"Besides Olga, how many other children do you have, Doña Antonia?"

"I've given birth to six, four of whom are still alive, *gracias a Dios,*" she said, making the sign of the cross. "Chepito, my eldest. Francisca, Ignacio and Olguita. I am thirty-six, old for sure. But perhaps not too old for God to again bless my womb."

Meg stared hard at Antonia. Only thirty-six! Only a year older than she was. She'd put Antonia at around fifty. Her hair, so carefully braided, was streaked with grey. Her paper-thin skeleton was covered by a mahogany flesh brittle to the touch. Her lips were cracked, and she had only a few teeth left.

"Do you and Chepe want more children?"

"*Si Dios quiere.*" She hesitated before continuing. "But I would be content as well with the children I already have. There is so little food, you see. I never know if I will have enough to feed them."

"But the land here seems quite fertile…"

"Ay, *Madre*, we don't own this land. We only rent a tiny piece of it, our *milpa*. It is just over there, only about five minutes from here. Right now we still have corn and beans and a few tomatoes. But the *milpa*, just like a woman, gets exhausted. And sometimes she can no longer give." Antonia's eyes filled with tears.

Meg reached over and patted the woman's hand. "You women seem to bear the brunt of so much of what isn't so good about your country. Do you think the farmworkers' union might be able to change things for your village? Owning your own land together, farming it together?"

"Yes, that would help solve our problems. And that is what my husband, Chepe, and Padre Rutilio want to get up and running. Such a union would mean that we could petition the government for land where we can plant and harvest together. It would give us a new way of being a people."

"And do you think the government would really give you the land?"

Antonia looked at Meg and shook her head sadly. "That's the problem with this dream. The government is not run by people who believe in us. But even worse, deep down we ourselves don't believe we deserve to own our own land. Many of us are so afraid, *Madre*. You see, we grew up believing that we were born to work for the *patron*—he is like a stern but just father. If we work for him, he will take care of us, baptize our children and take care of us when we get sick. But do *los patrones* really fulfill their promises? No. They never have. But going against them is so hard. You see, often their wives or their sisters are our godmothers, our *madrinas.*"

"But things have to change, Antonia. You are no longer children needing this father."

"I know, I know, *Madre.* Little by little we are realizing this. And our children, they will be different," she said in a determined voice.

Antonia stood up with a smile. "And now I must go off to the *milpa.* And you must have your class with the children."

Meg spent the morning with the children and noted that through Chepe's careful instruction, these scarecrow-looking kids had a very solid grasp of the life of Christ.

"And Jesus' spirit is with us still, right here in San Jacinto, helping us fight to have our own land," one little boy had explained to her while the others nodded in agreement. She noticed with amusement that in their drawings depicting their favorite scene in the life of Christ, all had Jesus looking remarkably like Rutilio Grande—even down to the white shirt and black pants.

Before she knew it, it was four o'clock and time for the meeting. Olguita, now proudly decked out in her pink dress, had stuck by her side the entire day. She took Meg by the hand and led her across the plaza to the low cement building beside the small church. The building, which served both as a school and as a meeting hall, was the community's pride and joy. It had been painstakingly built by the villagers over the past five years. But San Jacinto was still waiting for the government to send them a teacher.

The whole community had gathered for this afternoon's

meeting. Meg still found it difficult to accept the fact that the men sat on one side of the room and the women and children on the other. She noted that the men had left their machetes at home and appeared in clean shirts, as if they were going to Sunday Mass. The women, in their brightly colored homemade dresses, sat modestly on the benches with their perennial hankies over their knees. All were gravely attentive.

Chepe cleared his throat then began nervously:"*Hermanos, como todos saben*, we've asked Padre Rutilio to come here to help us understand how our cooperative can become part of the national *campesino* federation. He will explain the benefits that will come if we join. The federation will protect us from *los grandes señores*. But last night I had a long talk with our *compañero* Rutilio. He tells me that it would be dangerous to have our *comunidad de base* too closely associated with the federation, because the government and the landowners will say the church is getting involved in politics, that the priests are taking sides and are supporting an organization that they think is subversive."

Here Don Chepe paused to see if he was being understood. Most heads nodded in agreement.

The leader continued, "Padre Rutilio says he'd be glad to put us in contact with the federation's leaders. Probably they're his cousins from Paisnal." He gave the priest a theatrical wink. His audience laughed shyly. "*El Padre* says they will come and give us assistance on how to pressure the government for the things we need—and on how to protect ourselves against the landowners. Meanwhile, Padre Rutilio has agreed to reflect with us on why we must keep on struggling to get our lands back from the landowners. So I'll turn the meeting over now to our good friend and our pastor, Padre Rutilio Grande."

The chapel erupted in applause, and many of the men stood up clapping and smiling their toothless smiles. Meg could almost touch the expectation in the room. She looked down at her hands, somehow embarrassed to be witnessing such bare hope.

Rutilio now walked to the front of the room. "What Don Chepe says is true, my friends," the priest began. "As your pastor and your *compañero*, I am charged by God to help you in your struggle toward liberation, in your efforts to make God's kingdom more visible here in your village. A fundamental part of that struggle is reclaiming the land that is rightfully yours— because the earth belongs to all of us, not just to a few. But I am only your John the Baptist, the one who points the way. You yourselves must be the ones to put the message I bring you into practice."

The priest paused and looked out over the crowd listening so intently to his words. His eyes met Meg's and he continued. "Never think I am a coward, because I am not at your side every step of the way as you go about forging links with the peasants' federation. I believe in the federation, in our *campesinos*' right and urgent need to organize. But my role must always be pastoral; others from the community must be chosen to lead you forward as you confront your oppressors. Do you understand why this is so? Why it is so important that the church not be seen as being the motivating force behind the federation?"

Again, those present in the darkening little schoolhouse nodded solemnly.

Rutilio grinned back at them, relieved.

"Don Chepe has asked me to give you the talk I often give at the leadership training center in Aguilares on the history of the landholding patterns in El Salvador and reflect on that situation from the point of view of our Catholic social teachings. That I will be most happy to do for you, *mis amigos.*"

For the next hour, Rutilio traced El Salvador's history from the time of the ancient Pipils, the country's original inhabitants, to the present, showing the shifts in land tenure. He told of how the Pipils began to inhabit what is now El Salvador a few years before the birth of Christ. Then, the land was capable of supporting a large population—especially in the fertile highlands, where enough maize was grown to feed all. But when the Spanish arrived, they drove the Indians to the lower, less fertile coastal valleys and introduced a new concept—that land could be used for personal gain through the labor of others. The Spanish eventually wrenched the land from the Pipils and forced them to work on the large sugarcane, cotton, and coffee plantations. As time went on, the Indians' descendents became *peones* on the large haciendas, because the food they grew on the exhausted soil of their own *milpas* was not sufficient to feed their families.

"One hundred years ago, most of El Salvador was still owned and farmed communally and we were a self-sufficient people. But the conquerors from Spain needed labor. In 1880, the oligarchy, made up of the famous fourteen families, although there were many more—the Alfaros, Polomos, Regalados, Orellanas, Escalones, Prados, Meléndez, Quiñoñez, Dueñas, Sol, Calderones, Cristianis, Mezas, Alayas—names we know so well, passed laws to dispossess our *abuelos* of their land. They horded that land and created the great plantations we have to work on today. And they outlawed our right to organize, to form *campesino* unions."

Rutilio paused briefly to check to see if the villagers were following him. Meg could see that they were enraptured by the priest, taking in his every word.

"Fifty years later, in 1932, one of our own, Farabundo Martí, a charismatic young man, sounded the rallying call and sparked a massive uprising of our native people. But as we also know, the response by the military rulers and the oligarchy was what we today call *La Matanza,* the brutal slaughtering of more than thirty thousand of our people, our *abuelos.* The memory of that massacre still haunts our memories, still wakes us up screaming in the night. This is our people's great heartache."

He stopped and put his hand on his heart. One by one, others in the chapel stood up and also put their hands on their heart. No one stirred, no baby cried, no dog barked. For a moment, all was still and Meg thought she could hear the sighs of those killed a half century ago whispering through the trees. "We are here, we are always here…"

The spell lasted for about five minutes, then without any outward signal, those gathered sat back down on their benches.

Rutilio drew a huge circle on the school's chalkboard to show how the land was now divided: Over the years more than a third of all Salvadorans had become landless peasants, another half owned a few acres, but only 1.5 percent—a mere two thousand Salvadorans out of a total of four and a half million—owned large farms geared toward the production of export crops, mostly cotton and coffee.

The chart on the chalkboard visibly moved those present and many got up from their benches to have a closer look. It was dark now, but Chepe had produced a Coleman lamp that cast a dim light throughout the room.

"What you have drawn here is what I've always known in my bones, *compañero,*" exclaimed Doña Antonia, as she traced the circle's divisions with her finger. Others joined in with "yes, yes, it is what I've always sensed too." Still others spoke of how their parents and grandparents had told them of how they had once owned large, wonderfully fertile lands but had them stolen by *los grandes señores.*

In all the commotion of recalling the stories their ancestors had told them of the land's usurpation, the villagers didn't hear the men arrive until they sprang.

Meg would later try to reconstruct what had happened in some sort of logical sequence. There must have been several dozen of them, but it seemed like an entire army as the masked men burst into the schoolhouse cursing "down with commie dogs" and began shooting at random.

A bullet hit the Coleman lamp, plunging the room—and the entire village—into total darkness and pandemonium. Women and children screamed as everyone tried to escape the gunfire. The sound of running feet, of whimpering voices, both young and old, the sour smell of urine and shit. Like mice caught in a maze, the villagers splayed out of the meeting hall and into whatever hole they could find.

Through her terror, Meg was aware that Olguita had seized her hand and was guiding her toward the school's one, paneless window. How the child did it, Meg would never know, but she managed to push her new *gringa* friend up and through the window and run after her just as a shot ricocheted off the wall, a bare two inches from the window.

Then they were both running blindly away from the village, stumbling through the dark night. Bruised and perspiring, Olguita and Meg didn't stop until they reached the riverbank below the village. There they scurried into the surrounding brush, hoping they were hidden from view. Meg's heart was pumping so fast she thought she might be having a heart attack. She also realized that she was wet between her legs. She had peed her pants.

Above them, from San Jacinto, they could hear the incessant gunfire and screaming. Then more hoof beats.

Finally the village grew quiet. They began to hear other noises, the faint sound of bushes rustling, distant voices, quiet footsteps. The young girl and the woman crouched still deeper into the earth, Meg silently shielding the girl with her body. Hours went by as the two of them lay shivering in the wet grass beside the river, the damp night silence only broken by their own breathing. Gradually the sky began to gray and the lines of a shadowy landscape emerged. Yet the two continued to huddle silently together in the brush. Then suddenly, they heard a man's voice.

"Come, we must wait no longer. We must go back to the village and see what happened."

Meg's heart leapt with relief. "Rutilio," she called softly, slowly standing up from her hiding place.

Rutilio and two other men were walking cautiously toward them from further down the riverbank where, from the looks of them, they too had spent the night.

"Meg!" cried Rutilio. "Thank God you are safe. And Olguita, oh, *niña*, bless you, bless you." He ran over to them, embracing both of them in the same desperate hug. Meg took in the priest's face. His dark complexion was strangely white and splotchy.

"And *gracias a Dios* you are also safe, *compañero*," Meg burst out, returning the man's hug just as thankfully. Then she embraced Rutilio's two companions; both were boys in their teens, but as the nun looked into their faces, she gazed into the eyes of two very frightened children.

Together the five slowly climbed back up to San Jacinto. As they drew near the village's edge, they noticed the flock of buzzards hovering around the church tower. Meg swallowed down the bile rising in her throat.

"Black heralds of death," she heard Rutilio mutter to himself.

At first glance, the village appeared to be like any other sleepy hamlet in the Salvadoran countryside waking to yet another sunny day. But today the inhabitants weren't stumbling casually out of their huts to splash water on their faces or to take a morning piss. They came as disembodied ghosts, creeping out of the hiding places where they'd spent the night to slowly, wordlessly encircle the village plaza.

There, in front of the chapel, two sticks had been plunged into the ground. On the one, a pig's head was impaled; on the other, the sightless head of Don Chepe. His Cleveland Indians ball cap anointing him like a crown.

Four bodies lay motionless in the plaza's grass; one was the headless corpse of the village leader. A woman started to wail. Other women took up her cry until Meg thought her heart would stop from the grief exploding in her ears and reaching down to the pit of her stomach. She found herself numbly cradling Olguita in her arms in front of the corpses. The little girl was trembling from head to foot.

"*Papa, papito, porque te han hecho esto?*" she cried as she continued to stare at her father's head. "Why have they done this to you?"

"Why would they kill my father?" the girl sobbed, turning to Meg and searching the nun's face with her wide, dark eyes. "Why? He hasn't done anything bad."

Meg turned her own tear-stained face away from the girl. "They killed your father because they were afraid of him, the bastards," she muttered in English. "The dirty, filthy cowards."

Meg could feel nausea coming on. *Oh God, I'm going to throw up or pass out*, she thought in panic, finally aware that she was shaking as much as the girl. "Come, Olguita. Let's go find your mother. We must get away from here."

"I don't want to leave my father." She began to cry harder. "I won't leave my father."

"Hush, hush now, little one." Meg forced herself to focus on the child. She pulled Olguita to her feet. "It is your mother who needs you now," she said gently. She glanced once more at the sightless face in front of her. The flies were buzzing in and around the empty sockets.

"We can do nothing more for your father here."

As she led Olguita toward her parents' hut, Meg caught sight of Rutilio. He was sitting alone on a rock at the edge of the plaza, his head bowed as if he was praying.

The villagers spent the next few hours burying their dead and tending their wounded. Other than the four men who had been killed, two children had been felled by the assassins' bullets: a little girl, about five, and a one-year-old infant who had been playing outside the school house when the ambush occurred. The gunmen must have thought the boy would warn those inside, because he had been shot at close range in the back of the head. Miraculously, no one else had been seriously hurt.

Rutilio celebrated a hastily arranged funeral Mass out in the plaza. The priest trembled visibly as he spoke the words of consecration. "This is my body. This is my blood, which has been shed for you and for all so that sins may be forgiven." Then, his bloodshot eyes full of tears, he raised his arms toward the heavens and cried, "Father, forgive them, for they cannot know what sin they have committed! They cannot know that the blood of these martyrs will water the seeds of something that will grow into a giant mustard tree—a determination that will crush all those who do not work to make this land the land of all!"

Meg had never seen the priest so passionate or so angry.

After the funeral, Rutilio again gathered the community together in the plaza. "I know who is responsible for this," he said in a voice that sounded as if it belonged to an old man. "Only Don Fermin Alaya and his cronies could order such senseless cruelty as this. He is the largest landowner in these parts and owns the big sugar mill in Aguilares. They say he is also behind ORDEN."

He smiled bitterly. "The *patron* doesn't like the idea that you might not work in his sugar plantations during the next harvest because you are too busy working your co-op."

He paused for a long moment and toed the dirt with one foot. When at last he continued, his voice was shaking noticeably.

"I am your pastor, not your local leader. But Chepe was my dear friend, and I will take his place for the next few days. I am going to confront Don Fermin with his deed. Afterward, I'll return to San Jacinto and together we will seek the meaning of this tragedy in prayer and reflection. But know, my brothers and sisters, I am with you, the church is with you, every Salvadoran who loves justice and righteousness is with you in this moment of your crucifixion." He embraced them all, one by one, then signaled to Meg to get into the jeep.

It took them almost five hours to reach San Jacinto. They were back in Aguilares in three. Rutilio never said a word throughout the hair-raising journey down the mountainside. He let Meg out at the center of town. "Go tell the others what has happened," the priest said in a voice Meg could hardly recognize. "I am going to Don Fermín's hacienda, and then to the archbishop." He sped off, leaving her in a cloud of dust.

Meg walked the ten blocks to the parish house in a daze. She needed a cigarette badly. Just as she was opening the gate to the house, Theo rounded the corner, followed by her faithful dog, Shadow El Séptimo. She was loaded down with the notebooks and charts she used to teach first aid to her women's group.

"Hey, Meg! Aren't you still supposed to be in San Jacinto?" she called out. Then she stopped short, taking in Meg's mud-stained skirt and blouse, her white, tear-streaked face. Putting an arm around her friend's shoulder, she let out a low cry. "Good Lord, what on earth has happened?"

Meg buried her head in Theo's shoulder and began to weep. "Oh, Theo, Theo, this country is too barbaric, too brutal; it's nothing like Chile," she sobbed. "I don't think I can take it, honestly I don't. Let's go back to the States. I'll teach high school and you can work in a neighborhood clinic, okay? We can get involved in all those renewal issues the congregation and the church are debating up there: women's ordination, the celibacy question, how to minister to the gay community. What do you say? Let's just get out of this goddamn country while we still can—before it's too late."

She knew she was babbling. The image of Don Chepe's

sightless head crawling with flies would not go away. "Before they murder us, Theo, and stick our heads on a pole!"

"Meggie, Meggie. Don't you know it's already too late?" Theo said softly. "Take it easy now. We'll be okay," she said soothingly as she practically carried the weeping nun into the convent and steered her into their one and only easy chair.

Disappearing into the kitchen momentarily, Theo emerged with a half-filled bottle of whiskey and a glass.

"Here, drink this. Doctor's orders," she said, pouring a stiff drink which she pressed into Meg's trembling hands.

"Now tell me what happened."

***

Later that night, after Meg had repeated the gruesome story of the massacre to the other team members, Theo helped her now slightly drunk friend to her room and put her to bed. She stayed sitting there next to Meg waiting for her to fall asleep.

El Séptimo snored in the corner.

Just when Theo thought she had dozed off, Meg groaned softly and sat up

"What is it, Meggins?" Theo asked gently.

"My head's going around in circles—that's what," she said groggily. "We both forgot, I can't hold my liquor, remember?"

"Yeah, I do remember, now that I think about it." Theo smiled in the dark. "We've spent other nights like this, haven't we? It seems a long time ago."

"Almost ten years now since we were in the Novitiate. Can you believe it?"

Theo shook her head. The faint slashes of light that managed to slip through the blinds from the street outside bathed the two women in contrasting stripes of gray.

"We used to have those long, convoluted theological talks, remember? God's will versus the tide of history, which was actually propelling us into the future. Then you'd do your wizardry and press certain points on my head and I'd fall asleep."

"Want me to find those acupressure points now?" Theo asked, bending closer.

"No, no. If I lie back down I'll see stars—and faces of dead people."

"I'm sorry, Meg. I forgot how whiskey affects you. I should have given you a sedative instead."

"It's okay. It'll pass in a bit. It's nice to know I'll never become an alcoholic. It runs in my family, you know. Besides, it's so nice to have you here next to me—like in the old days." And she reached over and took Theo's hand in hers.

Meg played with the silver band on her friend's hand for a few minutes. "What on earth did we find to talk about hours on end during those nightly vigils back in the Novitiate?"

"Oh, we'd rehash the day, remember?" Theo laughed. "We'd talk about the different nuns, their quirks and foibles. Who we admired and who we thought was a phony. We'd share our plans for the future. How you'd be a razzle dazzle high school teacher. How I was going to be Sue Barton, inner city nurse, or Cherry Ames, jungle nurse."

"We sure never imagined we'd be working together in a banana republic on the verge of civil war."

"No, we didn't."

"Is it more than you bargained for?"

"I'd say so!"

"And if you had your druthers?"

Theo withdrew her hand from Meg's and smiled almost sheepishly. "But I haven't any choice, now, have I? This is where God plunked me, so this is where I try to be Sue and Cherry. But what about you, Meggie? Where'd you be if you had your druthers?"

Meg was silent for a long moment.

At last she leaned back on the pillow and let out a deep sigh.

"If you'd have asked me that yesterday, I would immediately have said Chile, but *sans* coup and with Alfredo still alive."

Sensing the clouded look in Theo's eyes, Meg quickly added, "Just working with him, being close to him, sharing in his magnetism and his enthusiasm, Theo. I-I'm not sure now about marrying him. I can't even imagine what it would have been like actually wed to him. Alfredo goes with Chile and La Bandera, just as Rutilio is only Rutilio if El Salvador and Aguilares are there as a backdrop. Anyway, yesterday I would have said to be working at Alfredo's side. But today, after what's happened, I… well… I just don't know."

Her voice started to tremble. "I'm not as good a nun as you are, Theo. Deep down, I'm horribly selfish and restless."

"Oh, hush, Meggie. Remember you're slightly in your cups. No crying jags now. Besides, you know that isn't true."

"No, let me admit it, so I can perhaps do something about it. You yourself said it. I'm constantly looking for perks. Forever falling in love. Forever looking for affirmation. You know,

'Mirror, mirror on the wall, am I still the fairest of them all?' If I don't see myself reflected back to me, I don't know who I am!"

"Then why don't you leave, find your mate, and marry?" Theo asked almost matter-of-factly.

Meg sat up straight in bed and gave her friend a startled look. "Leave? At this juncture? At this stage in the game? How could I ever think of leaving with the inferno of evil and oppression that is eating up this country? How can I leave after I saw an outstanding leader mutilated, his head stuck on a pole in his village's main plaza? After a ten-year-old peasant girl saved me and hid me through the night?"

"But you said just a little while ago that you wanted to go back to the States and teach high school. That El Salvador was too brutal—"

"Come on, Theo! Have some pity on me. You know that was just the initial shock. You know me better than that. Just like you, I'm in for the long haul."

Theo bent over and gave her friend a warm hug. "Oh, Meggie." She laughed sadly. "When all is said and done, despite your infidelities, I believe that you have the heart of one of God's very own. You keep on having these affairs—I suppose it will be Rutilio next—but in the end, my girl, they pass and you straggle back to Him whose ring you wear on your finger."

Meg rested her head momentarily on Theo's shoulder. "Theo-y, Theo-y, once again you're on the scene to help me wrestle with my demons," she said in a tired voice. "Sometimes I think you are terribly tough on me, but then I know you're my self-appointed guardian angel. I'm grateful, honest."

For a few moments the two women remained silent.

Finally, Meg said in a low voice, "I ask your forgiveness— and God's and the community's—for whatever wasn't quite right about my relationship with Alfredo."

Theo slowly released Meg and sat up straight in her chair. "Did you make love with him?"

Meg was caught off guard. She studied Theo's face in the dim light that slid through the blinds. "Why does it matter to you so much?"

"Did you?" Theo insisted.

Meg turned her face away from her friend's intense gaze. "It wasn't what you'd call a platonic relationship," she murmured almost inaudibly.

"What am I supposed to make of that?"

"You want specifics?" Despite the effects of the whiskey, Meg was becoming uncomfortable.

"Try me."

"Well, it wasn't exactly like what happened between Romeo and Juliet," she said lamely. She saw her friend was not going to let her off the hook, so she took a deep breath and began.

"Alfredo would generally come over to my little house in the evenings for a glass of wine. We'd talk over the day together, how the meetings had gone, what the problems in the barrio were and what could be done about them—always a lot about the political situation. One thing led to another. We'd hold hands, he'd kiss me goodnight, as is the Chilean custom, then the kisses were longer and more frequent." Meg looked over at her friend but couldn't make out her expression in the dark room.

"Well, keep going."

Meg hesitated a moment longer, then plunged on rapidly. "Well, remember I shared the house with Molly, even though we had different schedules. So we didn't have that much time alone. Still, we began to look for those moments to be alone, and when we found them, well, we were more passionate with one another, fondling and exploring each other's bodies. We never experienced complete intercourse, though," she laughed nervously. "So technically I guess I'm still a virgin."

"Why?" Theo's voice was low and gruff.

"Why?" Meg repeated, as if she hadn't understood the question.

"Yes, why?"

"I-I don't know, Theo. Maybe we wanted to save that for the future. Maybe he was afraid of getting me pregnant. It doesn't matter really. The feeling of connection and love was very deep and very mutual."

The woman beside her let out a deep sigh, and her body relaxed visibly. Then she stood up, bent down over Meg, and made the sign of the cross on her forehead.

"Forgive yourself, and if you are truly sorry for your infidelity, atonement will come on its own terms. We both know that. Meanwhile, in the name of the community, I too forgive you. As Mum would say, 'Become the Sister of Charity you were always meant to be.'"

"I don't think I have any choice now, not after today, not after all I saw..." Her eyes began to flutter.

Theo pulled the covers up. "Think maybe you can sleep now?"

"The spirit is willing, if the flesh is," Meg quipped tiredly.

"Well, give it the old college try," Theo said, adjusting the pillow. "Good night, Sister. I love you, too, you know."

"Night, Theo. Yes, I know. Thou art the best friend Meg Carney could ever have. Together we're invincible."

And she closed her eyes and tried to sleep.

Chapter 5

April 1976

San Salvador

Meg shifted her position on the straight-backed folding chair, crossed then uncrossed her legs, and looked again at her watch. The bishop had already kept them waiting a half hour.

Rutilio cleared his throat for the umpteenth time. Carlos' low, continuous whistling of the national anthem seemed to be getting on the priest's nerves

The whole Aguilares team was squeezed into the tiny parlor outside the bishop's office: Theo, Sister Bernadette, Rutilio, the four seminarians, and herself.

They all had to be there: Romero, as an auxiliary bishop of San Salvador, held jurisdiction over the parish of Aguilares. He had formally summoned them to answer some serious questions about their pastoral work.

Meg glared at Carlos who abruptly stopped his whistling and grinned back at her apologetically.

Thank you, *querido.*

It wasn't hard to guess the reason for the summons: Don Fermin Alaya had been furious at Rutilio for implicating him in the San Jacinto massacre. And maybe the priest *had* overdone it. Apparently he had stormed angrily through the gates of the Alaya hacienda raging like an Old Testament prophet.

"Fermin Alaya, your hands are soiled with the blood of innocent people. Before God, I hold you responsible for the deaths committed this day in the village of San Jacinto."

Don Fermin's henchmen finally managed to throw the raving priest off the property. Rutilio had then gone straight to the archdiocesan office in San Salvador and, unannounced, burst into a meeting the archbishop was holding with several of his vicars, including Bishop Romero. There, he poured out his story. Evidently Rutilio's disheveled hair, bloodshot eyes, and bloody clothes had scared the clerics half to death.

Old Archbishop Chavez had listened silently to Rutilio, then gone directly to the presidential palace. He refused to leave until he obtained a presidential promise to launch an immediate, nationwide investigation into the massacre. Chavez' statement to the press suggested that landowners in Aguilares might be implicated in the crime, causing a furious onslaught by El Salvador's infamous oligarchy against the church in general and Rutilio in particular. Ads began to appear in San Salvador's leading dailies warning the Catholic faithful that the church was becoming the pawn of "subversives and communists," some even accusing an "unnamed priest working in Aguilares" of being everything from a homosexual and a womanizer to an alcoholic and a cocaine addict.

Meg was sure this was what had sparked today's mandatory meeting with Romero. The bishop had a reputation for being an archconservative, although Rutilio insisted that he was a very prayerful and humble man. Shy and reserved, his deep compassion was not always visible at first blush. Rutilio had been close to Romero when the priest was rector of the Jesuit seminary in San Salvador. At that time, he once confided to Meg, Romero had been a spiritual father to him. But in recent years, they had drifted apart and the bishop had taken a dim view of his work in forming lay-directed grassroots Christian communities.

Bishop Romero walked out of his office forty minutes late.

"Please pardon the tardiness of your bishop," Romero apologized as he shook hands with each of the team members. "I'm afraid I dozed off while I was reading my breviary."

The greetings over, Romero vanished inside his office again and emerged seconds later with a folding chair and a large, worn three-ring red notebook. He squeezed the chair in between Carlos and Theo in the already crowded parlor. Waving a hand toward his tiny inner office, he said apologetically, "As you can see, my office is even smaller than this room, so I'm afraid we'll have to hold our meeting here."

No one spoke as the bishop sat down, opened the notebook and began to leaf through the contents. Romero was dressed in a black cassock, complete with the red sash of his ecclesiastical rank, but the cassock was shiny with age and the high rim of his collar was badly frayed. And his red biretta was on at a slightly crooked angle. He extracted several handwritten sheets of paper, cleared his throat, and without looking up, began to read:

"The mission of the church is to keep to the center, watchful, and in the traditional way, invite the flock toward salvation in Christ. The mission it enjoins on its priests and pastoral agents is eminently religious and transcendent—*not political,*" he stressed, raising his head and looking directly at Rutilio.

Then, for the next hour, the bishop expounded from the Fathers of the church, from papal encyclicals—both recent and from the distant past—and from the documents of the Second Vatican Council to support his vision of the church in the world.

At last, he closed his notebook, glanced around at the circle of faces in front of him, and delivered the ultimatum they all feared might come.

"From my examination of your work in the formation of so-called Christian base communities among the *campesinos* of Aguilares, I conclude that you are—however unintentionally—using your positions as pastoral agents of the Catholic church to promote certain political postures among the flock with which you work."

He cleared his throat and went on in staccato fashion. "Because this flock is almost completely composed of uneducated peasants, they revere your word as the word of the church, thus associating the church with several incipient *campesino* organizations declared illegal by the government. While the church has the right and the duty to work for social justice, it is not the church's place to become directly involved in organizing these *campesinos*. Nor is it in the church's interest to form lay-led Christian communities that are not closely supervised by proper church authorities which may become—and in fact, in your parish, probably *have* become—facades for suspect political groupings."

The bishop paused a moment then continued. "It is my wish, given the tense situation which the church in El Salvador is living through at the present time, that you discontinue all work, all preaching that has political implications. Let me be quite specific: distance yourself from the *campesino* federation. While it is not our place to judge the merits of such an organization, it is imperative that the church not be seen as one of its main supports. Second, keep close watch on the local Christian communities you have formed; remain in close contact with your lay leaders and make sure they only preach the doctrine Holy Mother Church has set down and do not use religious gatherings to discuss or promote political ideas. I have received many disturbing reports," the bishop concluded, tapping the red notebook, "that your work is much more political than pastoral. I hope that, after this meeting, I will no longer hear such reports."

He was about to stand up, but changed his mind. His fingers tapped lightly over the red notebook as if he were touching the keys of a piano.

"My dear friends," he sighed. "I know you act only out of great dedication to our people. I too share your dismay at their poverty and the seemingly endless tragedy of their lives. I too struggle with what Christ would do if he were alive in these times. But our savior was a peacemaker, not a revolutionary. So please, let me not have to call you together like this again."

Then Romero stood up and, with a gesture, indicated that the meeting was over and that they too should rise. "I'll be happy to give you my blessing," he said formally.

The Sisters and the seminarians rose automatically, but Rutilio stayed in his seat. "Excuse me, bishop, but for the record, I would just like to say that what we are doing with our people is studying the Bible. If doing that is becoming involved in politics, then, out of fidelity to the church we belong to and love so well, we must keep on being involved in political issues, because we only discuss Scriptural texts and their implications in the lives of the *campesinos* at our community meetings. Furthermore, in recent years the Latin American church has spoken again and again of its preferential option for the poor—"

Romero's face reddened. "I know perfectly well what the church teaches, Rutilio. And while it has a special love for the poor, its message is for all—its mission is to call all to salvation, including the rich." He shot the priest a piercing glance. "Including men such as Don Fermin Alaya. I want to be perfectly clear," Romero continued in a low voice. "Do not keep on working in the way you have been. You are engaged in pure politics, Rutilio! I don't want any more trouble with the government over you. And I want this newspaper campaign against the church to stop. That is all." He strode back into his office and slammed the door.

Stunned, the Aguilares team stood huddled together in the outer parlor for a few more minutes. It was Sister Bernadette who finally broke the silence. "I think we all deserve a good strong cup of coffee," she said, shooing them toward the door. "There's a cafeteria across the street. Come on, my treat."

The dejected group straggled down the steps of the archdiocesan building into the capital's central plaza. They lingered at the foot of the steps to discuss the meeting.

"Thank God he's not the archbishop," said Carlos. "We know Chavez supports our work and that Romero is just an old stick-in-the-mud when it comes to anything involving social justice or *campesino*-led Christian communities. Maybe with luck, they'll move him to Rome, where he can be secretary of some stuffy Vatican office for the rest of his life."

"He's the conservative's favorite candidate to replace Chavez when the archbishop retires next year," Ervi reminded them.

Sister Bernadette cleared her throat, clasped her hands behind her back, and rocked back and forth on her heals, just like she used to do when lecturing to the novices.

"As pastoral workers, we can't simply dismiss the bishop's point of view. We may not agree with it, but his point of view is a valid reading of the Scriptures and church teaching," she pointed out. "And did you all notice how he came to the meeting so prepared? He had taken the time to collect key documents from the church Fathers and revered theologians—that's probably why he was so late."

"Aw, Mum, he just wanted to impress Rutilio," Carlos cut in. "We just witnessed another Inquisition—and it was his protégé's head that rolled."

"Well, what are we going to do? We can't abandon our support for the *campesinos'* right to form a union and fight to own their own land," said Theo. "Land reform is way overdue here in El Salvador, and there are all kinds of church documents to support that position, even though Bishop Romero doesn't seem to have those at his fingertips as readily as he has other ones."

"Even if we could rein in the *campesino* leaders, we couldn't stop the people from continuing to gather to reflect on the Bible," Pablo added.

"Well, I think we should be honest and tell our leaders about the bishop's warning and see how they respond," Rutilio said. "That's the whole sense of what the Second Vatican Council meant when it said the church is the 'people of God.' Let's have faith in that 'people of God' and their ability to follow the impulse of the Spirit. It's they, not us, who must decide what to do with Romero's warning."

"I'll vote for that," Theo said. "And, Rutilio, I was proud of the way you stood your ground with the bishop. Thanks for that."

Her words made the priest blush. "I suppose I slammed a door shut on a relationship that can never be reopened," he said. "We were once very close. I had the greatest respect for his humility, his thoughtful scholarship—and I thought he felt the same about me. But now, we seem to be on a collision course about the church's role in this rapidly polarizing society. But it is a damn shame."

Meg was surprised to see how upset Rutilio seemed to be over the bishop's repudiation of his work. As they walked toward the cafeteria at the other end of the plaza, she pulled the priest aside.

"I too was very proud of you in there, and I want you to know it," she said. "And I-I just want to apologize for my sharp words to you during our picnic on the way to San Jacinto," she stammered, looking down at the ground.

"You're anything but a coward. And you certainly aren't positioning yourself for a comfortable place in the church hierarchy," she added with a laugh, finally able to meet his gaze. "After today's outburst, I'm afraid you've burnt your bridges once and for all for a red hat."

Rutilio gave her an embarrassed grin. "Now don't go making a radical out of me. In normal times, there is more of a separation between the church and political movements. They really are two separate playing fields. But then we aren't living in normal times…"

"My friend Alfredo would have said that politics and religion can't be separated. He believed socialism would shape theology, transform the church, and even change our concept of God. But since coming here, I'm confronted with a way of working that starts from the other way around: your sense of God and what God expects of His people, to build a compassionate society. Some people would call that Marxist, but you insist that all you are doing is promoting the Gospel. Rather than socialism, you're just telling folks about the teachings of the man from Nazareth."

She smiled and added, "If he were still alive, Alfredo would argue all this with you long into the night. I'm such a poor substitute."

"No you're not, Margarita," the priest assured her energetically. "Besides, Alfredo and I already had this conversation years ago in Ecuador."

"Really? You've got to be kidding,"

"No. Remember, I told you we were together at the training center in Riobamba. Alfredo produced a bottle of your fine Chilean wine and we sparred until dawn about this whole issue."

"Who won?" Meg was dying to know how Alfredo responded to Rutilio.

"We agreed to disagree." He shrugged. "Two different countries, two different approaches."

"Did you part friends?

"We parted with great respect for one another. It was hard

not to like Alfredo, was it not, Margarita? He had great charisma and zest for life."

"He was straightforward and sincere," Meg said. Then she added quietly, "But you, too, are a man of vision." They walked along together in comradely silence.

"But come now," she said, nodding toward the others up ahead. "Let's leave it at that so there can be peace between us. There is too much violence in the air to waste our energy over which comes first, the chicken or the egg."

Rutilio's face relaxed into a broad smile. "Thanks, Margarita. I couldn't agree more."

Meg smiled back, relieved.

"The others have probably ordered their coffee by now, and if I know your seminarians, they are also indulging in heaping bowls of chocolate ice cream."

With that, she guided the priest toward Queen Mum's cafeteria. Later that evening, curled up in their one easy chair, Meg wrote a long overdue letter to Rosa, her friend and mentor in Chile.

Dear Rosa,

    I can't believe it has been a whole year since I left Chile! I try hard to hold you, Molly, A, and the people from La Bandera daily in my heart, but I've been catapulted into such a raw reality.

How to summarize all that had been happening in this country, so different from Chile?

The whole country seems to be moving toward an inevitable holocaust. We hear of yet another massacre or assassination with each passing day. At the same time, more and more young people are taking to the hills to join the guerrillas.

Our parish team has become a prime target for this stepped-up repression. At present, the landowners and their cronies in the government are mounting a vicious attack against what they term "creeping communism" in the church. They've singled out Rutilio and the Jesuit seminarians working here in Aguilares for special attention.

She described the massacre in San Jacinto, how terrified she had been as she huddled with a little girl in the bushes along the river for an entire night, how Chepe's sightless head on a pole gave her nightmares, how their team was in trouble with the bishop. On and on she wrote, long after Theo and Mum had gone to bed.

Oh Rosa, what I wouldn't do to be able to have one of those heart-to-heart talks with you! I need you to help me understand what I have gotten myself into here in El Salvador—and to see if this is really where I belong!

When I see these things I feel so scared, so in over my head. Perhaps I should have returned to the States after A's death. And yet, everybody recognizes us as nuns, and knows we are on their side. Besides, at this point, I don't think I have any choice but to go on. Just like in Chile, we are a protection for the poor. They won't kill us gringas. That would not be politically wise.

She stopped for a moment, realizing that so far, the whole letter had been about her. Time to ask about her friends back in La Bandera, she thought guiltily. Their faces were slowly receding from her mind's eye.

> *Three years now of dictatorship and repression. How are you surviving? Surely the end is in sight?*
>
> *I do miss you and will come back one day. But my place is here for the moment, if only to bear witness to both the savagery and to the miracles taking place around me.*
>
> *Tell the community of La Bandera to pray for this tiny sister nation and for their old compañera. Hugs to everyone. I miss you very much.*
>
> *Lovingly,*
>
> *Meguita*

Ten pages. Meg slowly folded the letter and stuffed it in the envelope she had addressed earlier. She held it for a moment against her breast and murmured a prayer for her mentor and her friends back in La Bandera. Tired, but somehow more at peace now that she had laid her burden on Rosa's shoulders, she got up from the chair and stretched contentedly. As she turned off the light and headed toward her own bedroom, she noticed the first frail rays of white peeking through the blinds.

It had been a long day.

Chapter 6

January 1977

Aguilares

Meg burst into the tiny convent kitchen, where Theo and Sister Bernadette were having breakfast.

"Morning, Sisters. I've got a real treat to start your day with. I just have to share this letter from my old Japanese aunt in New York."

Meg wore a sheepish smile and her face was flushed. "It's downright preposterous, if not insulting, even though she swears she loves me," Meg said, laughing as she sat down and poured herself a cup of coffee.

"The famous Aunt Kay? The one who bowled you over with her oriental wisdom and the nudes plastered all over her apartment?" Theo asked. "I didn't know you wrote to her."

"We've been writing back and forth ever since I went to

Chile. Every now and then she sends me a check for what she calls a 'pagan baby.'"

"A pagan baby?" Mum repeated. "Why, I haven't heard that expression in ages. Years ago the nuns would ask the school children to save their pennies for the missionaries in China and Japan so they could baptize a 'pagan baby.' But goodness, dear, that theology went out with the Second Vatican Council."

"I know that, Mum," Meg grinned. "And so does Aunt Kay. It's a joke between us—she's poking fun at the church."

"Is she anti-Catholic, then?" the older Sister asked.

"Oh no, she's a Catholic all right. She converted when she married my Uncle Joe. But she sort of mixes Catholicism with her own beliefs—what you get is a free thinker. Listen to this."

My dear Meg,

Your last letter has given me much to reflect on—and to worry about. Your passionate description of the unjust distribution of land ownership sent me to the library to read all I could on El Salvador. I now know about the famous "fourteen families" who control most of the country's wealth. I also read with a good deal of trepidation about the peasant uprising against the landed aristocracy in 1932 that left 30,000 dead out of a population of barely one million. From what you describe, I bet conditions are ripe for another peasant rebellion. Would it lead to another slaughter?

As I devoured all I could on your little country, I couldn't help but be reminded of my own Japanese history—the terrible oppression of the peasantry in the early part of this century. A different situation to be sure, but so many similarities. If history teaches us anything, it shows us that such a skewed system cannot continue indefinitely. So I suspect, my dear, that—yes— there could be a violent revolution in El Salvador.

"That's quite perceptive," Theo said, as she gave Séptimo a piece of her tortilla. "Your Aunt Kay really has done her homework."

"I couldn't agree more," Queen Mum added. "Your aunt knows more about El Salvador than most of our Sisters at the Motherhouse." The old nun looked intently at Meg. "She must care for you very much to have gone to all the trouble of researching the history of this tiny, out-of-the-way country."

"She loves me a lot," Meg said, blushing as she met Mum's steady gaze. "I'm not sure why exactly—we only met that one time in New York—but ever since, she's written me long and challenging letters. Maybe I'm taking the place of the daughter she never had. She rakes me over the coals on kind-of off-limits topics. Just listen to this:

I worry that you think you can play a part in such a revolution. Clearly, my dear, when a human being (someone who happens to be my beloved niece), by an act of will—rather than by accident of birth—chooses to cast her lot with a people not her own, for a cause not her own, well, I very much want to plumb her motivations.

My challenge to you is both theoretical and practical. First, what do you really hope to accomplish as a missionary, Meg? And spare me the textbook response they taught you in the convent about bringing God's love to the poor. How many missionaries did we have to endure in pre-war Japan, intent

*upon converting us to a Christianity we didn't want or need?
As if God had never revealed himself to us in equally marvelous
ways as Christ did to you Westerners! And, there in El Salvador,
isn't God already present, revealing himself as he sees fit,
through those mysterious ways that you perhaps don't yet have
the eyes to see?*

*If these words give you pause, they are meant to. Meg, dear,
I wonder if you were honest with yourself you wouldn't have to
admit that you went to Chile—and now to El Salvador—to
save yourself. From what? Perhaps from dealing with the
ordinariness of life where YOU have been born. It's a tall order
to be a Messiah in dreary old Pittsburgh, isn't it? Not much
chance of being murdered by a death squad there!*

"Ouch," Theo said and put down the piece of tortilla she was
munching on. "Hitting you below the belt there, isn't she?"

"I'll say," Meg agreed. "She's an expert at touching a raw
nerve in me—and she zeroes in on my most vulnerable spots.
There's more:

*Answer me honestly, Meg. How much of your Chile
experience can be labeled adventure seeking—or even an
unconscious desire to win a martyr's crown? Is there not buried
deep within you the secret hope of having your icon hanging
alongside Maria Goretti's or Saint Teresa's, vigil light dancing
perpetually below in silent adoration?*

*And how much of this Latin American missionary business
is linked to the problems you've avoided facing as an adult?
I know you think I harp too much on the whole question of
celibacy and motherhood. But Meg, you entered the convent
when you were scarcely out of puberty. Your mother was so*

busy raising your brothers and you that she didn't have much time to really mother you. Besides, she was Irish, just like your Uncle Joe. Believe me, I know firsthand that sexuality wasn't addressed much, except in embarrassed whispers. Have you really ever picked up where your mother left off and dealt with your own sexuality, Meg? Are you comfortable with your body? Judging from your blushes at my nudes, my guess is that you have renounced an essential aspect of what defines us as human beings without ever knowing what you've given up!

"Now my dear aunt-turned-shrink goes on to give me advice about my martyr complex and my unresolved sexual problems." Meg laughed without looking up. She now regretted sharing the letter with her companions. Mum would no doubt be scandalized; even Theo might not be too comfortable with talk of glorying in one's body. She quickly read the end of the letter:

Come back to the United States, where you belong. As just as the Chilean struggle is, as righteous as the Salvadoran struggle is, it is not YOUR struggle. Be a prophet up here if you must. It's harder, but more authentic. Come spend some time with me here in New York. Let me teach you how to do yoga in the buff, to feel that marvelous oneness of body and spirit.

I again enclose something for ransoming one of those pagan babies—or for the farm workers union. Use it as you see fit.

Your loving aunt,

Kay

"When was the last time you did yoga in the buff, Sisters?"

Meg said with a shy laugh as she folded up the letter and put it back in the envelope. She expected the two nuns to be as embarrassed by Kay's outlandish opinions as she was but was startled to see the thoughtful expressions on their faces.

"Yes, it's far out to try to imagine any one of us doing yoga nude, I'll admit," Theo said, smiling, "but your Aunt Kay appears to have an uncanny sense of the devils we all wrestle with as consecrated women and as foreign missionaries, doesn't she? She goes right to the heart of our motivation for being here—our sense of ourselves, our identity as fulfilled sexual beings. I don't think she's much off the mark."

"How will you respond to your aunt?"

By the tone of Mum's voice, Meg knew the older woman wanted a serious response.

"Well, I-I don't exactly know, Sister. There are, ah, well, so many questions within questions, aren't there?"

"How would you answer the accusation that you've come to Latin America to seek adventure, to escape the ordinary—even to be martyred?" Mum persisted.

Meg took her time pouring herself another cup of coffee before she answered.

"I think, with hindsight, that there was a lot of romanticism in my decision to go to Chile. Yes, I wanted adventure. I wanted to be involved in a world-shaking event, like Allende's socialist government. I don't deny that. And then after the military coup, when so many of my friends were being arrested and even killed, I remember thinking that it would be easier to be dead than live through all the suffering those of us left behind had to endure. But that's not exactly desiring martyrdom, is it?"

"No, it isn't, dear. Not in the least," Mum said as she leaned forward in her chair and gave her old student a piercing look. "But why did you choose to come here to Latin America instead of plugging away with the down-and-outs in Pittsburgh?"

"Jeez, Mum, you're putting me on the hot seat again, just like back in the Novitiate. Ok, you get what you see—just like you and Theo, I just couldn't resist the invitation, the challenge of working in a foreign country, a chance to experience the rawness of life with an outsider's eyes, and see if I could help in some small way, the chance to share the story of Jesus, but certainly not impose it, like so many of our Spanish predecessors evidently did. And then, once in Chile, I began working alongside Alfredo—"

"So perhaps your Chilean experience was colored by the fact that you were attracted to him?" Mum probed.

"I suppose so." Meg shifted in her chair.

"But after he was killed, you stayed on in Chile, and then, instead of going back home, you decided to come here to El Salvador. Why was that?" Queen Mum asked.

"Well, because there in La Bandera where I worked, I think I became a sister to the people I lived with. I think I really came to share the ups and downs of their lives, their joys and sorrows." Meg suddenly found herself responding passionately to the elderly nun's questioning. "I've learned that being a missionary doesn't mean converting anyone. It means believing in the people's dreams and hopes, laughing and crying with them.

"A new definition of service, but maybe a very old one, too?"

"Yeah, that's it. The greatest gift I was able to give people back in La Bandera was to believe in them. And that's what I want to do here in El Salvador too—what I've been trying to do for more than a year now. Mirror back to the kids and their beaten-down moms and machete-swaggering dads their possibilities, their greatness of heart, their beauty. Does that make any sense?"

"Indeed it does. And I think that answer may give your Japanese aunt cause to reflect," Mum said, giving Meg a long look. "We end up being converted by the people we serve, time and time again, don't we? God's good joke on us, when we thought we'd be doing the converting."

"But what about your Aunt Kay's charge that you went to Latin America to avoid dealing with your sexuality?" Theo asked.

"Oh God, Theo," Meg snapped. "You should know better than anyone how I wrestle with dear ol' Brother Ass. All my romantic sexual fantasies that haunt me day after day after day. It doesn't matter if I'm in the United States or in Chile or in Timbuktu."

"Yeah, kiddo, nobody knows that better than me," she said, giving her friend a tired wink. "It's just that I wonder if those struggles might not be symptomatic of some deeper confusion— even fear—about being lovable."

"Hey, how about shoving the Psychology 101 stuff, okay?" Meg said in an exasperated tone. She gave Theo a sharp look and nodded toward Mum. It was one thing to mull over her sexual life with her friend. It was quite another thing to have this conversation in front of their old novice mistress. "It's only 7:30 in the morning, for heaven's sake."

Mum closely followed the exchange between the two younger women. "For everything your poor mother suffered raising you three kids alone, she surely might be forgiven for not having much time to be present to you in those crucial adolescent years," she said.

"Well, you've both met her. You know how cold and proper she is—she's like that all the time, not just when she's on public display. So yeah," she shrugged impatiently as she heaped fried bananas on her plate and reached for the cream, "I probably didn't get much mothering or sex education or learn to love all of me. But I can't exactly redo my childhood at this point now, can I? The mold is set, for better or for worse," she said, then poured a generous amount of cream on her *plátanos fritos.*

"As it is for all of us, I guess," Theo said. She reached across the table and squeezed Meg's hand. "Sorry to put you through the wringer so early in the morning—blame it on Aunt Kay," she laughed. "And hey, if you don't want to take her up on those yoga lessons, tell her I'd be game my next time in the States. I could learn a lot about myself under her sharp eye."

"God doesn't ask us to be perfect, remember. He just asks us to keep trying," Mum said. "Now hush, both of you," she commanded as she reached over to turn up the radio. She never missed the morning news.

The first news flash made them instantly forget the letter from Meg's aunt.

"Bishop Oscar Arnulfo Romero, auxiliary bishop of the San Salvador archdiocese, has just been named by the Vatican to replace Archbishop Luis Chavez y Gonzalez, who is retiring for reasons of age after thirty-nine years as archbishop of San Salvador," the voice announced. "The new archbishop will be installed February 23."

Theo choked on her coffee and Queen Mum let out a rare

"Oh Lord." Meg sat with her mouth open, a spoonful of fried banana between her plate and her chin.

Theo got up, switched off the radio, and sat back down with a heavy sigh. "Well, Sisters, now we're really in for it," she grumbled. "I can just imagine how the government and the plantation owners are jumping up and down with glee over this piece of news, including Fermin Alaya. In fact, I wonder just how much pressure he put on the papal nuncio get Romero appointed."

Queen Mum pushed her breakfast plate away. "The poor people! Now they'll have an uphill battle fighting for a voice in the church as well. What a shame Archbishop Chavez had to retire. He's such a young seventy-five, alert and on top of things, and always on the side of the poor." She sighed heavily. Suddenly she seemed to be the old woman she was. "God writes straight with crooked lines," she muttered as if she needed to convince herself that He really did.

Meg also pushed her fried bananas away. "Looks as if we've all lost our appetites," she said, as she placed her dish on the floor for Séptimo.

"It's the last straw. Since the beginning of the year, I've counted forty-seven paid advertisements and twenty-three editorials against the church, most of them veiled threats against Rutilio. Pablo and Ervi have been expelled from the country on trumped-up charges of subversion, Father Rafael has been tortured, Father Guillermo tortured and expelled, and Father Mario, after being picked up by security officers, disappeared for a week—only to show up yesterday battered and with amnesia in a detention center in Guatemala. Sisters, if we are not living through a witch hunt against the church, you can take me to the loony bin."

Just then Rutilio bounded up the parish steps, slammed the screen door behind him and called out his usual "Any coffee left?"

He stopped short as he took in their gloomy faces. "*Qué pasa?*"

"Romero's just been named the new archbishop," Theo volunteered.

"Ay, *Dios mío*," he said, sighing as he sat down with a thud. Mum poured him a cup of lukewarm coffee. "Most of the diocesan priests were pushing for Bishop Rivera y Damas. Even the old archbishop was grooming him for the job." Rutilio drank his coffee in one gulp and leaned forward on his elbows.

"I guess in the end, stronger forces than ours won out in Rome."

"I wonder how much longer we'll be able to work before he throws us all out of here—us back to the Motherhouse in Ohio and you to study patristic theology in some monastery in Constantinople," Meg said. She realized that she was desperately wishing for a cigarette.

"Now, now, Meg," Rutilio chided. "Romero's a holy man. His theology is up to date. He's an avid reader. He's intellectually honest with a penchant for logical frameworks. So let's not write him off once and for all. Besides, he comes from a peasant background himself."

"But the whole country knows he's in the back pocket of the landowners," Theo wailed. "He's had conflict with almost all the progressive priests and pastoral workers—not just with us. And most damning of all, the conservatives considered him the safest choice of all the bishops."

"Oh, Sisters, don't be so hard on the poor man," soothed Queen Mum. She came over and patted the priest on the back. "You know him much better than we do, Father. Let's hope he lives up to your faith in him. It's edifying to see such loyalty to your old mentor."

Rutilio glanced up at the matronly woman and gave her a grateful smile. "You'll see, Sisters. Mark my words. Romero just hasn't had the chance to shine yet." Theo shook her head at Meg but said nothing. "But I really dropped by to see if you wanted to go with me to Apopa," Rutilio said. "All the priests and lay leaders from this part of the country are going to celebrate Mass there this afternoon. We're joining the people to protest the kidnapping of their pastor, Father Mario. It will be a tense affair. The place will be crawling with ORDEN thugs and government security forces."

"When have henchmen ever held us back from being with the people?" Queen Mum huffed.

Rutilio chuckled. "Yes, when? Well, then, let's get going."

***

Rutilio had been right. The town square in front of the Apopa church appeared to be full of government informers. It was easy to pick them out—most carried tape recorders and cameras, wore dark glasses, and smoked Marlboros. Meg noticed that several large sedans, which could only belong to some of the landowners, were also parked on the town's side streets.

She spied Don Fermin Alaya and his bodyguards sitting on the balcony at the town's main hotel overlooking the plaza. The old man tipped his hat to the Sisters as they passed below him. He was dressed in his usual white, Colombian-style *guayavera* shirt and dark pants. With his iron gray hair and austere bearing, he was very distinguished looking. Don Fermin had always treated Meg with urbane charm whenever she ran into him. He had even invited her to his home for lunch and to the beach when she had first arrived in Aguilares, but she had always refused.

"Sister, please give me a minute. I need to speak with you urgently." Don Fermin leaned over the balcony and addressed her in a formal British English.

Meg stopped and squinted up at the landowner. She met his gaze in silence.

"Please meet me after this… this circus for a cup of coffee, if you still refuse to come to my home for a meal with my wife and me. I repeat, it is urgent, Sister, if you care for the safety of your companions."

Did she detect a threat in his voice? For a moment the nun hesitated. *Love your enemies, do good to those who hate you.*

Meg was aware that Theo and Mum had stopped and were listening to the exchange. She was also conscious that people in the plaza noticed that Don Fermin had stopped the newest of the Sisters of Charity and was engaging her in conversation.

"I don't think we have anything to say to each other, *Señor* Alaya," Meg finally replied in a stony Spanish. "Perhaps at another time in the future—"

"There is not likely to be much of a future for you Sisters here if you don't stop hanging around with subversives," Fermin said. "I won't plead with you, *Madre*, but this is your last chance. I thought you were different from your companions, more intelligent, more sophisticated politically, having come from

Chile."

Now the whole plaza watched the exchange.

Meg felt the adrenalin rise in her body. It was all she could do not to run away. Although slight in build, Fermin seemed so heavy. Maybe it was his After Shave, but to her he reeked of something stale, something that turned her stomach. She focused on the diamond-studded gold band on his finger as he gripped the balcony rail.

"*Lo siento, señor*. I cannot meet with you at this time. *Buen día*."

As she walked away, she heard him say softly, "You have been warned. Good day, my dear Sister."

"Good work," Theo whispered. "He's always trying to warm up to us—especially in public. He knows everyone is watching to see whose side we are one."

"I hope we are right in refusing to meet with him," Mum added. "I know he's trying to use us, but there just might be the slightest opening for a real conversion of heart."

"He'll have to make the first move, Mum. Meanwhile, it won't hurt to pray for him," Theo said as she tried to soothe her old spiritual director. "But now, let's hurry. The Mass is about to begin."

The three nuns stationed themselves as close to the church door as possible. A large outdoor altar had been set up on a platform in front of the church for the Mass. The plaza was now jam packed with people. Besides the parishioners from Father Mario's church, many people from other parishes had come as well, including a good representation from their own Christian communities in Aguilares. Meg recognized the faces of well-known members of the *campesino* union, who were circulating flyers, calling on those present to attend a general assembly the next day.

Electricity filled in the air as the Mass began.

"Doesn't this remind you of the pageants the Romans had before they threw Christians to the lions?" Meg whispered to Theo as they stood in the hot sun. The open-air Mass had begun. There were six priests concelebrating. Rutilio was among them.

"Fermin isn't too far off in describing this as a circus, all right," Theo fretted. "I just hope there's no spark that ignites this crowd. I can feel people's tension, can't you? I sense a seething anger."

Meg shuddered but didn't reply.

The Mass moved through the ancient rituals of *Lord have mercy, Christ have mercy. Glory to God in the highest,* and then the readings from Exodus, Isaiah, Matthew—*the people have seen a great light.*

Meg's heart stood still when she saw Rutilio rise to give the homily. "Please, please be careful what you say," she prayed silently.

The priest's skin looked so much darker, clothed as he was in the liturgy's prescribed white alb. His face appeared to be chiseled in granite. He began without any introductions.

"Jesus' message was utterly clear. He taught us that we have a common father, so we are all brothers and sisters. All of us are equal. But the Bible tells us that there was a Cain who killed his brother, Abel. Cain was an aberration of God's plan. Here in this country there are groups of Cains who invoke God's name for their own murderous deeds, which is much worse than what the

135

biblical Cain did. Beware, you hypocrites with clenched teeth who call yourselves Catholics but are full of evil. You are Cains who crucify the Lord!"

Rutilio looked up pointedly at the hotel balcony and continued, "Yet even so, Christians do not hate these Cains. They are, after all, our brothers, and we invite them to seek forgiveness for all they have done and to come to this common table and partake of this Eucharist. In God's kingdom there is food for all. Christ had reason for making a supper the sign of his kingdom."

The priest's gaze roamed over his listeners. He paused for a moment, took the crowd's measure, then went on in a loud, solemn voice, "It is practically illegal to be a Christian today in our country. Because the world around us is radically based on an established disorder, before which the mere proclamation of the Gospel is subversive. I am very much afraid that soon copies of the Bible won't be able to enter our borders. We'll just get the bindings, because all the pages are subversive. I'm afraid that if Jesus of Nazareth came back tomorrow, coming down from Galilee to Judea—that is, from Chalatenango to San Salvador—I dare say he would not get as far as this town of Apopa with his preaching and actions. They would stop him outside the city and jail him there. They would accuse him of being a rabble rouser, a subversive and a revolutionary, a foreign Jew, one who was confusing the people with strange and exotic ideas contrary to democracy, that is to say, against the minority. A clan of Cains hold sway over El Salvador today! Undoubtedly, that clan would crucify Christ all over again, because they prefer a Christ of the sacristy or the cemetery, a silent Christ with a muzzle on his mouth, a Christ made to their image and likeness and according to their own selfish interests. This is not the Christ of the Gospels! This is not the young Christ who at thirty-three years of age was murdered because he preached justice, humanity's most noble cause."

Rutilio sat down and the crowd exploded in wild applause.

Then the chanting began.

Viva la Federación!

Tierra! Salarios justos! Hombres libres!

Padre Mario, presente!

It only stopped when Rutilio and the other priests finally stood up and begged for silence.

Meg didn't notice she was trembling until she grabbed onto Theo's arm and felt the other woman shaking too. Looking up, she noticed that Don Fermín and his bodyguards had disappeared from the balcony.

Later, people would say Rutilio's sermon that day sealed his fate.

Chapter 7

March 1977

Aguilares

Later, Meg would recall other times she was awakened in the middle of the night.

The night *Madre* Rosa banged on the door of her pre-fab house in La Bandera to tell her that the secret police had just come for José.

The night they came to the house back in Pittsburgh to tell her mother that her dad's truck had jackknifed across the Pennsylvania turnpike. Somehow Meg knew that her dad had been drinking.

This time when the knock came, she had been dreaming about her mother. She was a little girl again and her mother was singing to her in the rocking chair.

Baa, baa, black sheep, have you any wool?

Yes, sir; yes sir; three bags full…

Funny. It had always been her dad who sang to her as a child and rocked her to sleep at night. Theo awakened her now. Meg took one look at her white face and hollow eyes and knew that Rutilio was dead. Theo was close to fainting as she gasped out the details of the priest's death:

Killed in an ambush…

His hometown…

Along with an old man and a kid…

Rutilio had been killed late that afternoon while driving through the cane fields on his way to say Mass in El Paisnal. Ambushers had opened fire on his jeep while he was still about twenty minutes away from the village. Along with Rutilio, an old man and a teenager had been killed instantly when high-powered bullets sprayed the jeep. Several children to whom Rutilio had given a lift managed to escape and make their way on foot to the priest's hometown to tell the people that there would be no Mass there that night.

It was Saturday, March 12, 1977.

The three nuns were waiting at the church door when the ancient blue pickup truck rumbled into the parish grounds bearing the bodies of the three slain men. It was El Paisnal's only vehicle and belonged to one of Rutilio's distant cousins, who ran a poultry farm in the village.

A small crowd of parishioners had gathered in the dark church yard. Meg recognized the faces of some of their most faithful community leaders. From out of the night other jeeps began to appear in front of the church. Priests from San Salvador; Father Julio, the Jesuit provincial; the Maryknoll Sisters from

Miramonte. Meg registered that Carlos and Ricardo, their young Jesuit co-workers, had silently joined the three women on the church steps. Carlos was weeping openly.

"*Vamos*, Carlos, we must help bring the bodies into church," Ricardo said, taking charge. "Sisters, go into church and turn on all the lights. Light the Paschal candle and tell the women to bring flowers, lots of flowers. We will exalt these martyrs for all to see." He was gasping for breath, fighting to hold himself together.

The seminarians, with the help of the visiting priests, brought the bodies into the church and laid them out on tables in front of the sanctuary. Rutilio was placed between the young boy and the old man. The people from El Paisnal had washed their wounds, put clean shirts on all three, and then carefully covered them with worn but clean white sheets.

Ricardo asked the arriving mourners to wait outside for a few minutes so the team could be alone with the bodies. Meg, Theo, Mum, Carlos, and Ricardo formed a fragile semi-circle around their dead pastor.

Linking arms with each other, they wept silently together.

Meg stared at Rutilio's face. Despite the large wound in the side of his head, the priest appeared only to be resting. His brow held the slight frown he always wore, and his wide lips seemed about to mumble some impatient phrase on how it was time to get back to work.

Theo was shaking like a leaf beside her. "Oh God, Meg, he doesn't look dead. Let's just try nudging…" She put her hand on the dead man's shoulder and shook him gently, then harder, more violently. She was sobbing openly now and had given up any effort at holding in her grief. Rutilio's hand fell from the table with a thud, and his lips parted slightly.

"It's okay, it's okay," Meg murmured, taking Theo in her arms and rocking her gently back and forth as if she were a child. "Come over here and sit down now," she said as she and Mum led the distraught nun over to one of the pews.

"How can he be dead?" Theo sobbed, rocking back and forth in the pew, hugging herself. "How can we go on without Rutilio—how can I? How... can... I?"

The three nuns huddled together and wept silently.

Throughout the long night, throngs of townspeople and *campesinos* formed an unending procession past the three white-robed men. Shock, grief, and apprehension washed over their faces. What would happen to these people without their pastor? Around midnight, Archbishop Romero arrived. The crowd made way so he could gaze one last time upon this former spiritual son of his who had, in his judgment, become too involved in politics. But the man who knelt and wept before the bodies was not the same stern prelate who had reprimanded them in his office a year ago for tainting the church's teaching with politics. Romero's face was gray. He had dark circles under his bloodshot eyes. He looked thin and shabby as he knelt there in his worn, dusty cassock.

Before leaving, the archbishop stopped to speak to them.

"I deeply regret that the last time Rutilio and I saw each other, it ended in a shouting match about how to proceed pastorally," the new archbishop said sadly. "Rutilio always managed to put me on the defensive theologically, even in the old days when I lived with him at the seminary."

Then, looking into Queen Mum's eyes, he asked anxiously,

"Do you think he will forgive me, Sister?"

"Perhaps you should ask his forgiveness in your prayers, Archbishop. And I suspect he will. He loved and respected you very much." Mum's face crinkled into a smile as she took Romero by the arm and walked him to the church door.

As the older woman and the man stood silhouetted on the church steps, heads bowed as they spoke softly, Meg had the impression that it was Mum who was calling down a gentle absolution on the archbishop.

All through the rest of the long night and through the funeral the next day, Meg stayed at Theo's side. She had never seen her friend so vulnerable. Theo's love for Rutilio was so evident, so genuine—and yet so unselfish. Nothing like her love for Alfredo had been.

She herself remained stoic, lost in her own thoughts. Rutilio was murdered exactly four years and seven days after she and Rosa had been called down to the police station to claim the bloated, mangled remains of Alfredo.

Rutilio's funeral Mass was held in San Salvador's huge cathedral on the central plaza. Archbishop Romero presided over the liturgy, accompanied by the Papal Nuncio, seven bishops, and more than a hundred priests. The crowd overflowed into the public square and out onto the adjoining streets—an estimated hundred thousand poor, downtrodden people had come to pay homage to this priest who had laid down his life for them—and for the growing number of their nameless countrymen who had died or disappeared anonymously and could have no funeral of their own.

Father Mario, shaken from his ordeal in Guatemala but more feisty than ever, recalled that Rutilio had once said that in El

Salvador, "a poor priest or a poor lay leader from our community will be lied about and threatened; they'll kidnap him under the cover of darkness, and they might even kill him."

"He always knew he'd be killed," Mario told the Sisters. "It was just a matter of time."

People who attended the funeral noticed how moved the new archbishop was at Rutilio's death. Later, many would link Romero's decision to "journey with my poor people" to the priest's murder.

Romero preached the funeral homily.

"At peak moments of my life, Father Rutilio Grande was very close to me, and those gestures are never forgotten. But this is not the moment to dwell on that friendship but to gather from this death a message for all of us who remain on pilgrimage," the archbishop began.

"Rutilio's faith in the God of life called him to preach liberation, but a liberation based on faith and because it is often misunderstood even to the point of murder, Rutilio died for that faith. But like this slain priest, the church's preaching is inspired by love and rejects hatred. If his murderers are listening to my words over a radio in their hideout, we want to tell you, murderous brethren, that we love you and that we ask God's forgiveness for your hearts, because the church has no enemies. Its only enemies are those who want to declare themselves so. But the church loves them and dies like Christ, like Rutilio, saying 'Father, forgive them, they know not what they do.'"

Meg wondered if Romero was reaching out to Fermin Alaya, trying even now to invite him to reconsider his understanding of Christ's message.

A lump formed in Meg's throat as she listened to the archbishop's homily. *God love you, Rutilio. You must certainly be astounded by this huge turnout in your honor*, she thought. She looked over at her tall, lanky companion sitting beside her with her head bowed, and squeezed her hand. "This is some bash, Theo. There are so many people that they can't all fit—even in this huge medieval cathedral. Wherever he is, Rutilio must be flabbergasted by the turnout," Meg whispered. But the woman at her side only smiled wanly.

Meg sighed and let her mind wander. If only Alfredo's friends could have gathered like this for his funeral, instead of hastily burying him in Santiago's general cemetery while security police looked on menacingly to see that they didn't make a "political event" out of the ceremony.

From a corner of her mind, she heard the final blessing. "Go forth and proclaim the Good News to all creation. And know that I am with you always, even to the end of the world."

The Mass was over. The funeral procession slowly wound its way out of the central plaza, out past the slums ringing the capital, through Aguilares and the cane fields, until it came to a halt on the low hill overlooking El Paisnal, Rutilio's birthplace—and his final resting place. The three caskets were buried to applause and song.

Padre Rutilio. Presente! Ahora y siempre!

Meg, Theo, and Mum stayed until the gravediggers finished covering the three mounds, then they prayed the rosary together.

When they finally arrived exhausted on the doorstep of the parish, they found a note attached to the door. "Go back to *gringrolandia,* commie nuns—if you don't, you'll meet the same fate as your commie priest friend."

Later, Meg would recall that Aguilares was given a respite of two months. Then they struck.

***

In mid-May, the army carried out a military sweep through the whole parish, which they code-named "Operation Rutilio." Hundreds of soldiers in helicopters and armored cars combed the region; they swooped down on El Paisnal, raided the villages and hamlets in the countryside, and finally descended on the town of Aguilares itself.

At dawn on May 19, soldiers surrounded the main church in Aguilares and knocked the door down. Inside they found the Jesuit seminarians, Ricardo and Carlos, along with some thirty peasant leaders. Despite Rutilio's murder, the team had been determined to continue its work with the Christian communities and had called the leaders together for a weekend retreat to strategize about the future.

Only after she gave him two tumblers of whisky, was Meg finally able to coax the details from Carlos, who for once could not make a joke out of a single filament of the story. Based on his halting account, Meg pieced together the awful truth of what happened that morning inside the church.

The group had been caught completely off guard. Most were still in their underwear, others were wrapped in their blankets, while still others groped helplessly in the dark church for their machetes.

"Hands over your heads, *cabrones*, all of you!" shouted the lieutenant who led the squadron. "If one of you so much as lifts an eyebrow, he gets his balls shot off."

One of the *campesinos* made a dash for the rope that would sound the church bell and alert the still sleeping town, but he was shot dead on the spot by two soldiers who fired simultaneously from different corners of the church.

The group of catechists drew closer together and stared at the body of their *compañero*, whose thin bare chest grew dark with blood before their eyes. Although he said his voice cracked, Carlos stepped up to the lieutenant and demanded, "What do you want here in this house of God? You tread on consecrated ground. If you have some complaint to make, please take your men and step outside and we will discuss it there."

"Why, you arrogant little bastard," the lieutenant sneered as he grabbed Carlos by his hair and flung him to the ground. "You must be one of the Jesuits—I can tell by the way you smell. Isn't it right that you are a motherfucking Jesuit?"

When Carlos didn't answer, the officer put his foot on the young man's chest and began to stomp on him. "Answer me, *carbon!*"

"*Si,*" Carlos screamed in pain. "*Si. Soy un seminarista jesuita.*"

"That's more like it," the lieutenant said, grinning. "We like a little cooperation, a little respect. Because we are here to make a little confession this morning, aren't we, boys?"

He turned to his men, who were obviously enjoying the way their commander was taunting the young seminarian. "But today, we're going to reverse the order. It is you who are going to confession to us—not the other way around." The soldiers behind him guffawed at his bad joke.

"Let's start by getting you to confess what you all happen to be doing here holed up in this church, more than thirty well-known commie agitators who take their orders from the Jesuits and from Cuba," the officer demanded, looking around the church, which was now beginning to brighten as the first pale streaks of sunlight shone through the tiny glass panes high above the altar encircling the sanctuary.

"We have nothing to hide, so we have nothing to confess," Ricardo said quietly. The seminarian was standing next to Carlos in his underwear and was shivering. "We were conducting a retreat, *teniente*. We hold one of these weekend gatherings a few times a year to reflect together on the Bible and to plan the biblical reflections we will conduct with our communities in the coming months."

According to Carlos, the lieutenant had no interest in debating the Jesuits. His orders were to raid the parish and put the fear of God into this town. The Salvadoran army high command had determined that the headquarters of the national *campesino* federation was located in Aguilares and the parish was providing a cover for the outlawed organization.

"We know better, you little bastard. You're using this church for a front for organizing a Moscow-funded *campesino* federation. The faces here are famous all over the country. You are the leaders of this organization, boy, and don't tell me anything different. And guess what, *compañeros*," he said, smiling menacingly. "We don't like it, do we, men?"

A chorus of obscenities from behind him signaled his soldiers' agreement.

"So we want you to stop meeting," the lieutenant said with mock sweetness. "But we're basically nice guys, see. We're not going to kill you if we can help it. We're just going to tickle you a little bit to make you more careful in the future. Go to it, boys," he ordered.

With shouts of glee the soldiers descended on the helpless men huddled together in the church. They stripped them naked, beat them, and then blindfolded and handcuffed them together in a circle on the floor.

Then, with surprising precision, the soldiers began systematically destroying the church. They smashed the windows, overturned the pews and statues, tore off the altar cloth, and threw the wooden altar against the stone wall until the finely carved piece of work splintered. Lastly, they shot open the tabernacle and strew the consecrated hosts over the sacristy floor.

Once the church had evidently been vandalized to his satisfaction, the lieutenant led his men outside, where they continued their pillaging through the town on their way to "Operation Rutilio's" second objective: the parish house. The soldiers shot randomly at the still burning street lights, fired at store windows and at the town's handful of ancient cars and pickup trucks.

The soldiers' shouting and shooting aroused the three nuns. Their simple one-floor convent was right next to the parish house. By the time Meg realized that the military were headed directly for the parish, it was too late to escape.

It was the lieutenant who first found the women huddled together in a corner in Theo's room.

"And now for a little *postre*." He grinned as he strode over to where the three women stood visibly trembling.

"*Tres virgencitas*," he said as he appraised them with a critical eye. "One definitely too old, but the other two should have

149

some honey in them if the Jesuits haven't already sucked it out of them—especially this little ripe plum here," he said, roughly squeezing one of Meg's breasts.

Meg felt a rush of hot rage. Why, how could they even think of violating nuns, missionaries from the United States?

"Get your hands off of me this minute," she said, her voice as cold as she could make it. "We are consecrated religious women. This is our convent and you are trespassing. Please leave at once."

"Ay, ay, ay. The *gringa* has a temper," the lieutenant said with a smirk. "Let's see what else she has."

Before she could grasp what was happening, the lieutenant was ripping off her blouse and tearing at her bra. Meg responded instinctively by hitting the man as hard as she could across the face. She was vaguely conscious that Theo too was trying to push her aggressor away.

"*Al ataque, muchachos*," the commander snarled to the soldiers behind him as he rubbed his face where Meg's blow had landed. "Have your fun, but don't kill them."

Then he lunged at Meg, pinned her arms behind her back, and threw her to the floor. "I'm first in line for this ornery white bitch," he panted. With his one hand he held the nun's arms against the floor over her head and with the other he pulled up her blue denim skirt and tore off her panties. As he reached to unzip his pants, Meg freed one leg from under her burly captor and kicked him with all the strength she could muster. The kick winded him for a moment and he let go of Meg's arms. Instantly she had her hands around the man's thick neck, digging her thumbs as hard as she could into his jugular. She caught the briefest glimpse of surprise in the lieutenant's bulging black eyes as he grasped for breath. Then, with almost effortless ease, he broke her grip with one quick chop to her forearms.

"You damn cunt," he spat furiously, slapping her hard across the face. The blow knocked her to the floor again, but the officer didn't stop. He slapped her again and again until she started to black out.

Then suddenly she was screaming. The pain between her legs was searing, as if someone were driving a cold pick into her. Again and gain came the thrusting, the bludgeoning. She opened her eyes a minute then quickly closed them again to shut out the sight of the man smiling down at her.

"So you were a virgin, after all, *amorcita*," he grunted with delight as he fell on top of her, his lust finally spent. "Well, no more. Now you are just a *puta*, a commie whore." With that, he spat in her face.

"You can have her now, Jorgito," the commander said to one of the soldiers standing behind him. He got to his feet, but before zipping up his pants, he urinated on Meg's face. "Thirsty, *Madre*? How about a little drink?" Then he stepped back to watch his soldiers rape the nun.

Meg lost count after the soldier called Jorge raped her. They laid on top of her in what seemed to be an endless stream of brown male bodies, crushing her body with their weight, thrusting as deeply as they could inside her, biting her breasts—some of them even shoved their cocks in her mouth.

She opened her eyes once or twice through the long ordeal and was terrified at the hatred and revenge she saw in the young faces above her. Yet all the time they were laughing and grunting with pleasure as they growled obscenities at her.

She was starting to lose consciousness. "Mom, oh Mommy, help me!" she heard herself cry out. "I'm so scared!"

Then, from somewhere far away, she heard the commander's voice. "*Basta ya,* she's had enough. My orders are to scare the shit out of this brood of subversives, not finish them off. You there, waiting in line, go take your pleasure with the other one," he said, nodding to the corner where Theo lay half naked. Two soldiers pinned the lanky nun down, while a third urinated on her.

Several soldiers went over to Theo, but only one unzipped his pants, roughly spread her legs apart and entered her. Another two lazily pissed on the nun's long brown stomach.

"Mission completed," the lieutenant said, signaling those in the room toward the door. "*Vamos, muchachos.* They'll never believe us back at the base when we tell them we fucked a couple of *gringa* nuns today," he said with a satisfied laugh.

They were gone as quickly as they had come.

Meg felt a soft, wet hand on her forehead. She knew it was Theo. She opened her eyes and slowly sat up. Theo's hair was plastered with urine and her face was streaked with it too. She was naked to the waist. Her skirt had fallen back into place, but Meg could see the blood trickling down between her friend's legs.

Meg was sore all over. Her face still smarted from the nameless officer's brutal slaps, and her head was pounding. She looked down at her bare breasts; they were bruised and raw. Her skirt was still above her waist. Like Theo, there was blood between her legs and she too reeked of soldiers' piss.

The two women stared wordlessly at each other for a

long moment. Meg saw the terror, the rage, the shame in her companion's eyes behind her broken glasses and knew those eyes were a dark reflecting pool of her own outrage. What had been done to these simple peasant boys, ordinarily so respectful of nuns and priests, to make them unleash such violence against defenseless American religious women? Who had taught them to hate so deeply?

And now, she hated them. She swore to herself that she would become some dark crone mother and seek each one of her violators out at night, lure them into the hills, then cut off their penises. Their worst nightmares come true.

Suddenly they became aware of a low moan coming from the next bedroom.

"Mum!"

They found the old woman slumped in the corner of her bedroom, a sizable, open gash over her left eyebrow. She was still conscious, but in a daze.

Together they helped her to a chair. "You'll be all right, Mum," Theo said gently. "It's only a surface wound, although I think you'll need a stitch or two. In the meantime, I can patch you up."

Mum slowly blinked at the two women as she took in their appearance. "And so they will even violate women of God," she said, tears welling up in her eyes. "May the Lord have mercy on them and forgive them."

The elderly nun reached up and feebly drew the two younger Sisters into her arms. She touched her dry, cracked lips to Meg's forehead and then to Theo's. "May you be made whole," she whispered. And in the age-old gesture of atonement, Mum made the sign of the cross on each woman's head.

Then she stood up, a determined look in her eyes. "We must get you both to the hospital at once for a D and C. And, yes, I could probably use a stitch or two," she said, tentatively touching her head. "But first, we must brace ourselves for the worst, Sisters. I think we will see death and destruction once we step outside these convent walls."

***

"Operation Rutilio" lasted five days. The toll: at least fifty dead, another two hundred disappeared, more than three hundred arrested. Most of the killings took place in the countryside, out of sight of the press or outside observers.

In Aguilares, the raid served to further terrorize the people. Worse yet, a right-wing vigilante group calling itself the White Warriors' Union sprang up as the self-appointed watchdog to guarantee the purity of the church against communist infiltration. Again, their special targets were the Jesuits: Paid ads started appearing in the local newspapers warning all Jesuits to leave the country within thirty days or face summary execution. Several bombs went off at the Jesuit university in San Salvador; another exploded outside the now boarded-up church in Aguilares' central plaza.

In early June Archbishop Romero came to Aguilares to celebrate a Mass of Atonement for the desecration of the church and for the other atrocities committed during "Operation Rutilio."

He arrived early, driving up to the parish house in his ancient white Volkswagen. The parish team was holding an emergency meeting with some of the village leaders to put together a pastoral strategy that would challenge the increasingly vicious campaign against the church and their Jesuit co-workers.

As soon as Meg saw the archbishop's car stop in front of the parish, she feared the worst. "Are we about to receive another dressing down for our 'overly political' pastoral work," she muttered darkly to Carlos, who had gone with her to the door to let Romero in.

But she was mistaken. The man came in and shyly apologized for interrupting the meeting. There were new wrinkles around the prelate's mouth, and he had lost the paunch he had had as auxiliary bishop. He wore the same dusty cassock she'd always seen him in and wondered if he even had another one.

"I have come here to ask your forgiveness," he said to those gathered in the room. He impatiently refused the chair Theo offered him and sat down next to Mum on the wooden bench against the wall. "I have been mistaken in my judgment of your work. You are truly preaching the Gospel here in Aguilares and, old fool that I am, I didn't recognize the word being preached even when I heard it."

He paused, and took the measure of each member of the group, looking each directly in the eye. He continued in a solemn voice: "From now on, I promise you that I will walk with my people. I will walk with the poor, the pilgrim church, and be with you in your difficult times as well as in your joyous and sad moments."

His audience sat absolutely still for a long moment, all of them staring in disbelief at the tall, thin man sitting awkwardly on the bench in their midst. Then they started to clap—softly at first, then louder and louder.

"*Viva Monseñor Romero!*" Carlos shouted, his eyes shining

with tears.

"*Viva!*" Those present responded enthusiastically.

"*Viva el pastor de los pobres,*" Ricardo chimed in shyly. Meg could see that this young man, the most reserved of "her" seminarians, was also close to crying.

"*Viva!*"

The archbishop smiled broadly, blushing with pleasure. He stood up and thanked them. "I must go prepare for Mass now," he said. "But I hope you will allow me to visit you more regularly and reflect with you."

"*Si, Si, Monseñor!*" they all shouted in unison. "Anytime," another added. "You are always welcome among us."

During the Mass that followed, Romero praised the people "as a light on a mountain for all to see" and counseled the packed church to be firm in defending that light—and their rights—but not to harbor any hatred in their hearts against those who had committed such terrible injustices against them. He also used the occasion to present to the parish their new pastor, Padre Miguel, another Jesuit and an old friend of Rutilio's who candidly announced to the people, "No White Warriors' threat is going to drive me out of my native land."

Meg would savor the memory of that June day of the archbishop's visit for months to come from her hideaway in the hills. It was the last time she was with the team in Aguilares.

The next day, she, Theo, and Carlos left for Chaletenango and a tiny village under guerrilla control called *Dulce Nombre de María,* Sweet Name of Mary.

El Salvador
June, 1977

Dear Rosa,

I am writing this in haste so that a trusted friend leaving the country tonight can send it on to you.
Where to begin? Events have moved so fast. Rosa.
Rutilio was murdered on March 12; the autopsy showed that the bullets that killed him came from the Magnum guns issued to the security police here.

Meg went on to describe "Operation Rutilio" with all its violence. It was harder to talk about the gang rape.

Oh Rosa, Rosa, until my dying day I will never forget the hatred I saw in those young soldiers' faces as they grabbed me and mauled me with such savage glee. What on earth do I stand for to have made them act with such animal-like rage?
The whole ordeal probably only lasted about fifteen minutes, but it seemed like a lifetime. Theo and I have tried to keep the fact that we were raped a secret. Our people would be enraged—and that would only breed more violence. Even the two of us haven't talked much about what happened; there hasn't been time. And now it seems only another piece of the surreal mosaic taking shape all around us. I'm very frightened. This is suddenly very serious business. I am in over my head.
Despite the archbishop's support, our team is dispersing. It's too dangerous here in Aguilares. Theo, Carlos, and myself are going deeper into the hills into one of the so-called liberated zones. I think it is relatively safe where we are going, because it

is deep inside guerrilla territory. We have also heard that they dearly need our pastoral presence, our health, and literacy skills. Queen Mum, bless her heart, is not retiring (for the third year in a row!) but is heading over to the growing number of refugee camps along the Honduran border to work with the hundreds of Salvadorans who are now fleeing this country for their very lives. Ricardo, the one Jesuit seminarian other than Carlos who was on the team when I first came, will stay on to help the priest who has been named as pastor to replace Rutilio here at the parish.

I can't believe all this is happening, Rosa—to me or to this country. Sometimes everything gets mixed up. Chile becomes confused with El Salvador, Salvadorans have the faces I've seen in Chile. Sometimes A's face blends with Rutilio's—and when I reach out to touch my lovely Chilean compañero, I find myself looking into the eyes of my dear Salvadoran brother.

Things are so mixed up right now. As soon as they calm down, I'll write you a long, reflective letter probing the meaning of this spinning journey.

In haste—

Much love,

Meg

Chapter 8

February 1978

Dulce Nombre de María

A motley group, Meg mused as she looked around at the two dozen or so children and the smattering of adults attending class at her open-air school.

Theo, Carlos, and she had been in Dulce Nombre de María for almost eight months. She ran her school, Theo her clinic, and Carlos helped the few remaining men to oversee the village's harvesting and planting.

Meg shifted to a more comfortable position on the rock, where she sat watching the literacy lesson go on. She sighed deeply and realized she was feeling very much at home. The villagers might be a ragtag bunch, but no one could outdo them in revolutionary enthusiasm and hospitality.

Tere Gajardo, her protégé, was winding up the lesson. She was so thin in her white t-shirt and faded blue skirt. Yet even by Salvadoran standards of beauty, which established light-colored skin as the norm, Tere was outstandingly lovely. She reminded Meg of the "Mother of the Streets" icon that graced the Motherhouse entrance back in Ohio. The young, brown Madonna with her gaze a dark pool of compassion and worry as she hugged the even darker Jesus to her check.

"*Muy bien, compañeros*, let's review what we've learned today," the girl said to the group under the sycamore tree.

In age, the class went from Tere's little five-year-old brother, Miguel, to her crusty grandmother, Doña Santos who had to be well over eighty.

"What is today's key word, again?" Tere asked the class, pointing to the piece of slate that passed for a chalkboard.

"*Frente*," the group chimed in unison.

"The '*Frente*' *de Liberación Far-a- bun -di Marti*, Miguel sputtered, beaming. The *Frente* that my brother fights with!"

The other children giggled at Miguel's mistake. "It's Farabundo, not Farabundi, *tonto,*" several of them corrected.

"Farabundo, Farabundo, Farabundo," the boy corrected, his lip quivering slightly.

"That's all right, Miguelito. That's a big word. A big name. A big, important name. Can anybody remember who this Farabundo Marti was?"

"Had to be some kind of hero from the olden days," Doña Santos said, as she peered at the other members of the class through her thick reading glasses. Meg wondered how she could see anything through them, spotted as they were with Baby Luz's fingerprints.

"Nobody's called Farabundo nowadays. Why, I've never known a Farabundo. But now that I think about it, my own grandmother had a cousin named Farabundo—or maybe it was Farabundi!" The old woman winked and gave her grandson a toothless grin.

Tere laughed along with the rest of her class. "Farabundo or Farabundi, what matters is that it is the name of the *Frente* that many of our brothers and fathers and cousins are fighting with. So this man must have done something really great, like Jesus, maybe. Now, who can give me the syllabic family of 'fren'?"

"I can!" piped up María. The little girl struggled to stand up on her gimpy leg, the result of a wound she received during an air raid six months earlier. As good as Theo's ministrations had been, she couldn't provide the child with the therapy she needed after extracting the shrapnel from her wound.

"Fran, fren, frin, fron, frun," María rattled off, obviously pleased with herself.

"Muy bien, María," Tere nodded.

"And who can read this next sentence?"

"I'll go for it," said José. He was the only teenage boy present. The village's other young men had joined *los muchachos* in the hills. José had to stay behind to take care of María after his parents were killed in the same air raid that crippled his little sister. He resented having to stay with the women, but the guerrillas had assigned him the important task of delivering food to them at intervals, so José consoled himself that he was contributing to the war effort. But in his dreams he saw himself soon joining the others in the hills, a rifle slung over his shoulder.

"En... las... tierras... de... Cha-la-ten-an-go," José read

slowly. "In the lands of Chalatenango, its men and women organize to bring about a new society." Those under the tree clapped enthusiastically both for the reader and for the message.

"And this sentence?"

"I'll try." It was Paulina. Meg's heart beat with tenderness as she watched the large-breasted, matronly woman in the faded green and yellow striped dress stand up. Ordinarily Paulina would have been stout, with her round endomorphic build. But her once-robust body now sagged in places that used to be filled out—her arms, her jowls, her girth.

Paulina had become the community's undisputed leader. The war had claimed both her husband and two of her children. Three of her sons fought alongside Tere and Miguel's brother, Raul, in the hills. She still had her five smaller children with her in the village. Unofficial mother for all Dulce Nombre de María's remaining children, she saw to it that they had enough to eat, that they were relatively clean, and that they ran to the shelter on time to avoid being hit by the deadly spray that came from the air raids.

"The mortars won't get me," she was known to boast. "But on the day of victory, I'm simply gonna expire from joy." That determination was reflected in the red bow she wore in her hair.

Paulina struggled to put together the words on the slate. "Long live… the northern… war effort of… Chalatenango. Long live… this, this liberated zone… and this liberated village!" Then she added her own *¡qué viva!* to the sentences. Again, the little schoolhouse exploded in applause.

Meg too joined the clapping as she got up from her rock. "A round of applause for your teacher, class!" she cried. The group began to shout and clap for Tere, who blushed furiously.

"How fast all of you are progressing," Meg said, smiling at the group. "Before you know it, you'll be reading Shakespeare."

"*Dios mio*, sure sounds like a fancy landowner's name," Paulina quipped as she came over and gave Meg a warm hug. "We only read the great writers in this village, don't we, *compañeros*? None of those reactionary fellows, please, *Madre*."

Tere signaled that the class was over for the day and gathered up her slate and her precious pieces of chalk.

"Great job, Tere," Meg said as she helped the girl collect the notebooks and pencils. "You're such a natural when it comes to teaching, young lady. Maybe one day you'll have a chance to keep on with your own studies and get a real teaching degree. If I had anything to do with it, I'd give you that degree right now."

Meg was working with Tere every afternoon, instructing her in the literacy training she learned in Chile from Paulo Freire, the well-known Brazilian educator. Freire had turned educational theory on its head with his *Pedagogy of the Oppressed*, a method where the poor themselves became the engineers of their own learning. Reading had to be relevant, he said, it had to involve the students—that's why today's lesson revolved around the passionate word *Frente*.

"Come on, *Madre*. You know I've only gone to fifth grade. Everything I know, you've taught me. Besides, you know my dream is to one day join my brother and the others in the fighting. There are more and more girls joining the *Frente*—"

"Ay, Tere, Terecita, I see I don't have all that much influence over you, after all," Meg said. She gave a light tug to one of the girl's long brown braids. "You're a natural community leader and can best serve the revolution by staying here and helping your village keep organized. Your work is just as important—if not more so—than being with the guerrillas. Even your famous brother, the *comandante*, tells you that."

"I know," the girl said with a sigh. "And I can't leave Miguelito and *la pequeña* Luz. I'm their mother now."

Meg thought how perceptive this young woman of seventeen was, mature far beyond her years.

"But don't forget that Theo and I are around to help you out."

"No, I don't forget," Tere said. "I still can't believe our village's luck at having you and Theo and Carlos here. You're teaching us so many things. How to read and write, how to get rid of the mosquitoes so we don't keep coming down with *paladismo*. Despite these times of trouble, God has seen fit to bless Dulce Nombre de Maria with your presence."

Meg smiled and took the girl's hand. "Come on. Let's go see if Paulina has any fresh orange juice for two thirsty teachers."

They climbed the hill toward the village in comradely silence. Meg glanced down at the brown hand in her own.

She remembered how, when they first arrived at Dulce Nombre de María, they had found a withdrawn, desolate young girl who spent her days helping her grandmother take care of her small brother and baby sister.

It was not long before Meg learned the tragic history of the Gajardo family: Both parents had been separately but brutally killed by ORDEN. Just like Don Chepe in San Jacinto, Don Ramón Gajardo had been the village leader and a protégé of the Jesuits. He too was promoting the *campesino* federation when he was killed. When Paulina told her that Ramón's sightless head had been mounted on a pole in front of the church, Meg had to sit down. Her whole body shook with the memory of Don Chepe and the massacre at El Jícaro.

"Yes, I too wonder what sort of human beings can carry out such atrocities," Paulina had said, sitting down next to Meg on the bench outside her hut. "I'm certain that it was seeing his father… like that… that made Raul join the guerrillas, even though he was only sixteen at the time."

"And now he leads the Chalatenango division of the *Frente*," she had added proudly.

It took Paulina a little longer to tell Meg the story of Doña Mercedes.

"Practically as soon as they could walk," she began, "Raul and Tere were sent to herd cattle at the Alaya ranch. Their parents were grateful to the ranchers who, in exchange, gave them a discount on the rent of their *milpa*—"

"Alaya? The ranchers are Alayas?" Meg had exclaimed with alarm. "Are they related to Fermin Alaya?"

"Don Ernesto and Don Lucho are Fermin's sons. Ernesto was the spitting image of his father. He was known as a playboy, loved fancy cars and clothes. Lucho must resemble his mother, Fermín's first wife, who nobody remembers much. Around here we all call Lucho 'Monkey Face.' Don't know why, really. Maybe he looks like a monkey." Pauline gave a short laugh. "I think he might have some of his marbles missing, but he is kind enough. In fact, he's become our own angel. Has a bad limp though."

Ernesto and Lucho. It came flooding back. The *patron's* kids that Rutilio had played with as a boy.

"Ernesto *was* the splitting image of his father? Where is he now?"

"Ah, I'm getting ahead of the story. *Paciencia, Madre*." Meg recalled how Paulina had smiled sadly at her companion sitting next to her. "Raul and Tere grew up, as children will do. Ernesto started violating Tere, as the bastards in these parts do to so many of our young girls. They think deflowering young virgins is their right, even their duty. Doña Mercedes eventually realized what was happening to her daughter. These things we mothers just know. She confronted Don Ernesto Alaya in the village's main plaza. Out of nowhere, the villagers appeared and one by one, began stoning him until he was surrounded, stripped naked and then run out of town."

Meg looked with disbelief at Paulina. Her mouth opened but no sound came out.

"That was a day no one in Dulce Nombre de María will ever forget, *Madre*," she said with proud glint in her eye. "A great wave of ancestral rage took hold of every one of us, from the youngest to the oldest. And we beat that *sin vergüenza* down."

But then Paulina's face had turned dark with anger as she described how Doña Mercedes was murdered a week later.

"Her naked body was found down by the river, her breasts cut off and the word *puta* carved on her stomach with a machete."

That horrible murder was followed by the Ernesto's mysterious death. "Could it have been otherwise? Most think it was Raul; some of us think it was Tere. Dona Santos believes it was Dona Mercedes and Don Ramon reaching beyond the grave to settle the score. Maybe it was Santos herself. She manages to be everywhere at once, that tiny woman, despite her years. No one will ever know for sure."

Hearing the story of Tere's tragedy had overwhelmed Meg. She sought the girl out and spent long hours with her, giving her a hand in caring for Miguelito and the baby. Then she asked the girl to help her start literacy classes for the villagers.

Meg and Theo had gratefully accepted Doña Santos' invitation to share her home with Tere, Miguel, and the baby. There was room. They could use Ramon and Mercedes' mattress that lay abandoned in the corner so they didn't have to endure the hammocks.

Meg chuckled to herself as she remembered how odd the family found some of their habits that for Theo and herself were so ordinary—like using sheets on the mattress and "making the bed" each morning, or carrying a roll of toilet paper in their pockets "for emergencies." She had been amused to find Santos fascinated with the fact that the nuns used bras and knew that the old women thought it strange that they were so modest about showing their breasts but never remembered their handkerchiefs. Didn't they know that every decent Salvadoran woman carried a handkerchief to place over her knees whenever she sat down? Modesty demanded it.

Such close proximity allowed Meg to observe Tere unobtrusively. She was amazed at the girl's leadership qualities, her instinctive understanding of the villagers' needs and hurts, her ability to gently prod the children out of their fears and nightmares, and her political savvy and cunning during the frequent air raids. If there were young women like Tere throughout El Salvador, then this country did indeed have a future. If the daughter had so much ability, what must her mother have been like? She found herself often talking to Doña Mercedes in her head. In her mind's eye, Mercedes looked like a younger copy of her mother, Doña Santos, and an older copy of this daughter of hers—tiny, with bright inquisitive eyes, full of energy and enthusiasm.

Meg sighed contentedly. She looked down at the brown hand she held in her own white freckled hand and gave it a squeeze.

"A penny for your thoughts, Tere."

"Do you really believe in the final victory, *Madre?*"

"Why, what a question to ask. You know I do! And the more I get to know the likes of you and Paulina and the other villagers, the surer I get."

Tere searched Meg's face for a long moment. "Sometimes you and Theo seem so depressed by all the killings and violence that I think you might die of sadness, or become so disheartened that you'll have to leave us for your own sanity."

Meg was caught off guard by the girl's words.

"It would be tragic," the nun said slowly, "if we allowed ourselves to die of sadness, believing as we do that the cross always leads to resurrection."

"Yes, *Madre,* we believe that—perhaps even more than you do. You two seem so awfully solemn to us most of the time." She added, "You should take time to have some fun!"

Meg stopped in her tracks and turned to face the girl. "Tere, *querida,* I'm sorry I'm not jovial enough for your liking. The circumstances of the past year haven't exactly inspired me to break into song, you know."

"Ay, *Madre,* now I have done it. I have offended you. I… I know how you and *Madre* Theo suffered in Aguilares, that you were part of Padre Rutilio's team … and, well, we have even heard that the soldiers committed a grave sin against you during the raid on the parish."

Meg blushed furiously then looked down at the ground. She

and Theo had made every effort to keep their rape secret. She never even talked about it to Theo.

"I-I'm not sure what you are referring to, my child," she stammered, "but even if I did, I cannot go there, I cannot… go… there…" Meg was finding that she was short of breath, although it wasn't from walking up the hill.

"Despite our being so different from each other, perhaps we are the same in our suffering."

Meg took several deep breaths, which seemed to calm her vertigo. "Oh no, Tere, your burden is much, much greater than mine will ever be. Sexually abused as a child, over and over again… I can only imagine … the shame, the disgust…"

Now it was Tere who was blushing. "I have never talked about these things with anyone. My mother tried; she guessed the truth. In the end, that knowledge killed her." Tere's eyes filled with tears.

"Ah, *niña, niñita*, I know."

"I am not a child, *Madre*."

The young woman finally met Meg's gaze directly. Was she defying her or inviting her to an intimacy she didn't know how to receive?

"Tere, we are not yet strong enough to have this conversation, you and I. One day, perhaps…"

"One day, yes, *Madre* Meg." Tere laughed her old laugh. "One day when neither of us is so proud. Now let's change the subject."

"Yes, let's." Meg gave a sigh of relief and they continued their walk up the hill, still holding hands.

"You and Theo don't seem to realize that this war isn't going to end in a year or two," Tere said, a trace of defiance still in her voice. "The landowners can count on the support of the army and the army can count on the support of *los yanquis*. The guerrillas won't be defeated, but they won't win either. This is going to be a long, long war."

"Hmm, it sounds as if you've been well briefed, dear," Meg said, looking sideways at the girl, relieved they were on a subject she could handle emotionally.

"Your own country, the United States of America, won't let a revolution take place in its own backyard," Tere said.

"Oh, Tere," Meg said in exasperation. "Where is your hope in the God of justice, your faith in your own people?"

"Right here," Tere said, solemnly placing her hand over her heart. "Of course I believe in the revolution, Meguita. It's just that before, when my father was killed and my brother went off to join the guerrillas, I thought the *Frente* would defeat the army within a few months, or at most, by the end of the year. But now… now I think it might take a whole lifetime."

"And all Theo and I want is to accompany you on that journey. Is that too much to ask?" Meg wished she could make this young girl, who had become so special to her, understand why she wanted to stay with them for her lifetime too.

"You see, my dear," she continued, "being with you and the other villagers is a conversion experience for Theo and me. We learn who God is by being with you. It's not just all the violence and the oppression you suffer; it's your joy too, the way you share the little you have with one another, the way you take care of one another, the way you pray. Theo and I consider ourselves very, very lucky, because we experience the presence of God among you. Now you wouldn't deny us that, would you?"

"No, no, of course I wouldn't, *Madre*." Tere impulsively reached over and hugged the older woman. "In some strange way, you and Theo make up for your own people's sins against us. And by knowing you, we also know that all *gringos* don't think we're misguided, ignorant *campesinos* duped by the Russians or the Cubans. But come now, I'm dying of thirst, and there's Paulina."

Tere and Meg reached the top of the hill and waved to the village leader. Paulina sat in the shade in front of her rambling shack, her perpetual red ribbon set jauntily in her thick, curly hair.

"Adios, madrina. You made it up the hill before us. You must have wings,"Tere called out. "How about some orange juice for two thirsty women?"

"For the two of you, there will always be orange juice." Paulina beamed as she welcomed them and drew up her only chair and a bench for her visitors to sit down. She bustled inside her hut a moment and emerged with a plastic pitcher and two chipped cups.

"You must be very proud of me, *Madre*. I'm a walking miracle. At forty-two, I'm finally learning to read!" she said, giving Meg a broad smile.

"Proud isn't the right word—I'm overjoyed!" Meg said, returning the smile.

The village leader served the juice, then gave the nun's hand a pat. "Forgive me, *Madre*, but I must go to the *milpa* and round up the crew picking corn or we won't have any tortillas tomorrow. Why don't you go behind the house and take a quick bath? No one is around at this time of day. You can use my hammock for awhile. A siesta would do you good. I know how this heat bothers you."

"Oh, I'm getting used to it. By the time I'm eighty I'll probably get goose bumps in the shade," Meg joked, touched by Paulina's thoughtfulness. "Don't be offended, but I think I'll take a stroll down to the river instead. Walking relaxes me more than a nap. But thanks for the juice," she said, getting up. "It's just what I needed. And Tere, we'll talk again."

"*Por supuesto, Madre.*"

Meg rounded Paulina's house and looked longingly at the barrel of water next to the outhouse. Maybe she'd just splash her face and arms to cool down in the ninety-degree heat. She turned back to ask permission but stopped short just out of sight of the two women.

Paulina and Tere were talking quietly together, but she could easily overhear their conversation.

"What were you two discussing that has given the *Madre* so much to think about?" Paulina asked.

"I think I might have hurt her feelings by telling her she might not be around for the people's victory."

"Who will?" Paulina snorted. "We say that they can't kill us all, but maybe they can."

"Those two women baffle me," Tere sighed. "And yet…"

"And yet they still treat us like children," Paulina filled in. "Am I not right? Oh, I love them too, *hija*; their sincerity and large-heartedness brings a lump to my throat just thinking about it. And what a blessing Theo's health clinic is, and Meg's school! But they will always be different. They will never understand us fully, just as we can never imagine how they ever grew up without having gone to the fields with their mamas to pick cotton or coffee, without having learned to curtsy properly before the *patrón*, without having awakened each morning to the smell of the lemon trees and the sound of the *clarinero* bird and the sight of grandfather volcano there in the distance."

"And in the end, they will go away," Tere said, "and they will go thinking they have understood us."

"Don't be so harsh on them. You've read too many of the *muchachos'* anti-*yanqui* pamphlets. Forgive them their unconscious need to feel they must save us, the pity they feel for us, even though they hide it so well from themselves. Let us learn from them while they remain among us—and cherish them."

"Yes, I suppose you're right, *madrina*. Besides, they try so hard to share our lives. Theo is especially sensitive, but then she has been in El Salvador longer. But it is Meg to whom I am attracted. If only she wouldn't treat me like a schoolgirl."

"Patience, Terecita. She is used to schools in America, remember, where girls have few responsibilities. She forgets that in El Salvador, we become women at fifteen. We don't have long girlhoods like they do. I counsel you to keep on talking with her. Who knows? One day she might play an important role in convincing her people that we are not the communists her government paints us to be."

"She doesn't want to talk about what the soldiers did to her during the raid in Aguilares."

"You brought that subject up?" Paulina asked, alarmed.

"*Sí* ... and it upset her a lot."

"Of course it would, *hija*. Let her have time to mend. She

173

will need lots of time, lots of *consejo* from wise friends. You are too young for her to lay her head on your shoulder."

"I understand that now. She will always think of me as a child."

"Maybe not *always*. Now run along," Paulina said as she shooed the girl on her way. "I must be off to the *milpa* and you must give your grandmother a hand with the little ones."

Meg dashed as quietly as she could into the outhouse. She cleared her throat loudly, then emerged. Paulina was heading off in the direction of the *milpa*, and Tere was walking across the plaza toward her own house. Neither woman noticed her.

She turned away from the outhouse and took the worn path leading to the river. Suddenly she felt tired and her shoulders ached. Almost a year now in this village, giving every ounce of her energy to these people, and still they didn't trust her. Nor Theo. It was always the same suspicion—they were *gringas*, they were from the land of the exploiters and could never be totally trusted, ever. She'd met the same reserve in La Bandera, despite her wholehearted commitment. What would it take to finally belong, either in Chile or in El Salvador? Do transplants ever really take hold, she wondered? Perhaps it is only by having children with a native—then the children would belong, and she would be the mother of the children.

She would need to reflect with Theo about this.

Meg breathed deeply, aware she was strangely peaceful, despite the overheard conversation. She would be content being a transplant for the time being.

Crazy, she thought to herself. Here she was, practically in the midst of a civil war, completely cut off from the mainstream of civilization, with constant air raids followed by army sweeps, and she was feeling a peace that she hadn't felt in ages. Meg sensed that part of it was the result of living in this village. She hadn't felt so much a part of a community since she'd left La Bandera, even though she was and always would be "*la gringa*."

Had she meant it when she told Tere that she would stay for a lifetime with the people of Dulce Nombre de María? It had come out without her ever thinking about it. But what about her promise to Rosa and the others back in La Bandera that she would return to Chile?

Oh heavens, she thought impatiently, she'd think about all this another day.

Yet, there was no denying it—in so many ways life here made her think of her shantytown back in Chile. Of course this village was so much smaller than La Bandera. There were only about two hundred people left now, most of them children, taken care of by a few dozen women and three or four old or sickly men like Don Augusín, their local religious fanatic. And Monkey Face, of course.

More than half the villagers had fled to the refugee camps cropping up in San Salvador or over the Sumpul River into Honduras. Most of those who remained had relatives fighting with the guerrillas and stayed on to be close to them, to provide them with food and information.

But she knew her mood also reflected her amazement and enthusiasm for what was taking place around her, the community's organization in the middle of war, the way they had organized the planting and harvesting tasks so they not only had enough corn and beans to feed themselves, but they were also able to send substantial food packages to the rebels, and sometimes those packages included oranges and bananas and maybe even a chicken or two.

Then there was the clinic where Theo nursed the kids and taught their mothers first aid, and she did what she could for those hit during the raids. Occasionally, Theo herself sometimes disappeared into the hills with one of the *compas* who had come for her. Meg's heart would be in her mouth the whole time her friend was away on one of these "sick visits."

Carlos, Theo, and herself also took turns guiding the community's biblical reflection. And all three of them took turns "keeping revolutionary watch" to alert the village and the guerrillas about troop movement in the area. Most of the time, the soldiers stayed clear of the village, because the surrounding area was known to be crawling with members of the *Frente*. But air raids were more and more frequent, and the planes and helicopters that swooped down on them rained small but deadly cluster bombs that, if they got under your skin, caused huge, gaping sores that burned the flesh.

When the planes came, the whole village ran to the shelter down the hill behind the chapel. It was nothing more than a large underground hole covered with wooden beams and stones, but it gave them relatively secure shelter.

It was the children Meg worried about most when she heard the planes' distant humming. War is always at odds with children, she knew, because they will continue at their play no matter what. She marveled at the way they made their own toys to give wing to their mighty imaginations. Little pieces of wood became oxen that pulled a cart or a plow. One of their favorite games, of course, was playing "war." They simulated ambushes, took over towns, tracked the enemy—and of course it was always the *muchachos* who won!

Little María and Miguel were fond of fashioning mud donkeys and pack horses loaded for an escape into the mountains. How graphically they reflected village life, Meg thought. Because, as often happened after an air raid, word would come from the hills that the soldiers were making massive sweeps of the area on foot. Then the villagers would have to quickly pack what they could and go on what had come to be known as the *guinda,* a massive withdrawal into the surrounding countryside. Meg and Theo learned that retreating to the hills was deeply imbedded in the Salvadoran psyche. They, like their Pipil ancestors, believed in the magic of the earth to protect them, even more than their Mayan neighbors in Guatemala.

Traveling by night and hiding in the deep ravines or caves found in the mountains, the villagers would be forced for days on end to try to avoid being discovered by the army. And when the guerrillas finally sent word that it was again safe to return to Dulce Nombre de María, they would find upon their return that the army had burned many of their homes, destroyed their crops, and run off with their tools and cooking utensils.

Yes, Meg reminded herself as she reached the river and settled down on a smooth rock near the bank, there was nothing to be joyful about when one took account of the terrible toll the ongoing war was having on these hardened *campesinos.* They lived constantly on the edge and were grateful for just one more day of life. Yet it was their determination that elevated the woman's spirits so! As grateful as they were to still be alive when the sun came up the next morning, they were at the same time convinced that, sooner or later, the *muchachos* would win and better days would be in store for Chalatenango and all El Salvador.

That hope had also infected Meg, even though she knew Tere was right. Victory was still a long way off. Through the guerrilla radio broadcasts, she knew that the army was getting more and more training, ammunition, and war planes from her own country. Why couldn't they just leave them alone, instead of always imposing the Big Stick?

As she sat there watching the river flow by, she fantasized how Raul would be minister of justice and Tere minister of education in a new revolutionary government. And Paulina wouldn't "expire from joy" on the day of victory, but go on to be president of the new republic. And Carlos would become archbishop and preach a whole new way of being a revolutionary Christian.

She and Theo, what would they do? Stay on, surely, and help wherever they were needed. And whatever they did, they'd do it together, she was sure of that. They worked so well together that they could almost read each other's mind. Yes, whatever lay down the road, Theo would be a part of it.

Meg suddenly realized she was daydreaming and glanced around guiltily. No one was in sight. She was tempted to strip off her clothes and dive into the cool, beckoning river, but modesty checked her. Although, God knows she didn't have much to be modest about these days. She shivered as she recalled last year's rape.

She knew the rape had traumatized her, but she tried her best to suppress her feelings. She and Theo didn't have the luxury right now for counseling. But the exchange with Tere had revealed how deeply she was hurting.

Just then, she spied Theo coming down the hill toward the river. She sat up and waved an eager greeting. Meg admitted that her present feeling of peace and wholeness had a lot to do with the growing tenderness she felt for this friend of hers.

Ever since they had held each other, trembling and weeping, after the soldiers raped them, a new bond had been forged between them. An intimacy, a oneness that bound them to these people, this village, this country. Their violated bodies, the violated and tortured bodies of this country's poor, all somehow merged into Christ's own mangled and crucified body. And ever since, it had felt right to taste the tears and the smells and the blood that came forth from those bodies and to bind up wounds and hurts. In the end, it was all poor humans could do for one another. So she held Theo close to her, and sometimes in the night as they lay next to each other in the bed Mercedes and Ramon had once shared, she gently caressed Theo's body, now, through some mystery she could not explain, an extension of her own.

Theo arrived at the river and sank down beside Meg on the rock. "Phew, eight years, and I'm still not used to this heat."

"I was sort of entertaining the idea of taking a dip in the river," Meg smiled mischievously at her friend. "Why don't we be a bit wicked and do a little skinny dipping? People won't be coming back from the fields for another half hour or so. What do you say?"

Theo gave Meg a surprised look. "What would these very religious *campesinos* say if they saw us splashing naked in the river? They'd be scandalized."

"Oh, beans they would. The women and children do it all the time—and so do the men, but at different times. It's called a real bath, rather than that exercise they do every morning with a pail outside their shacks. Come on, Theo. We're both as sweaty and as dirty as two old Pennsylvania coal miners."

Meg could see that Theo was tempted. "How about if we take turns, while the other stands guard?"

"What? And take all the risk out of the adventure? Come on, you wet blanket. A five-minute dip won't bring the banshees out." And Meg stood up, took a quick look about, and then deftly unzipped her skirt and let it fall to the ground and hurriedly unbuttoned her blouse and slipped it off. She stood a minute before Theo in her bra and panties, then stripped them off too. Theo stared at Meg for a brief moment, then modestly cast her eyes down.

In three long strides, Meg was into the river splashing around. "Oh, this is heaven. Come on!"

Theo hesitated another minute, then stood up and undressed as quickly as Meg had and made a long dash for the river.

The current was gentle and the river low at this time of the year. The two women kept everything but their heads under water, even though the water was only waist deep. After five minutes of swimming a few yards from Meg, Theo called out, "This is as far as my courage goes. I don't know about you, but I'm getting out, delightful though this is."

Meg watched her friend as she waded out of the water. No, Theo wasn't in the least bit good looking, she had to admit. Too tall and thin to be thought sexy. Her thighs and buttocks were lean enough to be a boy's; her breasts appeared to be no more than two brown buttons. But a deep warmth spread over her as she watched Theo dress. *Not pretty, but oh, so lovely*, she thought. That body was as straightforward as her soul, reflecting Theo's no-nonsense commitment, her spontaneous openness to both pain and joy.

Meg took another dive under water and soaked in its

coolness. Then, heaving a resigned sigh, she too waded to shore. After another glance around assured her that they were still alone, Meg plopped naked down on the grass at Theo's feet. "Will you allow me two minutes in the buff to dry?" she said as she looked laughingly up at Theo's face.

"I'll keep an eye peeled for you, but I think you're tempting fate."

"Oh, quit acting like an old prude. We've seen each other naked before."

Theo reddened. "I know." Her tone suddenly changed. "We manage to avoid talking about that, don't we?" she mumbled.

"Well, yes, I guess we do. It's our way of trying to forget it ever happened, I suppose."

"I certainly haven't forgotten."

"Do you think I have?"

"What… what did you feel, Meg, when those soldiers were on top of you?"

"I felt what I think every woman must feel at being raped. Outraged, vilified, dirty. Why, I dream of meeting that lieutenant some dark night and pouring a bucket of boiling oil on his cock." Meg shivered as she tried to push down the memory of the officer's triumphant look as he thrust deeper and deeper inside her.

She reached over to her pile of clothes and retrieved her skirt. "How often I've fantasized about what the 'first time' would be like," she said as she sat up and wrapped the skirt towel-fashion around her. "Most of those fantasies revolved around Alfredo, but we've all had our sexual fantasies, despite having taken the vow of chastity. Even you'd have to admit to that, Theo."

"I've always been curious about intercourse," Theo said. "Ever since I was a little girl I've been fascinated by the human body, how it works, how all the systems complement one another. That's probably why I became a nurse. I love to touch, to soothe, to heal. Technically—even more so, aesthetically—the female body matches the male's so perfectly. I know all that. I've done my share of gynecological duty. But I was curious about what penetration would feel like. I've so often wondered about that ecstasy the poets and songwriters go on so about."

"And instead of ecstasy, that repulsive, traumatizing, violent act…"

"I can't say I'm traumatized—or even angry."

"Well, you should be," Meg cut in impatiently. "My God, we were raped, violated! Sinned against. And it's even worse, because we're women of God."

"Seems like you have enough anger gnawing at you for both of us, Meggie," Theo mused. "But I don't know, I only feel a great sadness. A tremendous loss. Not just the loss of my physical virginity—that's the least of it—but somehow the loss of part of my vitality, my energy source. I-I would have preferred going to my grave still fantasizing about intercourse rather than having only that senseless mauling burnt into my heart."

Theo's face twitched. "It seems like a cruel joke: The only man I ever loved never knew it—or if he did, he never acknowledged it." She turned her face away, but Meg still saw the tears splash down her friend's cheek. "Then he was taken away from me, when all I wanted was to work by his side."

Theo's voice was shaking. She went on in a defeated tone. "And then, after such a great loss, I must also bear this terribly stupid, childish rape by soldier-boys who only went after me because they wanted to brag to their buddies that they fucked a nun—a *gringa* at that. They won't mention that she wasn't very sexy in the first place."

"Oh Theo, you loved Rutilio, didn't you?" Meg said gently, as she scrambled to her knees and caught the tearful nun's hands in her own.

"Yes, with all my heart." She gave her friend a long, almost defiant look. "But not the way you loved your Alfredo—or the way Rutilio was starting to love you."

"No, Rutilio never—"

"Wait a minute before you object," Theo said, squeezing Meg's hands emphatically. "He was falling in love with you, although he didn't even know it. Believe me, Meggie, I knew the man so well. I loved him like a mother, like a sister—and I saw it happening before my very eyes."

"But you know I wasn't falling in love with Rutilio, surely!" Meg cried, reproach and anger in her voice. "He was like a brother to me too, and… and besides, compared to Alfredo, well, no offense, but there was just no comparison. And furthermore, Theo, you are my witness: ever since that night after the massacre in San Jacinto I've tried to play it straight. What you see is what you get: Sister Meg Carney, consecrated virgin with the perpetual vows of poverty, no problem; obedience, no problem; and chastity, problematic, yes, but a cross that I must shoulder for the sake of God's kingdom. You know that's true, Theo, you of all people!" She looked at the other nun, her eyes begging for affirmation.

"Perhaps I am jealous of you," Theo whispered, smiling her old, sad smile. "I'm jealous of your loveliness. I'm jealous of Alfredo, perhaps. I'm jealous of this wonderful body of yours."

She reached over and untied the knot that held Meg's skirt around her. The cotton fabric fell down around the nun's waist, revealing full white breasts crisscrossed with light blue veins and topped with dark, pink nipples.

Theo shyly cupped one breast and then the other in her hands. "How does it go?" she murmured softly. "'You are all-beautiful, my sister, my love. Your breasts are like twin fauns, like clusters of the vine. Your breath is the fragrance of apples, your mouth the taste of excellent wine…'"

"The Canticle of Canticles"?

Theo nodded.

Meg gently pulled Theo toward her breast and held her friend tightly against her. The warm, wet cheeks and the feel of Theo's soft breathing filled her with delight and she felt weak with joy. "My love, my dove, my beautiful one," she whispered, tilting the other woman's face toward her own. Then she softly brushed her lips to Theo's. "Be healed, my lovely one," she whispered. "Believe in other connections. Believe in the love we share, my Theo-y…"

Just then, the sound of voices reached them. Meg looked up and spied a group of women and children making their way toward the river bank.

"Heavens, have we forgotten that I'm stark naked?" she said as she began to search for her underwear.

"No, I haven't anyway," Theo said gently as she freed herself from Meg's embrace. "But hurry now, duck behind that tree and get dressed," she said, throwing Meg's bra and panties at her.

Meg emerged from behind the tree still buttoning her blouse

as Paulina and some of the other women trudged wearily up to the nuns' perch by the river, balancing bundles of freshly shucked corn on their heads.

Paulina took one look at the two nuns and grinned conspiratorially at Meg and Theo. "From the looks of the wet hair, I guess you two have finally crossed the barrier and become genuine *campesina* women by bathing in the river." Turning to the other women, she said, "Anyone want to follow the *Madres'* example and do the same?"

Giggling shyly, the women chorused a hearty "*Sí.*"

"Keep an eye out for Don Augustín," Paulina directed the tongue-tied Americans. "He's forever spying on us, the old fool. Bathing women and reading the Bible are the only delights he has left in life these days, it seems." Then she and the others quickly stripped to their rough cotton drawers and plunged into the river.

***

Dulce Nombre de María, Chalatenango
May 1978

Dear Aunt Kay,

After all these years—and all those obligatory Christmas cards—Mom finally decided to let bygones be bygones and visit you. I would like to think that I might have had something to do with it; in my letters home, I've often mentioned your generous contributions and warm letters to me—and how close I feel to you. But as I'm sure you've discovered, Mom has a mind of her own. She may indeed think that, as she "goes into the homestretch," it's time to put her house in order and do some reconciling.

I never really understood what the rift was about in the first place. Anyway, I think it is wonderful that the two of you have become friends again after all these years.

My one concern is that you might share what I have told you in my letters. There's something about you that has made me spill out my guts. But I'd be very upset if you ever told Mom about all the raw experiences I've faced. I think she believes I'm at some sort of glorified Girl Scout camp here in the hills of El Salvador—it would be kinder to keep her in the dark, especially about "Operation Rutilio."

Mom is a real rock, and I admire how she raised us kids all by herself after Dad died. But we're really not all that close— not like other mothers and daughters are. Yet she's so proud of me! And that stops me from letting down my hair with her, from showing her my warts.

I'd be so embarrassed if she knew about my struggles with celibacy, for instance. Sex is one topic that has always been taboo between us. I don't really know why. Maybe it has to do with our Irish Catholic background, which equates sexual passion as somehow beneath us—except for creating more children for God, of course!

That's why I'm constantly caught off guard by your persistent probing into my own sexual feelings. But while I find it disconcerting—even disturbing—at one level, on another I catch myself being terribly eager to discuss feelings and anxieties with you that have been off limits for so long.

Take your last letter. I appreciated your blunt questions about the rape—yes, thanks to Queen Mum, we went directly to the hospital and received the necessary treatment. And yes, I know it is important for Theo and I to talk about it—together and with trusted friends. Counseling, at this point, is out of the question here in the foothills. But Theo and I have begun to talk about our feelings surrounding the violation. Basically, I'm just really angry, but Theo is very depressed; there have been too many losses in her life of late, and she still mourns so for Rutilio.

Strange as it may seem, experiencing the terrible violation together has drawn the two of us very close. Here at last is a love that is as deep as the sea and as wide as the heavens. I don't know what I'd do without my Theo.

I'm also grateful for your counsel about not becoming repulsed by sex because of the rape, although I can't quite take your advice about gentle masturbation as a way of healing a battered body. Some things are off limits to us nuns, and I'm afraid gently massaging one's private parts, no matter how lovingly performed, is one of them. But YOU know that, Aunt Kay, so I suspect you are just trying to test the waters and see how deeply I'll let you probe.

I do admit, however, that it is essential for all of us poor human beings to be in touch with our bodies, and not simply repress our deepest urgings. But that mandate takes on an entirely different meaning here in El Salvador, where one comes into contact with so many broken and violated bodies. It breaks down all prudishness and false modesty. Suddenly, there are no "private parts" anymore, and in some awful and awesome way we find ourselves, mangled and wounded, being forged into the one broken body of Christ.

Thanks again for the "pagan baby" donation. It couldn't have come at a better time. We were able to buy some essential *antibiotics for Theo's little clinic here. Thanks to you, some of our villagers wounded from aerial bombings are alive today.*

Bless you, Kay.

Lovingly,

Meg

Chapter 9

November 1978

Dulce Nombre de María

As long as she lived, Meg would never forget the air raids and the resulting *guinda* of that autumn.

The rains had finally come to Dulce Nombre de Maria, bringing relief and joy to the villagers. Not only did the onslaught of the downpours mean the beginning of a new planting season— and, with luck, a new harvest of beans and corn by July—but it also meant that visibility would be poor, making it harder for the planes to spot them. The army battalions too would be slowed down now as the dried river beds would once again turn to swollen streams and the dusty paths in and around the village would become slippery and dangerous.

So she, as well as the whole village, was caught off guard when the raids began on that otherwise ordinary Monday in November.

Meg watched the lone plane appear on the horizon. For several hours it circled almost lazily around the sky, checking for signs of life. It swooped down for a closer look at a recently furrowed patch of land, pointed its nose at the smoke curling upward from the fire one of the women had lit to cook the day's tortillas, buzzed a clothesline where faded homespun skirts and pants swayed tiredly in the morning sun. Then, its peek-a-boo mission done, it flew away just as unhurriedly as it had come.

Later that afternoon, as the villagers were returning from their *milpas,* the spotter plane returned, feistier this time. Behind it, three U.S.-made A-37s flew in tight formation high over the village before circling around and zooming in for the attack.

The planes' roar served as the villagers' warning signal; adults and older children seized the little ones and raced madly for the bomb shelter down the hill behind the chapel before the planes turned around. Those too far away dove for any nearby ditch or boulder that would offer them some protection from the attack.

Meg and Theo had made it to the shelter and tried to help the other women calm the terrified children. "Don't worry. They can't hurt us here. We're really safe here; I promise you," Theo whispered over and over again as she crawled through the dark, suffocating cave comforting the shivering, whimpering children.

"Thank God keeping the children quiet takes all our attention," Meg said in a low voice to Theo as she also tried to keep the kids quiet. "That way we don't have time to fall apart ourselves."

But even the adults went rigid as the attacks began.

Whomp! Whomp! Whomp!

Over and over the shrill whistle came, followed by an ear-shattering thud as the bombs exploded on the village behind them. One. Two. Eight. Ten of them. Meg lost count. She lost all sense of time as well.

Finally, after what seemed to be many hours later, the hum of the planes grew more distant and finally stopped altogether. After waiting another twenty minutes or so, the people wearily began to crawl out of their homemade cave.

To their surprise, it was not yet dark. The attack had lasted less than an hour.

Paulina and Carlos began to take count. Most of the children had been rounded up and taken to the shelter; they could only hope that those missing had found a makeshift trench that could at least protect them from becoming open targets.

Slowly, cautiously, the villagers climbed the hill and surveyed the damage. Mothers hastily put handkerchiefs or their skirts over their children's and their own noses and mouths to ward off the stench from the brown, dusty smoke that swirled around the plaza. The church, the village's largest building, had been hit once again and was smoldering there in the twilight. Small fires glowed here and there from the dying mortars, and smoke from several charred huts formed a tangled series of black halos that hung low in the sky above them. But the village still appeared to be in one piece. Either, Meg thought, because God was merciful or because the A-37s' crew had bad eyesight.

Then they saw them. Dona Angelica and her three children, Gustavo, seven, Isabel, four, and Lety, six months, were huddled in the shade of the burning chapel's east wall, where they apparently had been spotted by the planes as they groped their way toward the shelter. Theo reached them first, with Meg right behind.

Meg's eyes filled with angry tears and she forced herself to swallow down the nausea rising in her throat as she took in the mangled bodies.

"Sons of bitches, sons of bitches," she swore as she gritted her teeth and helped Theo separate the bleeding children from their mother. Gustavo and Isabel were still alive. The boy's left leg looked strangely twisted and was bleeding profusely. Isabel's hip was a bright red gap of sinew and muscle. Dona Angelica clasped tiny Lety in her arms. The child was dead, her back a pool of blood. She rocked her baby back and forth, back and forth, coaxing it to suckle the offered breast.

"Meg! Carlos!" Theo ordered. "Help me get the two children to the clinic, if it's still standing." Then she gently touched the grieving mother on the shoulder. "We will save them, I promise you, Angelica. Gustavo and Isabel will live, little mother." And she signaled Paulina to take charge of the moaning woman.

Two hours later, Theo had Gustavo's wound dressed and his leg in a splint. She had also put fourteen stitches in Isabel's hip. Both children were weak from loss of blood, but with luck they would recover.

Carlos held a simple burial service in the shadow of the still smoldering chapel for the slain infant. Then the villagers joined the stricken mother in a procession up the hill to the cemetery where so many of their loved ones had been laid to rest. But that night, around midnight, the planes, like lethal mosquitoes that never go away, returned for more target practice. Meg couldn't tell whether they were the same three planes from the afternoon's raid or different ones. Neither could she tell how many there were; the planes flew without lights and dropped parachute flares to detect any traces of human movement. But darkness had always been the silent shield for the civilian population and the guerrillas in their efforts to elude the army. And once more tonight, its black, engulfing womb offered the villagers the needed cover to steal silently back to the cave below the chapel.

This time Meg made sure everyone was accounted for, including Dona Angelica and her two wounded children. After consulting with Paulina and herself, Carlos quietly announced that he thought it would be wise to spend the night in the shelter, even though it was damp and unbearably crowded, with the villages' entire population of 206 crushed into the long, shallow dugout. She was gratefully aware that Theo had taken time to grab some tranquilizers from her clinic as she helped carry Gustavo and Isabel to the cave. Now she helped Theo to mash them up and dilute them in water, adding a bit of flavoring from two oranges Grandmother Santos produced out of nowhere. The nuns administered the brew to most of the frightened children and one by one, they fell into a fitful sleep while the adults kept vigil through the endless night.

Meg spent the night next to Gustavo. Theo had given him a powerful sedative and the little boy slept peacefully. His wound had turned out to be superficial, and the break in the leg was clean. Theo thought it would mend nicely in a month or two, and she doubted that the boy would have a limp. Isabel's wound had been deep, but it too would heal with time, although the little girl would bear an ugly scar. Theo stayed near the child, who, despite heavy sedation, continued to toss and turn in her sleep, crying out occasionally.

Meg whispered a silent prayer of gratitude when Theo told her that neither of the children's wounds were a result of the white phosphorus rockets that the army was using with greater and greater frequency. When you were hit with the *fuego blanco*, not only did the shrapnel become embedded in the deep tissue where it continued to smolder long after the initial hit, but sometimes it reignited spontaneously, causing excruciating pain and almost inevitable death.

Once during the long night Meg reached over the two sleeping children, found Theo's hand, and held it tightly. "Hey, Doctor Dooley, you're fantastic," she whispered in English, only to be reprimanded with a chorus of *shhs* from her frightened neighbors.

Some time in the middle of the night, the overhead hum of the planes subsided; they had heard only three *whomps*, and Meg guessed by their distance that the planes were having difficulty spotting the village in the dark. But toward dawn, those who had not dozed off suddenly froze at the sound of footsteps. At first they were far off, but then they became steadily louder until they were right outside the cave.

Both Carlos and young José had their revolvers cocked when those in the shelter heard a low bird whistle, the signal the guerrillas used to alert the villagers to their presence. Then Don Lucho Alaya stooped down and ducked into the cave.

Old "Monkey Face" had become the villagers' go-between with the guerrillas. When Tere first told Meg that the taciturn cattle rancher was "on their side," she found it hard to believe. How could the son of Fermin Alaya, Rutilio's intellectual if not actual killer, possibly be trusted? How could the brother of Ernesto Alaya, the man who had raped Tere and engineered her parents' murders, be considered anything less than a bastard cut from the same cloth as the rest of the family? But Tere had impatiently insisted that her old *patron*, through some fluke, some twisted miracle, had indeed come to sympathize with their struggle and could be counted on to relay messages back and forth between the rebel units and the beleaguered civilians.

Meg wondered if Monkey Face guessed that she and Theo knew about the relationship between Rutilio and Ernesto and himself while growing up. The only mention he ever made of the slain Jesuit was that his hobby of whittling miniature animal figures grew out of a boyhood friendship. "A kid I grew up with would bring me these tiny wooden animals as a gift. He received them from his father, but instead of keeping them, he gave them to me." He said he played with his collection of tigers and dogs and donkeys for hours on end. Then he tried making them himself.

"Whittling is something a man like me can do," he said, looking down at his gimpy leg, "and then I can give them away as gifts."

Every child in the village possessed a Monkey Face miniature. Some hung their animal around their neck, while others kept it deep inside their pocket. The kids were superstitious—the gift from the rancher was a lucky charm, a talisman.

During her months at Dulce Nombre de Maria, Meg reluctantly came to accept Don Lucho's loyalty. He would advise them of army movements in the area and often passed on strategic information about upcoming military sweeps they suspected he picked up from his father's cronies whenever he traveled down to Aguilares. He also quietly smuggled them medicines, seeds and newspapers, and the villagers had come to look forward to the sight of the man with the crooked leg limping up the hill toward the village.

Once Don Lucho had even gruffly presented Theo and Meg with an out-of-date copy of *Newsweek* he'd picked up in the capital, "since you probably don't get too much news from home these days." Meg suspected that the rancher's behavior was somehow linked to his need to atone for his brother's terrible sins, but it was only a guess. She also noted the deep trust that existed between Tere and her former employer and was baffled by it.

This time Don Lucho's message was brief—and depressing. *Comandante* Raul had stopped at his ranch a few hours ago with the message that the army was conducting a massive sweep of the area and that they were to evacuate the village immediately. They were to trek over the mountain range that lay directly to the east of them as quickly as possible and hide out in the ravines along the Sumpul River that bordered Honduras.

If they left at once, they would have about a day's edge on the soldiers. The guerrillas would also try to stall them. But an estimated fifteen-hundred-unit force of crack U.S.-trained men was spreading out to form a pincer movement around the area and clear it of civilians suspected of supporting the guerrillas. It was part of the much-heralded counterinsurgency initiative of "taking the water away from the fish" that Don Lucho told them about after one of his recent forays down to visit his father.

It took a few minutes for the villagers to digest the rancher's message. Then they sprang into action.

Their experience of four previous *guindas* had taught them how to prevent the village from being completely destroyed by the invaders. The children were quickly dispatched to bury each family's most prized possessions—cooking utensils, tools, even a few precious toys—in well-secluded holes in the nearby woods. The village's few men took charge of scattering the village's chickens and milk cows in the fields, while the women hurriedly fried and packed as many tortillas as they could to feed the villagers on what they hoped would be a short absence from their homes. Meg and Tere buried the school's notebooks, pencils and chalk under the rock from which Tere usually conducted classes, while Theo hid her clinic in a nearby tree trunk made invisible by a clump of brilliant bougainvillea bushes that surrounded it.

Within two hours they were ready to evacuate.

They formed a single column, with Carlos in the lead. Between them, Meg and Theo shouldered the hammock that served as a makeshift stretcher to carry the two injured children. Tere, with one-year-old Luz on her back, helped Paulina marshal the school-age children, while Doña Santos and the elderly Don Agustín kept four-year Miguel and several other toddlers in tow. José trotted at the rear, carrying his crippled sister, Maria, in piggyback fashion. The motley contingent struck out toward the mountains in the distance.

The women and girls set a determined pace as they carried infants in their arms or on their backs and balanced jugs of water or food provisions effortlessly on their heads. Despite their lack of sleep the night before, the column tramped along at a good clip during most of the morning. Meg caught herself almost enjoying the walk through the woods and then on up through the winding grasslands toward the still distant hills. The air was fresh from the recent rains, and although the land was just beginning to show a few new sprouts after the long dry season, Meg could sense the definite change in the weather.

When the sun was high above them, the column halted for a quick lunch of beans and tortillas. Then they pushed on toward the foothills, their objective for the first day's trek. Don Lucho had told them that once they made it to the slopes, a guerrilla squad would join them and help them find their way over the mountains under the safety of darkness. Meg knew that they had been lucky so far because the spotter plane had not returned, but she and the others expected it at any moment. For that reason, Carlos kept the caravan on the less direct but wooded paths that provided some covering.

As they trudged along, the anticipated storm clouds gathered on the horizon. Another hour or so and it would begin to rain. Just as Meg felt the first drop of rain on her arm, she heard the still far-off hum of the engines. The column was spread out now, a half kilometer long, as it wound its way up the shady incline to keep their rendezvous with their rebel guides.

"Whoever's commanding this damn war sure is stupid," Meg muttered to Theo as they struggled along under the weight of the hammock. "What a silly time to send the spotter out to look for us, with a downpour about to start. Anybody with any brains would have taken advantage of the morning sun and the shrub lands to sniff us out."

"But they don't know we've gone on a *guinda,* Meg," Theo reasoned. "They probably don't want to alert us to the upcoming sweep, so they are just trying to keep us uneasy by a little reconnaissance."

Meg thought she was probably right. Theo followed these things closely and prided herself in being an amateur military strategist. Still, as the hum of the engine drew nearer, Carlos signaled a halt and instructed the villagers to scatter among the large boulders, now more and more in abundance as they drew near the hills.

"Even with the rain and the forest covering, they might still detect our movement," he warned. "Best not to take chances, even though it will slow us down somewhat." Meg noted that the young seminarian, once so jovial, was now the community's undisputed leader.

He checked his compass, then his watch. "We've got another six or seven kilometers to go before reaching the foothills. Even with the rain, we can cover that distance in another hour or two. We'll take a short break and then plunge on."

The exhausted villagers scattered among the rocks to take advantage of the respite. Meg marveled at their endurance, especially the children. Even the smallest ones had grimly marched along throughout the long day's journey with barely a whimper. What stamina these people had! She collapsed behind a boulder and began to massage her sore, swollen feet. She tried to imagine what her mother would think if she could see her daughter at this moment, or the nuns back at the Motherhouse in Pennsylvania or, for that matter, even *Madre* Rosa and the community back in La Bandera.

After about fifteen minutes, the sky was silent. The planes had vanished. "Let's go," Carlos commanded.

For the next two hours, the villagers picked their way up the slippery paths toward the hazy mountains, now barely visible through the torrent of rain. Some of the children began to cry softly. In the hammock, Isabel and Gustavo moaned whenever Theo or Meg inadvertently jerked the improvised stretcher when one of them lost her footing in the slimy mud.

Finally, just as darkness was descending, they reached the abandoned hamlet of La Unión, where a half dozen guerrillas were waiting to take them over the mountains. The villagers quickly took shelter in what remained of the hamlet. Three huts were still relatively intact after last year's raid that had forced the hamlet's residents to flee over the Sumpul and into the refugee camps along the Honduran border.

The guerrillas had built a small fire next to the wall outside one of the huts and were warming a large pot of hot *atol,* the sweet drink of corn mush that Salvadoran *campesinos* are accustomed to drinking in the evening. The soaked, bone-weary villagers gratefully accepted the mugs of *atol.* Then mothers nursed and bedded down their children as best they could on the damp dirt floors before joining the guerrillas, Carlos and the others gathered around the fire.

Meg guessed that Benjamin, the contingent's leader, wasn't more than eighteen. But he seemed to be the oldest, while the others appeared to be fourteen or fifteen. No wonder the villagers referred to the guerrillas as their "*muchachos* in the hills." They really were no more than boys.

Benjamin addressed the group solemnly. Meg could see he was nervous. "*Comandante* Raul sends all of you greetings and wants you to know how much he holds you, his family and his neighbors, in high esteem." The guerrilla cleared his throat and hurried on. "Our plan is to go to sleep now. We will wake you up at around two in the morning. By that time, the rains will have stopped and we will be able to see by the waning moon." He sought out Don Agustín in the crowd, who nodded back to him. The boy was correct about the moon's cycle.

The guerrilla leader straightened his hunched shoulders and spoke with more confidence. "We guess it'll take us about five hours to cross the range and get down into the ravines along the river. That's longer than it should take us, but we've got lots of kids and wounded people to take care of." Meg wondered if he really felt for the kids, or if this was some sort of rehearsed speech he had memorized because this was his first *guinda* and he didn't want to make any mistakes. "The plan is to hide out in the caves there 'til we hear that the coast is clear to return to Dulce Nombre de Maria. Any questions?"

No one spoke.

"The army will begin its sweep early tomorrow morning. And knowing our great army, that means they'll get started about nine o'clock," Benjamin said with a wry smile. "So, unless something goes wrong, we should be over the mountains and into the ravines by daybreak." Meg caught his eye and nodded back to him. She thought she saw a look of relief flash over his face.

"The soldiers will arrive in transport helicopters. They'll have a network of fancy air cover and get information from smaller, faster helicopters that act like flies. But these flies are deadly in tracking anything they spot. Besides that, the Honduran army has posted a heavy guard along the Sumpul to stop anyone who might try to cross the river into Honduras."

"So, you see," he continued, "our safest strategy is to make it to those caves on the other side of this mountain. Once there, we'll break up into small groups of no more than ten or fifteen, and it will also be necessary to keep the children quiet at all costs and to stay well hidden until we get word to return home." He cleared his throat and spat on the floor, then wiped his mouth with his sleeve. "Our *compañeros* will be ambushing the battalion like pesky mosquitoes, and knowing these dogs the way we do, they won't last more than a couple days out here without their chicken dinners and their soft beds." Then he told everyone to try and get some sleep and that he and the other rebels would keep watch.

After checking on Isabel and Gustavo, Theo flopped down next to Meg in a corner of one of the huts.

"Do you think we can trust these *muchachos* to get us out of this in one piece?" Meg whispered.

"What other choice do we have, Meggie? Let's hope so. Remember Rutilio's prayer: '*That the poor may become a people, and that the men who are not men will become men.*' May it come to be. Now get some sleep."

Both women fell into an exhausted sleep as soon as their heads touched the floor. When they were awakened six hours later, the rain had stopped and ribbons of moonlight filtered through the hut's open windows and doors. The villagers breakfasted hurriedly on cold tortillas and water. Then they silently took their places in the column to begin the long, slow march they hoped would bring them to the safety of the ravines along the river by dawn.

The column snaked up and around the mountain, a human mass of slipping, stumbling feet and hands inching to the cover of the ravines on the other side. As the first faint streaks of daylight appeared in the sky, they reached the crest, and just as the sun burst through the cloudy horizon, they half tumbled–half rolled down the other side toward the rushing waters of the Sumpul.

There, on the other side of the river, what looked like the entire Honduran army stood poised. They were pointing their guns directly at them.

The soldiers opened fire. The scattered column broke and people ran frantically for the cover of the shallow caverns that yawned in the folds of the steep mountain they had just crossed. On instinct, Theo and Meg let down the hammock. Theo took Isabel in her arms and began running in the direction Carlos was pointing out.

Meg hoisted Gustavo on her back and yelled, "Hold on as tight as you can and keep your head down." She stumbled to some nearby underbrush and crouched there until she caught her bearings.

Below her, along the river, women and children were dashing frantically for cover. The six guerrillas had posted themselves above the caves and were returning the soldiers' fire. Thank God the river was wide at this point, she thought, as she realized that most of the bullets fell far short of their mark.

Meg spotted a small fissure of rock directly below her. "Gustavo," she whispered, "I'm going to drop you down right into that crack. It'll be easy, but you must land on your good leg. Then slide down into the crevice, okay? I'll be right behind you."

Meg lowered the boy down toward the crevice, a good fifteen feet below, and held her breath. As she had instructed, the boy used his good foot to brace himself on the steep hill and then slid down the rest of the way on his behind, landing right in the middle of the fissure. Meg came sliding down behind him and they jammed together in the tiny hole that would be their home for all that day and on into the night.

The heavy gunfire trailed off, replaced with only an occasional shot. The only other sound Meg heard was the drone from the helicopters that patrolled the river banks on the Honduran side. No hint of her companions; it was as if they had vanished into thin air. Yet she knew that they, like herself and Gustavo, were crouched inside the many adjacent caves. She prayed fervently that there had been no casualties and that they had a little more room to breathe than she and the boy had. They were wedged into a space about the size of a baby's playpen, except that the walls were much higher and the floor was made of stony, wet sand pebbles. A faint light filtered down from the sky far above, revealing their predicament. For the time being, they were trapped.

As the hours passed, Meg had time to recover from the shock of the Hondurans opening fire on them. She knew that the soldiers could legitimately prevent them from crossing the border, but it was totally against international law to fire upon citizens of another country, even if that country's government said those citizens were "subversives."

"If I get out of this alive, I'm going to raise all hell about this," she whispered to Gustavo.

"But, *Madre,* everybody knows that the two armies work together in these operations," the boy replied matter-of-factly. "Besides, no one will believe you when you say the Hondurans fired on us; they'll just say we had already crossed the river when they attacked us, or the Salvadoran army will say it was they who attacked us. So you see, you just can't win."

The boy was good company for the long hours the two of them were crammed together in their crevice. He seemed to be rallying, despite the splint on his leg. Meg wondered if the impact of his little sister's death had really hit him yet, as he had been given no time to grieve. Then her thoughts turned to the last time she had been forced to hide out like this, that long night—it seemed like a lifetime ago now—when she had crouched with Olguita along the river below the village of San Jacinto, the night of the massacre that took the life of the little girl's father and their best village leader. Was it really possible that this was happening again?

As the day wore on, Meg's thoughts turned even gloomier.

She wasn't a military strategist like Theo, but she knew that if the Honduran army had spotted them, then the Salvadoran battalion had been advised of their position. Right now that battalion was probably infuriated, because the villagers had escaped their dragnet, and to save face the soldiers were probably destroying anything they could lay their hands on back in Dulce Nombre de Maria.

"Oh, please don't let them find the medical supplies in the tree trunk. They can find anything but that," she pleaded silently to a God she hoped was listening.

Meg still had her ration of tortillas. Around four in the afternoon she produced from her skirt pocket the soggy, mashed-up treasure for her small companion and refused his offer to share them with her, even though her mouth watered as she watched him gulp them down hungrily in the cave's increasing darkness.

She guessed that as night descended, the guerrillas would signal the villagers to move downstream to a safer hiding place. It began to rain again, and the sound of the downpour pounding on the rocks above them was somehow comforting to them as they waited.

Gustavo heard the soft bird call first and alerted his companion. Slowly, stealthily, Meg and the boy climbed up the jagged wall of the cave. Gustavo's nimbleness astonished her; before her eyes, he turned into a one-legged tightrope walker. He crawled out of the crevice before Meg was even halfway up.

After her eyes adjusted to the darkness, she spied movement along the path next to the river's edge. Their column was reforming! Meg quickly hoisted her charge on her back, and after an initial stumbling, she adjusted to the boy's weight and quickly covered the distance between the cave and the gathering villagers.

No one spoke. The villagers pressed one another's hands and arms as they realized that everyone was still alive. After a frantic search, Meg finally stumbled upon Theo and Isabel; she blinked back tears of relief and gave the other nun a quick hug.

There was no time for rejoicing. Despite the rain and the mud-clogged path, Benjamin started the column off at a brisk march north. The pace never slackened until they reached a wide bend in the river several hours later. There, the column veered to follow a tributary that turned them back from the border and deeper into Salvadoran territory again. A short distance in, the guerrillas called a halt and hustled the villagers into a wide, deep cavern well hidden from the main river.

Once inside their new shelter, everyone—even the guerrillas—dropped exhausted to the ground and slept.

***

The first rays of dawn were filtering into the cave when Meg awoke. She was half sitting–half lying against an old, rotting log near the front of the cave. Gustavo slept soundly beside her, his pale, pinched face on her lap. She became aware of the dull pain in her feet and looked down to find that her tennis shoes had disintegrated; all that was left were patches of navy blue cloth flapping around her ankles and the last wisp of a shoestring. Her feet were caked with mud, but as she examined them more carefully, she realized that some of the mud was dried blood. She had some nasty gashes that would slow her down during the long hike back to the village.

Others were starting to stir. Meg spied Theo on the other side of the cave ministering to several children who whimpered in their sleep.

Carlos saw that Meg was awake and crawled over to the log.

"How are you, *compañera*?"

"Okay, except for some scratches on my feet. And you, *compañero*?"

"Okay, too, just tired—and scared." The seminarian gave Meg his familiar boyish grin. "What I wouldn't do for a Havana cigar," he joked tiredly. Then more seriously, "And to see my mother…"

This young Jesuit was such a gem, Meg thought, with his gentle leadership, his optimism, his easy laughter. "You'll be seeing her very soon now. She'll dance at your ordination next March. Keep dreaming of that day, Carlitos. It will help you get through this *guinda*. Surely we've passed the worse part by now, don't you think?"

"I hope so. The army usually gives up after one or two nights of trying to round up civilians in guerrilla territory. Let's hope that by now they're bored with the whole operation and are packing their bags and heading back to their bases. Still, I wish we had stuck with the original plan and hidden in small groups. I don't like the idea of waiting it out all together like this. It makes us too vulnerable."

No sooner had he spoken than they heard the hum of distant helicopters. The sound was much louder than the din that came from the smaller ones that patrolled the banks of the river throughout the previous day. "Transport 'copters," Carlos muttered. "They're letting them off further up the river. Their Honduran buddies must have told them where we were hiding."

The noise had awakened most of the other adults. Benjamin

addressed the villagers in a low, hoarse whisper. Meg could see that he too was nothing more than a very tired, frightened child.

"Stay calm, everyone! The dogs don't know which direction we've gone! The rain has erased our footsteps. But we must keep absolutely quiet. Mothers, keep your children from crying!"

He was pleading with them now. "They'll be listening for that, the sound of children crying. They won't stay out here very long, these rats; they'll want to get home to their hot soup and whiskey before the afternoon rains start. We, we must go into hibernation. We've all heard the stories about the bears up there in the North Pole, how they go to sleep for the whole winter when it is snowing. And when they wake up it's spring! So everyone, please, please to go back to sleep now. Tomorrow it will all be over—you'll see."

But the noise from the helicopters grew louder. They were having trouble finding the cave, but they had somehow picked up their scent. Scattered gunfire sounded in the distance, and Meg wondered if guerrilla units were harassing the army from behind.

Benjamin and two of the other guerrillas kept guard at the mouth of the cave while another three went out on a scouting mission.

Ten minutes passed, then twenty. Then they heard footsteps, followed by a shaky bird whistle as one of the guerrillas from the scouting party came running breathlessly into the cave.

"We're surrounded," he gasped, as he fell sobbing to his knees. "They're right over the ridge opposite the cave!"

Meg's heart stood still. From her vantage point near the

cave's entrance, she could see the soldiers taking up positions above them on the ridge on the other side of the tributary. They were trapped! Any second the army would storm the cave, killing them where they crouched or forcing them down stream toward the raging Sumpul.

Bedlam broke out in the cave as people started screaming and running in every direction.

"Try to break through the enemy's line, break through the enemy's line, it's the only way!" Meg thought it was Carlos' voice, but she wasn't sure. She grabbed Gustavo, who clung to her hip and started to run blindly along with the others.

Machine-gun fire splattered above her as she splashed through the stream and rounded the side of the ridge. She dashed wildly through the underbrush, the instinct to live driving out every other thought. The helicopters swarmed like gnats above her. Out of the corner of her eye she saw a woman throw up her arms and fly into the air before crashing to the earth, a wet mass of blood and flesh.

And still Meg ran, in doubled-up fashion, as if she were carrying the football down the field in a wild fifty-yard dash that went on and on. The boy and she were one, his fingers gouged so deeply into the flesh around her neck that she thought the two of them could never be separated again.

Finally she could run no longer. "This is it," she thought, the sudden serenity of defeat sweeping over her. "Dying is better than running. I can't run one more step," she gasped out loud as she flung herself into a shallow ditch, furrowed by some unknown farmer in another age. There she stayed, waiting for death, the boy under her, until the rains came and the night slowly descended.

The two of them lay frozen in mud. Gustavo scarcely breathed beneath her, but she knew he was alive, and that she was alive, but barely. Her body ached all over; she wasn't even sure whether she had been wounded.

She must have dozed off, because when she awoke the moon was out. But she still heard shots, and now flickering shadows cast by the moonlight played tricks on her. Everywhere she saw movement. Specters surrounded them, then backed off, then came again. They were wearing her down—all part of the strategy of psychological warfare. Or had she been banished to some underworld where only phantoms dwelt? She sank into an exhausted sleep.

She was dreaming that she was back home in Pittsburgh, in bed with her brothers, Micky and Tommy. But they were cold, and they needed a blanket. Yet as much as she called out to her mother to come with the blanket, she never came…

Slowly Meg became aware of the arm gently shaking her awake.

"Mom, you finally came. What took you so long?" She opened her eyes and looked into the mud-streaked, worried face of *Comandante* Raul.

"*Madre,* are you all right?"

Meg raised her head and squinted at the blazing sun high in the sky. She stiffly rolled over on her back. Raul helped her sit up. Then he bent over the child beside her. "Still alive, thank God—just sound asleep."

The events of the previous day rushed through Meg's mind like a cold fire. "Raul, the others, where are they?" She said in a voice she didn't recognize.

"They are scattered all over the river bank," Raul replied in a low voice. "Come, we need you to help us find them."

As he helped Meg struggle to her feet, she saw that he was accompanied by a large guerrilla column that had fanned out and was slowly pressing toward the ridge in the distance. Had she really run so far? Where were the others?

Throughout the morning, they found what was left of the village of Dulce Nombre de Maria. Among the dead: Carlos. Doña Angélica. José and Maria under a rock at the ridge, their arms entwined around each other.

A total of twenty-six bodies.

They also found Don Agustín sitting near the bank of the stream, his eyes glazed. In his arms he held the remains of Paulina's youngest child. Something had blown the child's head off; it lay by the old man's side.

Further down the river they found Paulina, two of her children asleep beside her. "Oh, I'm so glad you've finally come," she said in a high, shrill voice. "I had to stop. I've been wounded, you see." Blood gushed from her shoulder, soiling her once gay green-and-yellow striped dress. What remained of her arm dangled from its socket.

Raul found Tere, Santos, Luz, and Miguel huddled under a rocky ledge behind the cave where the army had cornered the villagers. His family had survived the massacre! And Raul, *comandante* of the guerrilla-controlled territory of Chalatenango, wept loud, raw tears.

About mid-morning, Theo appeared out of nowhere, limping up to the exhausted group of survivors as they regrouped in the very cave where the army had trapped them. She still clutched the wounded little girl. Theo had been hit in the leg as she dashed from the cave but had managed to crawl with Isabel to the cover of some underbrush where the tributary curved into the Sumpul. When Meg saw her gangling friend, she wept as freely as the *comandante* had.

They also found the bodies of their protectors. Benjamin and the other five guerrilla fighters had been killed while providing what cover they could while the villagers scattered. As Meg observed their mutilated, decapitated corpses, she could only hope that they had been killed instantly and that the macabre carving up of these once young, athletic bodies—the gouging out of their eyes—had happened after their souls had already winged to heaven.

Two hundred and six of them had set out on the *guinda*—one hundred and sixty-five survived it. The villagers laid the bodies they recovered in nearby ditches or in the bushes, knowing the vultures would eventually sniff them out. There was no time to bury their friends.

"The vulture should be declared the national bird of El Salvador," Raul muttered through clenched teeth after they had hidden the last corpse. "The best and bravest among us always end up in a vulture's gullet."

Fifteen people were still unaccounted for. Most were children. The villagers were forced to assume that the swollen Sumpul River had claimed them, but they hoped against all odds that the missing might have made it to the other side of the river and would find their way to one of the refugee camps in Honduras. Or maybe a miracle would happen and they would be impatiently waiting for their mothers back at the village.

Theo had quickly cleaned her own wound in the stream. "Just

a little badge of courage so that I never forget what happened to us," she said with a shrug as she limped back to the village unassisted.

Yet even with the guerrillas' help, it took the survivors four days to make their way back to Dulce Nombre de Maria. Only Paulina was seriously wounded; the rest were badly bruised and scraped from the falls they had sustained while escaping the battalion's fire. Most, like Meg, walked home on cut and swollen feet. They would mend physically, but Meg knew that the overexposure and the psychological exhaustion the massacre dealt to the remaining villagers would take a long time to heal.

That gloom deepened when they finally reached the village. When the battalion found Dulce Nombre de Maria empty, the soldiers had taken out their anger by smashing furniture, turning over water barrels, burning the remaining stores of corn and beans. The village was strewn with debris, and when Meg went into Tere's house, she found that soldiers had urinated on the mattress where she and Theo slept. The huge poster of Christ the Good Shepherd, which hung on the wall above the bed, had been smeared with mud, and someone had scrawled across it, "He doesn't help Commie pigs."

But the holes where they had hidden their possessions had not been found, even though the soldiers discovered one of the cows out in the pasture and had slaughtered it and left it to the vultures.

Raul and the *muchachos* stayed for a few days and helped the villagers clean up and repair what could be salvaged. Several guerrillas disappeared mysteriously one morning and then returned with three donkeys laden with corn, beans and fruit. One of the rebels led a new milk cow into the plaza, a gift from

Monkey Face, their silent benefactor.

Theo never left Paulina's side as the woman hovered between life and death. Meg knew the clinic's supply of penicillin was running dangerously low, and Paulina also desperately needed blood transfusions. The community leader's only hope was that she would be strong enough, with the penicillin shots, to fight the blood loss resulting from the hemorrhaging she suffered when her arm was blown off. Theo had done her best to dress the bloody stump, but she complained to Meg that the woman should be in the intensive care unit of a hospital. Since that wasn't possible, they could only hope that her body would be able to fight off the infection.

Late the next afternoon, Meg took a few minutes to sit beside Theo at Paulina's bedside. She watched Theo gently massage the area around the bandaged wound.

"Where does such love come from, Theo? You get inside the hurt, inside the throb in the sprained leg or the crushed heart. You reach into its hot center and heal it."

"Some of us are born to be Cherry Ames, I guess. You learn how to meet the pain, engage it."

"Yeah, I can see that. But me, I try to void pain with everything I've got. I've always been so scared of it." Meg shut her eyes tightly. "I could take being a martyr as long as I didn't have to suffer, as long as it was over quickly."

"It has something to do with 'vocation,'" Theo grumbled. "I doubt if you will be called to be a martyr. Now get back to your own tasks, Sister." And she sent Meg packing.

As Meg went about helping to clean up the village and assisting Theo in treating the minor injuries and the inevitable colds and fevers that caught up with them, she was dimly aware that the guerrilla radio station had been broadcasting news of the massacre. Yet she was totally unprepared for the visit this news would provoke. They had been back for three days when the guard stationed at the edge of the village sounded the alert that a caravan of men on horseback was approaching. Panic-stricken mothers quickly rounded up children and were scurrying down toward the shelter when Raul shouted, "Stay calm, all of you! It is some sort of delegation."

Fifteen minutes later, as people peered curiously from inside their doorways, a horse bearing a mud-splattered Archbishop Romero trotted into the plaza. He was accompanied by two men, Padre David from Chalatenango and a doctor from the International Red Cross, and several pack horses loaded with provisions.

As she watched his approach, Meg thought there was something familiar about the doctor. Why, yes. The man in the three-piece suit who had given her his card in the airport the day she arrived in El Salvador. What was his name? Ah, yes, she remembered, Gomez.

"So you didn't heed the custom officer's warning and stick to teaching First Communion classes," he said, shaking her hand.

"No, I guess I haven't," Meg answered, smiling broadly.

"Well, I still don't discuss politics with strangers," he said with the faintest hint of a wink as he went off to examine Paulina's wound.

When Romero saw Meg and Theo, the archbishop's face lit up. "So this is where you have fled to."

They nodded.

"I suspect Rutilio would be proud of you," he said. "As for me, well, I too am glad you are here. Will you stay on now, at my personal invitation, and replace Carlos and continue to serve these suffering people?"

"You know we will, *Monseñor*," Theo replied for both of them.

He thanked them and added, "These days I walk the roads gathering up dead friends, listening to widows and orphans and trying to spread hope. Pray for me, *Madres*." With that, he turned away to attend to the long line that had formed to seek his blessing.

He spoke for a long while to Raul. Afterward, when she saw his face, Meg knew the young guerrilla commander had been deeply moved by whatever it was that the archbishop had told him.

Tere too came away with her eyes shining after her brief meeting with Romero. "He reminds me so much of my father," she told Meg later.

Although they were grateful for the food and medicine he brought, Meg noted that it was the way the man seemed to enter into their pain, his sad, compassionate eyes that appeared to read their very souls, the weary face, the faded, dusty cassock that the people would remember. And when he was martyred a few years later, they would revere him as a saint.

Meg knew she didn't have to be a prophet to predict that Romero's visit to Dulce Nombre de Maria would be described for years to come—around guerrilla campfires, during the Masses celebrated by the priests who accompanied the civilians inside guerrilla-controlled territory, in the refugee camps in Honduras, at gatherings of the Christian communities back in Aguilares and throughout El Salvador. Perhaps the story would grow with the telling, but the kernel would remain true—how the archbishop had knelt down and kissed the ground in the village plaza and called it holy ground and its people a holy people; how he said Mass for all those who had been slain; how he wept when people described the massacre; how sad he was when he told them that the government had scoffed at the guerrillas' newscasts and assured the country and the international news media that no massacre had ever taken place, that it was only "guerrilla propaganda;" how he had eaten and even sang with them as the afternoon wore on; how he seemed so reluctant to leave them.

Then there was the "miracle." Paulina seemed to rise from the grave itself as soon as she felt Romero's hand on her head. "He laid his hands on me and I got right up and danced," she would tell anyone who'd listen to her when she was once again well. After Dr. Gomez examined her and consulted with Theo, however, they decided to take advantage of the archbishop's jeep waiting down at Padre David's parish in Chalatenango and get the woman to a hospital. But the doctor was amazed at Paulina's progress and laid the saving of her life clearly at Theo's feet. "You have the gift of healing, *Madre*," Meg heard him tell Theo with admiration in his voice.

"I don't like the look of Sister Theo's leg," Dr. Gómez said to Meg after he'd finished examining Paulina.

"But she said it was just a scratch and that she'd removed the bullet when she washed the wound at the river that morning after the massacre," Meg said, astounded.

"Well, she hasn't told you the truth," the doctor said. "Something is still there, deeply embedded in her calf. And it is infected. We'll have to operate—and fast—to remove it."

"But she'll be all right, Doctor, won't she?" Meg asked, mildly alarmed. She had been dimly aware that Theo's limp had not gone away, but then everyone was suffering from sore feet after the exhausting *guinda*.

"I think we can halt the infection, but I need your help to convince her to come down with us. Today. She doesn't think she can leave the people here after the, ah… after what's happened to you all here," he stammered, looking down at his feet.

"Don't worry, Doctor. She'll go with you; I'll see to that," Meg said in a determined voice. Then she added, "We'll be okay here. We're pretty tough people, you know." And she went off to find Theo.

It took some convincing—and a good deal of reassuring—to make Theo see that they could get along without her for a couple of weeks. "Besides, we need you whole if you're going to be a guerrilla nurse," Meg joked as she helped her pack her belongings.

In the fading light of the setting sun, Romero blessed the villagers and promised he would come back "at harvest time" to visit them again. Then he and his caravan set off, more slowly than they had come, with two of the guerrillas carrying Paulina in a hammock and Theo riding behind the doctor.

Meg watched them until the caravan faded over the horizon.

Chapter 10

Christmas 1978

Dulce Nombre de María

"I don't care if it isn't the custom here. It just won't feel like Christmas if we don't have a Christmas tree," Meg complained to no one in particular over breakfast.

"Look," Meg announced to her adopted family as they dunked yesterday's tortillas in mugs of warm milk, "how about if we do a little cultural fusing and I make a Christmas tree out of one of your own native trees instead of mooching around because there's not a pine tree within seventy miles of here? How about if I decorate that old banana tree in front of the chapel? The poor thing's been bombed so many times it's been traumatized and can't grow bananas anymore, so if it becomes the village Christmas tree it will feel it still has some purpose in life. What do you think?"

The little group around the breakfast table stared at her. Their friend, ordinarily so cheerful, had grown moody, even touchy in Theo's absence. Meg was aware that she was being difficult and suspected they had agreed to humor her.

"But, *Madre*, what is a Christmas tree?" Miguel asked between mouthfuls of soggy tortilla.

"Ah, Miguelito," Meg grinned, her eyes lighting up. "A Christmas tree is truly magical. It is trimmed with lights and ornaments and tinsel and strings of berries and popcorn—and on the very tiptop of the tree is a bright, golden star that shines out for all to see."

"Does it glow in the dark and shoot off fireworks?"

"Well, no, not exactly. Let's just say it has a magic all its own. And if you want to, you and your friends can help me make the ornaments and—and yes, that's it, tonight after our Christmas celebration in the chapel, we'll invite everyone to gather round the tree for some dancing and singing." Meg was becoming enthusiastic. It was the first time she felt somewhat like her old self since Theo had been taken to the hospital three weeks ago.

"But, Meguita, what does this tree have to do with Christ's birth?" Tere asked. "The children and I have been putting so much work into making the *Nacimiento* in the chapel. We have to finish it today."

"Oh, how could I forget?" Meg gulped guiltily.

Under Don Lucho's direction, Tere and the school children had been whittling figures and animals for the crib scene for over a week now, and she realized she mustn't divert the kids' attention with some sort of *gringo* wonder that spouted fire and popcorn. "It's just that it's hard for me to really get the Christmas spirit without a Christmas tree—that's just the way I was brought up," she said too brightly, ignoring the quiver in her voice. "A family tradition."

"We understand about traditions, Meguita." Tere smiled, but there was a worried look on her face. "How important they are, how they express the very soul of a people. Tell us more about your Christmas tree tradition."

Meg shot her a grateful look. "Ever since I can remember, my brothers and I would look forward to going out with my dad—then, after his death, with my mom—to track down a pine tree out in the countryside somewhere," Meg reminisced. A faraway look spread across her freckled, sunburned face. "When we found the perfect tree, we'd chop it down and drag it home through the snow and store it in the garage. Then one night right before Christmas, we'd all decorate it with things we'd been making for weeks—just like you've been getting ready for Christmas by making things for the crib. You can hang just about anything on a tree, you know—and we did! Gingerbread men, candy canes, cutout reindeer and snowmen and elves, plus the special ornaments that had been passed down in my family from generation to generation, which my mother hung so carefully on the tree each year. Then we'd turn off all the lamps and light the tree and just sit there and admire it. My mom and dad would have a glass of 'Christmas cheer'—which is what they called a shot of whiskey—and we kids would eat Christmas cookies and drink hot chocolate and lie down underneath the tree and look all the way up to that star on the very top."

Meg looked at the confused faces around the table and was suddenly aware that she was not making any sense. She realized she was homesick for the smells and sounds of her home in Pennsylvania. Her mother would still have a tree, and maybe some of the grandchildren would help her trim it. Her brothers,

Micky and Tommy, and their wives and kids would all gather in Pittsburgh for Christmas dinner. She hadn't been at that dinner for many years now.

"Listen, Meguita, I have an idea." Tere brought Meg's thoughts back to the breakfast table. "The children and I will work on the crib scene and try to finish it by early afternoon. Then we'll all help you with the tree. Meanwhile," Tere added authoritatively, "you can be excused from helping us with the *Nacimiento*. In fact, I *commission* you to work on the tree, because it means so much to you. We want you to be happy on our Lord's birthday, *compañera*." Tere gave Meg a smile that registered both understanding and concern. "Besides," she added, "I think you might like to have some time to yourself today."

The withered old banana tree didn't offer a lot of possibilities. Its giant-sized, mud-streaked leaves were a poor substitute for long-needled pine boughs. Instead of coming to a point at the top, the tree spread out into three separate stocks. But Meg remained undaunted as she puttered about collecting odds and ends that might be used for an impromptu ornament. The day was cool and sunny and the *nortes*, the name the villagers gave to the breezes that came from the north at this time of year, blew gently through Dulce Nombre de Maria this Christmas Eve day.

Meg hummed "Oh Tannenbaum" as she scavenged items to decorate the tree. A few oranges, an ear of corn, a sprinkling of the dark red blood flowers El Salvador was so famous for, a sugar cane stock, ripe coffee beans for a chain that she could loop along the tree's massive leaves, cotton balls that could pass for snowflakes.

"Homegrown ornaments, all right," she said to herself, grinning.

What to do about the star and the three-pronged tree top? Meg quickly dismissed the Father, Son, and Holy Ghost motif as well as a Jesus, Mary, and Joseph arrangement. Then she had an idea. She would cut out stars and put on them the names of all those who had died "giving light" to the village. The Christ Child would still hold the center spot, but he would be flanked by the "Don Ramon" and "Dona Mercedes" stars. Immediately below them would be stars for Carlos and the others who had died in the Sumpul massacre. She would hang stars for Rutilio and Don Chepe from El Jícaro—and maybe even one for her dearly beloved Chileans Alfredo and José.

It took Meg most of the day to make the stars and string the tough little coffee beans into a chain long enough to be respectable. She kept humming away—snatches of old Christmas carols—while she worked, pleased with her progress.

The guerrillas had declared a Christmas truce and the army was expected to honor it. That probably accounted for the villagers' festive mood. Meg felt part of an age-old drama as she sat in the shade of the chapel next to the banana tree stringing her beans and cutting her stars. The village women were bustling about preparing a special *atol* to share after the evening's liturgy, while the kids scurried hither and yon tracking down yet another item for the ever-expanding Christmas crib inside the chapel. Tere had given orders that the adults were to stay away from the chapel until the children had finished the crib. "And that means you too, *Madre*," she said firmly.

Meg was dotting the tree with her last handful of cotton balls when Tere and Grandmother Santos came over to inspect her masterpiece.

"Well, what do you think?" Meg turned and faced her two

friends.

Tere giggled and Santos smiled her wide, toothless grin and clapped her hands.

"You've made what we call a harvest tree, Meguita," Santos cried. "It's what we make to honor the Lord's blessings, to thank him for a plentiful harvest for our crops." She paused, walked over to Meg, and grasped her hands. "You have given our harvest tree a new meaning. Your stars show our gratitude for the sacrifice of our loved ones. They have watered our land with their blood so that we might live more abundantly."

"It's really lovely, *Madre,*" Tere said, hugging Meg. "Maybe we'll adopt it as our national symbol in the new Constitution we'll write after the victory."

"You'll be accused of 'cultural imperialism' if you do."

"Not if we use banana trees!" Tere laughed. "But your tree has given me an idea for our reflection tonight. We can meditate on how all these 'stars' of ours have brought light to the darkness, made the crooked ways straight, the valleys smooth, the Kingdom of God more present among us. What do you think?"

"You're our village leader until Paulina returns, Tere, so I'll let that be up to you."

"And I think the crib scene will also add to the reflection," Tere said with a twinkle in her eye. "Come along. I've been sent by the children and Don Lucho to bring you to see our finished work of art."

Tere led the nun into the chapel. It took Meg several seconds to adjust to the darkness. At first she didn't see the children gathered in front of the far wall behind the table that served as an altar. She heard a few muffled giggles before Don Lucho ordered them to move back from the wall and make room for her to take in the scene.

Meg let out a gasp. She had been prepared for a greatly "enlarged" rendition of the Nativity scene, with many contemporary figures mixed with the traditional shepherds, wise men and angels, but the kids had expertly reproduced the entire village of Dulce Nombre de Maria in miniature, including the main plaza and the chapel, which not only housed Jesus, Mary and Joseph, but the villagers themselves had become modern-day shepherds gathered around the newborn Savior. The homes, the fields, the river, the mountains in the distance—all were faithfully depicted.

Deeply moved, Meg drew closer to study the crèche more intently. She took in the airplanes and the helicopters that had been painted in the sky above the village. Her eye followed the tiny path behind the chapel that led to Don Lucho's ranch, where "Monkey Face" had expertly portrayed himself standing by his corral whittling. Beyond him, in the forest, a guerrilla unit camped—Meg supposed it was Raul who was in the lead.

But it was the scene beyond the forest that brought tears to her eyes. There, graphically re-enacted, was the massacre: the dead bodies of the children, of Carlos, of their six guerrilla companions. There she was, hugging Theo and the two children, Gustavo and Isabel. Theo's leg was red from her wound. And there was Paulina, her shoulder all bloody. And the soldiers retreating in the distance.

"Oh, dear Lord," Meg whispered, as tears trickled down her face. "This is more a crucifixion scene—our own!"

Her eyes shifted to the other side of the crèche. There, in a small clearing at the village entrance was Archbishop Romero,

Padre David, and Dr. Gomez with donkeys bringing supplies to the village. And at the very end of the Nativity scene, way to the left, was a gravesite with Rutilio Grande's name on it and people kneeling before it.

Meg sank to her knees before the scene, buried her face in her hands, and wept.

"Oh, Meguita, what's wrong? We thought you'd be pleased with what we've done!" Tere was down on her knees, holding her.

"But don't you like it, *Madre?*" said little Miguelito.

"Hush, child. I think she's crying because it is so real," Santos said, bending down to where the crying nun knelt. She patted the dark blond head. "Death has been so much a part of our lives this year. It is only right that we show all of that in our homage to *el Salvador y su Madre* this Christmas. It is our way of remembering our loved ones, just as you remember them with your 'stars.'"

Meg was trying to get a grip on herself. "Oh, no, forgive me, children. Forgive me, all of you," she gasped. "I... it's just that it's so, so graphic, so real... and so very lovely. All the work that's gone into it... it's just that I've never seen anything quite like it before, or ever had such a sense of the link between birth and death. Christmas and crucifixion—even resurrection. I'm just overwhelmed. Can you understand that?"

The children solemnly nodded, reassured by Meg's smile. Their *gringuita* did indeed like their hard work, even though she had a funny way of showing it.

Meg was aware of Don Lucho beside her. Looking into his eyes, she was startled to see the deep pain reflected there.

Wordlessly, he placed his hand on her shoulder. Then he limped back toward his post in the corner of the chapel.

"Children, go out and bring in the other adults so they can see your fine creation," Tere said, swishing them out of the chapel. Then she turned to Meg. "I know how you feel, *compa*. I cried all the time we made it."

"You did?" she said with relief. "That makes me feel better. Not like such a wet dish rag."

"How strange," she continued softly. "I, who always thought of myself as your big sister, even a substitute for your mother, I find myself suddenly needing your support and nurturing. Thank you, Terecita," she said simply.

And as she spoke, she knew deep down that, although she was loved, she was no longer needed in Dulce Nombre de Maria.

The evening's Christmas celebration was a simple affair. Tere surprised the villagers by having the children read from the prophet Isaias as he told of the child, the Wonder Counselor who would be born of a virgin, a sign of contradiction. Then they read the story of Christ's birth and sang "Adeste Fidelis" while they led the adults over to the *Nacimiento*, now shining brilliantly behind the altar in the glow of a dozen candles.

Gathered around the crib that told their own journey as a people, the villagers, led by Tere, prayed for all those portrayed in clay and wood before them. A litany of loved ones, living and dead:

Don Ramon
Dona Mercedes
Padre Carlos

227

Dona Paulina
Raul y los muchachos en la montana
Dona Angelica y su hijita
Los pequenos Maria y Jose
El companero Benjamin y sus valiosos companeros quienes
murieron protegiéndonos de los soldados
Madre Theo, que se mejore pronto para estar con nosotros de nuevo
Padre David
Madre Meguita
Todos nuestros hijos, vivos y muertos
Todos nuestros amigos en los campos de refugios en Honduras
QUE DIOS LES BENDIGA Y PROTEGA AHORA Y SIEMPRE

When the liturgy was over, Meg was cajoled into leading everyone outside to behold the old banana tree, which even under the full moon looked woebegone compared to the Nativity scene inside the chapel. Her friends patiently listened as she sheepishly explained the Christmas tree tradition in her country.

"Children, look at the stars on the tree," Tere interrupted. "Each one has a name of one of our martyrs. See how the moon plays on them and illuminates them? Well, these people are Dulce Nombre de Maria's shining stars that light up our life, give us direction and hope, just as the star of Bethlehem did for the wise men long ago. Like them, we too are being led to Christ by our stars. That is why Meg wanted us to sing and dance and be happy around her tree. So what do you say?"

Someone produced a guitar and the singing and dancing began. The piping hot *atol* appeared, along with oranges and apples and homemade candy made from the sugar cane harvest. Meg led the children in an improvised version of the Virginia reel around the Christmas tree, to the giggles and hand clapping of the adults.

Later that night, just before she dropped off to sleep on her mattress in the corner of the hut, Meg reached over to nudge Theo. "Wasn't that one of the loveliest Christmases you've ever had, dear?" she whispered happily before she realized that she was alone in the bed.

Throughout the celebration, she had kept an eye peeled for Theo, but her friend had not appeared.

"Tomorrow perhaps, on Christmas Day. That would be just like her." Then she rolled over and went to sleep.

***

The day after Christmas was laundry day. Meg was kneeling in the mud along the riverbank washing out her clothes with the other women when she spied Don Lucho limping down the path.

Here comes our guardian angel," she announced to her companions. "Let's hope he's bringing good tidings this time."

Their taciturn informer slowly picked his way through the drying clothes laid out on the grass until he reached the spot along the riverbank where the women knelt. He greeted them formally, then turned to Meg. "I have a message for you from some of your friends down in Aguilares," he said, clearing his throat. "They say to tell you that the *Madre* has taken a turn for the worse and that a visit from you might cheer her spirits."

Before Meg could absorb the full impact of Don Lucho's message, Tere bounded to her feet and threw a protective arm around her shoulder.

"But the *Madre's* wound was only superficial, *patrón*," Tere cried. "What happened?"

The rancher thrust his hands into his pockets, shifting his weight from his good leg to his lame one and back again. "I was only told that she has taken a turn for the worse, and that *Madre* Meguita is to go at once," Lucho replied gruffly, his eyes avoiding Meg's. "Ah, yes, and that a guide has been stationed over by my ranch ready to take the *Madre* to Chalatenango as soon as she is ready. From there, the priest will give her a ride to the capital." He stopped a minute, then added, "The message is to hurry."

Without saying good-bye, "Monkey Face" turned on his heels and hobbled off in the direction he had come.

Meg felt rather than saw the women's grief-stricken eyes on her. She fought down the panic that was rising from the pit of her stomach.

"Theo's probably just feeling lonely in the capital. We all get homesick at Christmastime. We mustn't sound the alarm." Then she added with a voice beginning to quiver, "Still, I don't think it would hurt to pray."

In fifteen minutes, Meg gathered what she needed, soothed the villagers as best she could, assuring them of her speedy return, and set off to meet her guide. In another hour and a half—instead of the two hours the hike usually took—she and her guerrilla companion were sprinting up the path leading to Padre David's house in Chalatenango.

The priest knew no more about the state of Theo's health than Meg did. But he too had received word that the *Madre* had taken "a turn for the worse". He took one look at Meg's face and immediately headed for the shed to ready his rickety old jeep for the drive down to Aguilares and on to San Salvador.

Meg was grateful for the priest's silence as they inched their way over the mud-clogged, rutted road leading to the capital. David was a Belgian priest. He'd been at the parish for five years now, and every month she, Theo, and Carlos had made the trip to Chalatenango for a pastoral meeting with the village leaders and the handful of other priests and Sisters who were working in the guerrilla-controlled areas in the eastern half of the province. Although she didn't know him well, Meg had the greatest respect for the gigantic red-haired man bouncing along next to her in the old Land Rover. It was from him that the villagers of Dulce Nombre de Maria had learned that God did not want them to remain enslaved to the landowners, that He wanted them to stand up and break out of their oppression. It was David who helped them start their cooperative and went with them to present their land claims to the government. It was he who insisted on sending village leaders such as Don Roman to church-run centers in other parts of the country, where they could learn more about community organizing, agricultural techniques, the ABCs of forming a cooperative.

Meg's thoughts returned to Theo. What could have gone wrong? Meg turned her conversation with Dr. Gomez over in her mind. They would have to operate at once, he said. The wound had become infected, but he was confident that they could stop the infection. Had there been complications? Perhaps the doctor felt that Theo needed to have someone to wait on her and cheer her up while she recovered. After all, Meg was the only other member of the Sisters of Charity in El Salvador since Queen Mum had gone to Honduras. The congregation's custom was to have a Sister at the disposition of a fellow Sister whenever there was a crisis.

She blamed herself for not even thinking about accompanying

Theo down to the capital. She had been so sure that it wasn't serious! Theo would have been embarrassed if she had offered and would have told her in no uncertain terms that she was to stay and tend the need of the villagers

"Let this not be serious," she prayed as they crawled down the mountain road toward the pan american highway.

It was almost midnight when they rumbled up to the parish gate at her former mission station in Aguilares. After ten minutes of pounding on the door and the barking of Shadow Séptimo, they finally roused a sleepy Ricardo.

"But we weren't expecting you until tomorrow at the earliest," said the surprised seminarian. "How did you manage to get here so fast? We only sent the message yesterday afternoon!"

"We flew," Padre David replied dryly.

"Ricardo, what's wrong with Theo?" Meg demanded, as she gave him a bear hug and Séptimo a quick scratch under his chin.

"Come in out the drizzle. Let me pour you a hot cup of *atol*. You must be exhausted. And don't worry, she's going to be all right."

Ricardo ushered the two visitors into the familiar parish house and sat them down at the kitchen table. Meg noticed that things were mostly just the same as when they had left over a year ago now, and yet there were subtle changes—different smells, no sign of Mum's treasured spice rack, no homemade cookies in a can on the table, Rutilio's napkin ring gone, another in its place. Theo's old dog still made his home under the table. He was a comfort to her now as he laid his head against her knee.

"Theo's going to be all right," Ricardo repeated as he served

David and Meg steaming hot cups of *atol* from the thermos on the table. The tall, thin seminarian seemed much older than his twenty-five years. His eyes held a resignation that was new to Meg; he had seen too much, chronicled too much, and now he was becoming a Man of Sorrows just like the master he served.

He sat down across from Meg and took her hands in his. "Meguita, the leg had gangrene. They had to amputate above the knee."

Meg's whole body winced. "Oh no, Ricardo!" she cried. "Oh, my poor, poor Theo." She pushed away the *atol* and put her head down on her arms. "God damn it," she moaned through clenched teeth. "It's so unfair, so bloody unfair!"

"No, it is surely not very fair," Ricardo said, as he laid his hands on Meg's trembling shoulders. "Things haven't been fair for a long time now," he mumbled, more to himself than to his visitors.

"The operation took place two days ago. Our ever gentle, compassionate Theo is in deep need of some comforting herself. We sent for you because she needs support, Meg. That hospital is so dreary and the staff so suspicious—if not outright hostile—of anybody they think has 'connections' to the *compas*."

Meg lifted her tear-stained face. "What about Paulina?" she asked in an alarmed voice. "Is she all right?"

"Yes, thanks to Dr. Gomez. With his Red Cross connections he was able to have her moved to a church-run clinic, where she's recovering nicely."

"Oh, and I haven't even mentioned Carlos—forgive me!" she said in a stricken voice. "Your beloved classmate and best friend. You were to be ordained together next year." Now it was her turn to give comfort. She got up and took the young man into her arms and held him for a long time. Both of them wept silently.

"So many deaths. I wonder if it's worth it?" Ricardo pulled his handkerchief out of his pocket and blew his nose. He sat back down and stirred his now cold *atol.*

"I don't know anymore. I just don't know…" The three of them sat for a long while in silence, each caught up in their own memories.

Finally Meg asked, "And Theo, is she terribly depressed?"

The seminarian shrugged. "Yes, I'd say she's depressed. Who wouldn't be? She'll have to spend months in rehabilitation, which means she'll have to go back to the States and probably never return to those she now calls 'her people' up there in the mountains."

"I must go to her at once," Meg cried, standing up. "David, can you take me?"

"I'll take you over first thing in the morning," the huge Belgian promised. "You can't go now—it's curfew, remember? Besides they'd never let you in. Let's get some sleep now. We can be there when the doors open in the morning."

"Right. Get some sleep now, *Madre.* You need to arrive fresh and cheery at the hospital tomorrow—for Theo's sake," added Ricardo, standing up to show the distraught woman to her bed.

"By the way," he said as he led her down the hall toward the guest room, "I also notified your Mother Superior about… about how the operation turned out."

"But why did you do that, if she's going to be okay? It will only alarm the nuns unnecessarily," Meg said crossly.

"Well, maybe I shouldn't have," Ricardo answered in a hurt voice. "I just thought she could use all the prayers she could get."

Meg lay awake throughout the long night trying to absorb the shock of the amputation. She tried to come to grips with what being an amputee now implied. But Theo was a nurse and knew better than any of them about how long it would take to recover—and what limitations she'd have to live with for the rest of her life. Could she ever hope to come back to El Salvador to work? If she couldn't, it would break her heart. And what about "their people" up in Dulce Nombre de Maria? And if it wasn't so serious, why had Ricardo felt it necessary to inform the Motherhouse? Mother Ursula would be frantic. She had better call herself, once she'd seen Theo, and assure the community that she would recover. Finally, Meg turned to prayer, beseeching the Lord over and over again and his holy mother, patron of all who suffered, to heal her Theo, her lovely, dearest, precious Theo.

Morning dawned at last and after a quick cup of coffee, David drove Ricardo and Meg to the hospital.

"I-I'd like to be alone with Theo awhile," Meg said to the two men as they pulled up in front of the hospital entrance.

"I thought you might," David said, giving her a sympathetic look. "I have to go back to Chalatenango this afternoon and I want to take word back about how Theo's doing to the people. But I have some errands to run in town first. I'll come back in a couple hours."

"I'll go with Padre David," Ricardo said, "but let me at least go in with you and show you the room."

Ricardo and Meg were met at the door by a police guard who demanded to see their identification papers. The guard only admitted them into the hospital after Ricardo told him that he was sent to visit the American missionary at the personal request of Archbishop Romero.

But that didn't work at the hospital desk.

"Absolutely no visitors are allowed to see the patient," snapped the officious-looking intern behind the desk.

"But I've come all the way from my parish in the mountains to visit my colleague," Meg said, the blood rushing to her face. "She sent for me, and there is no way you are going to keep me from seeing her!"

Ricardo squirmed beside her. "Now you've done it," he whispered.

A small crowd of hospital personnel had gathered near the desk and were staring at Ricardo and Meg. "They're sympathizers," muttered one. "The *Madre's* one of those crazy foreign nuns who stirs up the *campesinos*, filling their heads with notions of forming cooperatives and such things," a white-clad man who Meg presumed was a doctor added in a loud voice.

"Please," she pleaded, turning to him. "I must see my friend. She's sent for me! She's just had her leg amputated and, and..." Meg was on the verge of tears.

"The order is for no visitors." But he seemed to relent somewhat as he glanced quickly away from Meg's face. "You'll have to wait until the doctor in charge of the case arrives and gives you permission."

"When will that be?" Ricardo asked.

"Dr. Gomez should be in sometime this morning." He turned on his heels and marched away.

"Meg, calm down, calm down, do you hear?" Ricardo pleaded as he guided her toward the sorry-looking cluster of chairs that served as a waiting room. "These people are very suspicious of us. You must remember that. Be extremely careful of what you say."

"But listen, I have an idea," he said. "I'll have Padre David drop me at the archbishop's office. Romero is taking a special interest in Theo's recovery. I'm sure he can make a few calls and get you in. Stay here and wait for Dr. Gomez. He'll be here shortly—he knows you are on your way. He was the one who advised sending for you. It's just that no one expected you to arrive so quickly. So just be patient."

Without waiting for a reply, Ricardo was off, almost running down the hall toward the hospital entrance.

In the waiting room, Meg paced back and forth in front of the desk in full view of the scowling intern. Neither spoke. Finally, after an hour or so, her name was called over the hospital loudspeaker and she rushed to the desk. There, the doctor who had told her to wait for Dr. Gomez was furiously writing out a pink slip, which he practically threw at her.

"Here, this will get you in to see your friend. A favor to the archbishop, although it is highly irregular," he said coldly.

Spying a nurse nearby, the doctor brushed by Meg and accosted the young woman, who appeared to quake in his presence.

"Show the *Madre* to Room 3-F," he ordered. Without looking back at Meg, he set off down the hall. Meg would later learn that he was the head of the hospital.

The young nurse accompanied Meg to the third floor and guided her to a small, out-of-the-way room past the main ward.

The door was shut and a "no visitors" sign had been posted. Meg thanked the nurse and was about to enter, when she felt the woman's hand on her arm.

"*Madre,*" the nurse whispered softly as she glanced around nervously, "stay with your friend as much as you possibly can. Sometimes—well, you see, they know you work with the guerrillas—and so sometimes care isn't what it should be and… and accidents can happen…"

"Whatever do you mean?" Meg turned around and faced the nurse, giving her a sharp glance. "What are you implying?"

"Nothing, nothing, *Madre*. Forget it, please," the nurse said as she looked anxiously toward an orderly coming down the hall. Then, in a louder voice, she announced, "This is the room. The patient is weak, so please don't do anything to excite her." She hurried off.

Meg paused before she turned the doorknob, disturbed by the nurse's warning. She made a mental note to query Dr. Gomez about the hospital's efficiency. She knew that hospital care left a lot to be desired in El Salvador, as well as all over Latin America, but she had never heard any tales of outright neglect as a result of a patient's political leanings.

Her misgivings mounted as Meg pushed open the door and let her eyes adjust to the darkness. The tiny room was dingy and smelled of medicine and urine. In the corner was a narrow bed. There, lost in the yellowing sheets and soiled pillowcase, Theo lay sleeping.

A sharp pain shot through Meg's chest, and she bit her lip to hold back the cry rising in her throat. Was this wan, pale woman lying there so silently with a tube in her arm and another in her nose really Theo?

She tiptoed up to the bed and studied the gaunt face for a long moment. How hollow her cheeks had become. And the dark circles under her eyes—when had Theo become so paper thin, so pale? What had happened to her fantastic tan, her rugged leanness?

Meg bent down and softly kissed the white forehead.

Theo's eyes fluttered open and Meg heaved a sigh of relief at the sight of those same deep pools of dark brown.

"Hello, pal," she whispered.

Theo had trouble focusing for a minute. Then a look of recognition flooded her face and she smiled her old familiar grin.

"Meg, bless you. You've come!" she said in a faint voice.

"Wild horses wouldn't stop me."

"I-I've lost my leg, Meggie," she said, her face twisting in agony. Theo's whole body began to shake as she broke into rasping sobs. "I won't ever be able to run across a field again. Or chase one of our little rascals and make him take his medicine…"

"Oh Theo, favorite Musketeer, it's going to be all right—you'll see." Meg gathered Theo in an awkward hug. "It won't slow you down much. You'll do more as a peg-leg than the rest of us do with two legs. You will!"

Theo slowly calmed down, but the uncharacteristic shadow of fear was still present as she gazed back at Meg.

"But what will become of me?" she moaned. "How can I go back to Dulce Nombre de Maria? I'm useless now as a 'guerrilla nurse,' as you always called me. What will I do during the air raids, the *guindas*?" She began to weep again.

"Well, kiddo, as Ruth said to Naomi, 'Wherever you go, I shall go,' so you're stuck with me—forever. If we can't manage back at the village, maybe we could stay with Padre David at the parish in Chalatenango. You can set up a clinic there for the whole eastern part of the province. Or maybe it's time to go back to Aguilares. Or perhaps Archbishop Romero might offer us some sort of special assignment we couldn't refuse. So you see, *compa*," she said, gently cuffing Theo on the chin, "there is no end to the possibilities for this fantastic three-legged team."

Meg had managed to bring a smile to the sick woman's face. "Ah, Meggie. You're such balm for my spirit. What a wonderful, out-of-the-blue surprise," she said with a contended sigh.

"You weren't expecting me?"

"No, of course not. They told me I couldn't have visitors. I only see Dr. Gomez. He's been wonderful to me, but he only comes in the mornings. So you are like a breath of spring in the middle of the darkest Ohio winter."

"Well, your spring is here to stay. She's not leaving until you are well enough to leave this God-forsaken hospital."

Meg looked around in disgust at the dreary cubicle that had become Theo's temporary home. "Our place back with Tere and her family is much more hospitable than this," she complained.

"And the people much friendlier," Theo added. "The staff seems so stiff and formal. As if they didn't know what to do with me. Guess they don't get very many wounded *gringas*." She winked weakly at Meg. "But as you say, Sister, it's only temporary."

Theo's eyes began to flutter and then her eyelids drooped. "I think I'll just take forty winks, Meg. You're being here is more than I could have ever wished…" Her voice trailed off.

Meg was sitting in the straight-backed chair beside Theo when Dr. Gomez opened the door.

"Ah you've come," he said, satisfaction in his voice as he motioned to Meg to step outside the door. "I sent for you because I thought you might lift her spirits," he explained as he closed the door behind them. "She's suffering the normal depression that comes after an amputation—and that can work against her chances of recovery."

"But surely those chances are excellent, aren't they, Doctor?" Meg asked, swallowing down the panic she felt rising from her stomach.

"Her body must fight the infection," Dr. Gomez said, directly meeting Meg's troubled eyes. "I think we got most of the gangrene. But now it depends on her own resistance. You can see for yourself that she is run down—her diet has been woefully inadequate for a long period of time—so all we can do is hope, bolster her spirits, and pray."

Dr. Gomez turned to go into the hospital room, but Meg stopped him with another question. "Doctor, is she getting the best possible care here?"

"Why do you ask that?" he asked sharply.

"Well, it is probably nothing, but the staff seems so hostile. They evidently know we work up in Chalatenango. I have the distinct impression that they don't like the work we are doing or the people with whom we associate."

"Look, *Madre*," Dr. Gomez said in a low voice. "The staff here is divided and the police watch the hospital like hawks to see if any wounded guerrillas are brought in for treatment. I'm sure they won't try to interrogate Theo or you, since you're

Americans, but it's best not to say anything about your work up there in the hills, agreed?"

"Agreed," Meg said, "but the staff can be trusted to take proper care of Theo, can't they?"

"I will make sure they do," he said curtly, and before Meg could ask another question, he entered the room and began to examine his patient.

Once the doctor left, Meg resumed her post beside Theo, who was now sleeping peacefully. As she studied her friend's face, a new wave of panic rushed through her. Just how serious was this? What were Theo's chances of not getting better?

"You can't have Theo, dear God, you can't," she prayed fervently. "It's not part of the program. You've taken Alfredo and Rutilio and so many others. Surely you have to leave some of us around to nurture the struggle, to water the shoots, to celebrate with the people when the victory comes. You who are the source of all wisdom, the fountain of all mercy, let Theo get well!"

Meg realized she was praying harder than she ever prayed in her life. She would do like her Irish ancestors before her and make some sort of promise to God in exchange for her friend's recovery.

"Save Theo's life and I-I promise you..." But what did she have to barter that wasn't already His?

She was thinking hard on what sacrifice she might promise when she was startled by a familiar whisper.

"Why bless my heart, you're here too, Sister Meg!" Queen Mum swept quietly into the room and hugged her. Then she bent down and made the sign of the cross on Theo's forehead. In a low voice, Mum explained how Mother Ursula had urgently sent word to her at the refugee camp in Honduras to go at once to be with Theo. The message was that Theo had been badly wounded. Yes, the whole Motherhouse now knew that Theo had lost a leg and the nuns were keeping a round-the-clock vigil in the chapel for their Sister's recovery. Mother Ursula herself was getting ready to fly down to El Salvador and was only waiting for a final call from Mum to update her on Theo's condition.

As glad as Meg was to see Queen Mum, she felt an unreasonable twinge of resentment at her arrival. She yearned to be alone with Theo, to nurse her back to health, to sit quietly at her side, holding her hand day in and day out until she was dismissed from the hospital. But now that Mum was here, she would have to share those tasks and bow to the older woman's decisions, according to the well-established rules of the community.

When she awoke, Theo was overjoyed to see Mum. And she was deeply moved that both of them had come to take care of her—and that even Mother Ursula was thinking of coming down to be with her.

"Oh please, Mum, tell Mother it isn't necessary," she said in a weak voice. "I already feel guilty for taking you away from the refugee camp, and Meg away from our village." Then she added ruefully. "I'll be seeing her and the other Sisters soon enough. I know enough about this… this process… to realize I have many months of therapy ahead of me."

For the next ten days, Meg and Queen Mum took turns keeping watch at Theo's bedside. They stayed out at the Aguilares parish, where they were daily showered with humble gifts of food and flowers and scrawled notes full of best wishes and prayers that the *campesinos* sent to their lovingly remembered *Madre Teo*.

Meg kept Theo company in the mornings and evenings, while Mum stayed in the afternoons.

Meg also managed to track down Paulina. Dr. Gomez had personally taken the village leader to a small clinic run by British Quakers. She knew that the staff was taking a risk in caring for Paulina, because the army was deeply suspicious of anyone who had been wounded from Chalatenango. But once she found the simple, out-of-the-way clinic and spoke to several of the nurses, she was sure that Dulce Nombre de María's charismatic leader was receiving both excellent medical treatment and would be protected from any attempted harassment from the army.

Although Paulina was weak, she appeared to be recovering from her amputation more rapidly than Theo. As a sign of her determination, she had defiantly donned an even bigger and brighter red bow.

The Quakers told Meg that their patient's recovery was quite amazing.

"I'll be mended in no time, and I'll manage just fine with one arm—you'll see. In the midst of so much death and destruction, there must be a reason why my life has been spared, so I must get well quickly and get back home," she told Meg. "And yes, these nurses are taking splendid care of me, even though they say they are pacifists. But by the time I leave here, I think I'll have convinced them of the righteousness of our struggle," she said, the old twinkle back in her eyes.

"Now tell me about home."

Meg had to give a detailed account of all that had happened in Dulce Nombre de Maria during the past month.

"And Theo, is she back yet?"

"No. Theo has been having a hard time of it. Her wound became infected and they had to amputate her leg."

The woman remained silent for so long that Meg wondered if she was all right. Paulina had aged in the last year. Why hadn't she noticed it? The round face was marked with creases; the black wavy hair, cropped so short here in the clinic, was streaked with gray. Yet she was only a few years older than Meg.

Paulina might still be bearing children if her husband hadn't been killed. And now she was mourning the death of yet another of her children. Thank God she hadn't witnessed the grizzly scene next to the Sumpul River, the blood-soaked little body of her youngest lying in Don Agustín's arms, its head blown off. The old man hadn't been in his right mind since. Meg had to force herself to erase that ghastly scene from her memory. In fact, there were many details of the Sumpul massacre that she could not recall at all—she had suppressed them deep inside her, where she supposed they would one day catch up to her and make her remember and grieve.

"You know," Paulina finally said, "you *Madres* did not have to come to live among us—and in some ways we felt it was foolish of you to do so. After all, this is our struggle, not yours. My wound here," she went on, putting her hand carefully on her bandaged stump, "well, you could almost say it was inevitable. I know I'm lucky to be alive. I've always been resigned to getting wounded, even killed. Life is cheap here, as I'm sure you've realized."

"Yes," Meg acknowledged.

"But the fact that Theo's been wounded, well, that's different. Can God really want even the blood of a dedicated *gringa* nurse—a *Madre*—to water this afflicted land? It gives me much to think about, I tell you."

Paulina's words troubled Meg. She turned them over in her mind long after she had bid her friend goodbye. Why did Paulina and Tere have lingering doubts about their commitment to the Salvadoran people? Why was it so hard for them to understand God's call to religious women from the rich North to go and minister to his poor, suffering people south of the border? Their lack of understanding after all they had lived through together puzzled and depressed her.

As the days passed, Theo seemed to be rallying. After a good deal of persuasion, Mum had finally convinced Mother Ursula that it wouldn't be necessary for her to fly down, that the doctor thought Theo could withstand the flight back to the United States in about a month's time if she continued to recover at the same rate. But as much as Meg wanted to convince herself of her friend's recovery, she also noticed that Theo remained weak and feverish. She was also deeply troubled by the strange content of some of their conversations.

One evening, Theo looked sadly at Meg. "Sometimes I worry that I love you too much."

"What on earth do you mean?"

"That my love isn't... how can I put it... that it isn't as pure as it should be, as detached as it should be." Theo struggled to sit up.

"Hey, take it easy, Cherry Ames," Meg was alarmed by the strain she saw in Theo's face.

"No, let me say this. I've wanted to for so long now. You see, you've become so much more than a friend, so much more than a fellow Sister to me. Sometimes I feel as if I'm a part of you and that you're a part of me—a union that is so unique, but also so exclusive, so special that I want to protect it at all costs. And, well, I fear that maybe I love you too much..." She reached out and touched Meg's face.

Meg took Theo's hand and held it firmly in her own. "Oh, for heaven's sake, Theo-y. Will you can all those old 'particular friendship' taboos from Novitiate days once and for all?" She pressed Theo's large yet thin hand and rubbed it gently up and down her own face.

"Surely you know that I love you fiercely—so much so that I'm even jealous of the time Queen Mum spends with you. I love your long, lanky body, and I love to hug you close to me. But even more than that, I love your soul, your unique Theo-ness." Meg grinned crookedly, her eyes bright with tears. "I can't live without you, Theo," she said, her voice breaking. "That's why I'm here, and that's why you have to get better. So go to sleep now, and don't worry about loving me too much. You can't ever love me too much, okay?"

"Okay." And the sick woman gave Meg a relieved smile.

Another night the topic was life after death.

"Do you remember your crisis of faith back in the Novitiate, Meg?"

"Which one? I had about one a week," Meg laughed.

"The one about heaven. About how it couldn't be a place, that maybe it was right here on earth. You were half convinced that we were reborn after death, that in an instant, we saw all the lives we had lived already and were given to see how we had contributed in our own small way to the coming of the kingdom; but we would also be shown at that instant all that yet had to be done and were given the choice to come back for yet another lifetime and keep on contributing to the kingdom."

"Ah, yes, I guess I did entertain the idea of reincarnation a bit back in those days, didn't I? I can't believe you've remembered all those crazy meanderings." Meg chuckled.

"So, what do you believe now?"

Meg was struck by the urgency in Theo's voice.

"If you want the honest truth, I don't think much about it anymore. There just hasn't been much time to philosophize during these years."

"But you always talk about one day joining Alfredo across the horizon when your journey here on earth is over."

Meg shifted uncomfortably on her chair beside Theo's bed. "It's true, Theo, there's some deep yearning in me that I'd describe as a desperate hope—rather than a firm belief—that when we die we are somehow reunited to those we love."

She paused a minute, groping for the right words.

"If I know anything about who God is, it is because I've been known and loved by people like you and Alfredo and Madre Rosa. If God is the one who has spun and fashioned these great loves of mine, then this Great Weaver must have purposely entwined our lives together, not just for now but for all eternity. And only in dying will we be given to see how the pattern all fits together. Whether or not we get the chance to be refashioned and return, I don't know. I just fall back on Paul's 'eye has not seen, nor ear heard, nor has it entered into the heart of man what God has prepared for those who love him.'"

Theo was listening intently to Meg's every word. "What a lovely image! God the weaver, the old, wise spinning woman. Yes, that does appeal to me." Theo's eyes grew bright.

"And what do you think about the afterlife?" Meg asked

reluctantly.

"Oh, I certainly believe in life after death. Although it's a bit sacrilegious, I toy with the idea of reincarnation. I suppose you never realized that your Novitiate philosophizing had an effect on me, Meggins." Theo laughed softly as she looked up at her friend. "But it did. Even now, I sometimes think that this life is just another time around. I'd like to hope that I'll be present in the next generation, plugging away in a new body—but with some of the old Theo genes still present—and have another chance to live and love and connect."

Meg leaned forward and brushed Theo's stringy brown hair back from her forehead. "And in your new body, would you also maybe meet a new Meg along the way?" she asked in a low voice.

"Oh yes. A new Theo would always seek out her Meg. It's part of the Weaver's eternal pattern, you see." And she reached out, found Meg's hand, and held it tight. "Now run along back to the parish and leave me to my dreams." Then her eyes closed and she slept.

And finally, there was the night Theo confessed that she was jealous of Alfredo.

"Oh, Theo, don't. We've been over this before. There's nothing to forgive, for heaven's sake."

She went on, troubled by her friend's uneasy conscience. "There are many different ways of loving. We've talked about this that afternoon down by the river in Dulce Nombre de Maria. The love between a man and a woman is only one way; there is the love of a mother for her children, and there is the love that can exist between two women. All these ways of loving are holy, and if we are gifted with any or all of them during our lifetime, we are indeed blessed. You never, ever have to be jealous of Alfredo, my Theo. I love you both with all the love that's in me. It's just a matter of different ways of loving, you see; and I don't think one excludes the other."

The words seemed to comfort Theo, and she slept.

But the next morning when Meg arrived to keep vigil by Theo's side, she found her delirious with fever. She also found Dr. Gomez down the hall waiting for her.

"I'm sorry, *Madre*," he said, looking compassionately into the nun's pale, frightened face. "The blood tests show that the gangrene has spread throughout her body."

For the next forty-eight hours, Meg never left Theo's side. Only twice did she regain consciousness.

"I can smell the *kielbasa* and the *golumki*… Mom's cookin'… and she's singin' to me," she mumbled softly the first evening. "Now everybody's singin' round the piano… "

"Do you want Mum and me to sing to you, Theo?" She seemed to nod.

Mum intoned the ancient hymn the Sisters chanted each evening at Vespers:

Salve, Regina, Mater misericordiae,
vita, dulcedo, et spes nostra, salve.

The older nun's strong alto voice filled the room. Meg joined in, her own lighter voice following Mum's.

ad te clamamos

exsules filii Hevae,
ad te suspiramus, gementes et flentes
in hac lacrimarum valle.
Eia, ergo, advocata nostra, illos tuos
misericordes oculos ad nos converte;
et Jesum, benedictum fructum ventris tui,
nobis post hoc exsilium ostende.

Theo opened her cracked lips and weakly sang the last verse with her Sisters.

O clemens,
O pia,
O dulcis
Virgo Maria.

"Our Lady is right here with you, Sister Theo. Take her hand. She'll guide you home," Mum whispered into the dying woman's ear. Then she bent down and kissed her.

Theo moaned softly, then sank again into a deep sleep.

On the second night of their vigil, Theo awoke one last time. Her bright, feverish eyes fixed for a moment on Meg's face, and she smiled her old grin.

"No death scenes, Meggie," she rasped. "See you next time round."

In the early hours during that second night's watch, with Meg and Mum at her bedside, Theo died.

According to the Sisters of Charity's custom, the two nuns kept vigil by their dead companion's side through the rest of the

251

long night. Queen Mum led Meg in all fifteen mysteries of the Rosary and after each decade they prayed:

> *Lord have mercy on our dearly beloved Sister.*
> *Christ have mercy.*
> *Lord have mercy.*
> *Oh Lord, hear my prayer.*
> *And let my cry come unto Thee.*
> *May she rest in peace.*
> *May her soul and the souls of all the faithful departed rest in peace.*

Queen Mum continued to finger her rosary beads, while Meg sat silently with her head bowed and her hands folded until the first dim rays of light broke through the hospital room's grimy windows.

"In another hour or so, it will be time to call Mother Ursula," Mum murmured.

Meg slowly raised her head. Her red-rimmed eyes blinked several times, as if she were trying to comprehend Mum's words.

"Isn't this just a cruel joke by some Dionysian God who enjoys playing with his creatures' emotions?" Meg pleaded helplessly.

Mum shook her head sadly but said nothing.

Meg's eyes continued to search the old nun's face for a few more minutes, then let her gaze fall again on the white, still face in the bed. She got up from her chair and went over to the dead woman.

"So now I have to bear witness to the deeds of yet another martyr. Damn it! As if Alfredo's and Rutilio's weren't enough," she said with a bitterness that brought Mum to her feet. "Now

Theo's name will be on the holy cards, on the stars hanging from the Christmas tree. They always leave me, these loves of mine. Inevitably, they leave me all alone."

She was suddenly shaking the still body before her. "It's not fair, Theo. It's so easy to be the martyr, the one prayed and wept for, the one whose memory is held in benediction. But it is so hard to be left behind! Why have you left me behind? What is Meg without her Theo?"

Mum's arms were suddenly around the sobbing nun, pulling her back to her chair.

"Stop it, Meg. Stop it at once! Get a hold on yourself, Sister, for heaven's sake," she said sternly, forcing Meg to sit down.

Meg looked up and saw the deep pity and sorrow reflected in Mum's faded blue eyes.

"Meg, dear," she said gently as she lifted the nun's chin and forced Meg to meet her gaze. "Yes, Theo is dead. She has given her life for El Salvador and its poor, suffering people. And yes, she wears the martyr's crown, although she never sought it and must be wearing it rather sheepishly. You, on the other hand, must go on living. You now must take the time to discern what it is that God calls you to do next. Remember that age-old lesson: His ways are not our ways."

Meg turned her face away and stared down at her hands folded in her lap.

There was only silence for a long moment.

At last Meg looked up. "Where does this all end?" she muttered in a hoarse voice. Then she struggled wearily to her feet, crossed the room and, without looking again at Theo's lifeless body, and went out the door.

Chapter 11

January 15, 1979

En route to Kennedy airport

Meg lit another cigarette, the third since they had taken off. Her hand shook as she struck the match. She wasn't used to flying on U.S. military planes, or accompanying martyred Sisters of Charity from foreign lands.

Theo had a sad though impressive send-off for her final journey. Even Archbishop Romero had come to the airport to bless the casket before it was loaded onto the waiting plane.

It had been because of Romero's homily last Sunday, which was broadcast over national radio, that Theo's body was on board a U.S. military plane. The archbishop had again condemned the Sumpul massacre and laid Theo's death directly at the door of the Salvadoran army and their U.S. military advisors. Although the embassy had issued a carefully-worded disclaimer insinuating that Theo was working with the guerrillas, the officials promised to investigate the murder and provide a plane to take the body back to the States. Theo was the first U.S. citizen to die in the growing conflict engulfing the country.

But in the end, it was just Sister Bernadette and herself who stood on the runway and watched the cranes lower the casket into the plane's baggage section. Then it was her turn to board.

"I'm not sure I can get on that plane," she had said in a quivering voice to Mum. "I don't know where it will be taking me." To her embarrassment, she had begun to sob uncontrollably.

"Hush, child. You are going home to a whole community of Sisters who love and cherish you more than you yourself do. They will know how to heal you, to help you find your way again. Believe me, dear," Mum whispered as she embraced Meg and led her toward the waiting plane.

Meg tried to calm down. "Yes, Mum. I do so want to believe that." She swallowed the knot in her throat. "This is good-bye then, isn't it? How strange. It was you who was supposed to retire to the Motherhouse after I arrived. I was to replace you, remember? And now it's me who's going back and you who will carry our love to our friends in the Honduran refugee camps."

Queen Mum had blessed her then, making the sign of the cross on her forehead.

Then Meg was on the plane flying over the low, lush hills of El Salvador. Somewhere down there lay what was left of her village: Tere and the children struggling with a new phonetic sound, the women down at the river sneaking in a bath on their way home from the fields, Paulina and Santos chatting over a glass of orange juice. Don Lucho might even be losing his shyness and join them. Raul might be looking up at the plane from his hideout, checking its passage with the hour on his watch.

Meg sank into her seat and took a last drag on her cigarette before putting it out. She tried to avoid thinking about the possibility of never going back to Dulce Nombre de Maria or never seeing Tere and Paulina again. Of course she'd go back one day!

But without Theo? Meg shut her eyes to hold back yet another avalanche of tears. Her eyes burned from so much weeping.

"Oh, Theo," she whispered as she laid her head back against the seat. "How am I going to make it without you? I have no patience, no staying power, no real courage or compassion—those were your virtues. If anyone had to die, it should have been me."

She opened her eyes a moment and saw her drawn, tear-stained face looking back at her from the plane's window. She had aged since she last appraised herself from the reflection of a plane window. The face she saw could have been that of an Irish washerwoman a century ago, the face of a harried mother of five, wife to a steelworker, a generation ago. She squinted harder. She was nowhere near being a younger version of Madre Rosa or an older version of Tere. She wasn't Chilean. She wasn't Salvadoran. She wasn't even a good missionary; she could never keep up with Theo when it came to dedication. Always the romantic, the adventurer, forever having to hold down center stage, come what may.

Why had it always been more appealing to be a missionary in Chile or in El Salvador rather than teaching and mothering high school girls back in the United States? Aunt Kay's eternal question. And the answer, if she was honest with herself, was that she didn't like to mother.

In fact, everywhere she went, inevitably she was the one who was mothered. Poor Mom probably didn't love her enough. So she could blame it on her, this greediness for love, this unconscious need to be the love object wherever she went. Yet the whole idea of the vowed life was to turn any attractiveness people find in a Sister toward God. To love always with a disinterested love. On that score, she had failed miserably.

She smiled ruefully at herself in the window. She was slowly getting it: the reason why she'd been left behind was because she had a lot of growing up to do yet. A lot of demons still to wrestle with. Isn't that right, Theo? You see the pattern now from the other side. Meg Carney's mosaic is far from fully fashioned. Will you be helping our Great Weaver friend as she spins and bends me into shape?

Again Meg felt the tears running down her face, but this time they were tears of a muddled sense of belonging. "Believe in the connections," Meg had told Theo that day they held each other by the river in Dulce Nombre de Maria. "Believe that our lives are entwined for an eternity," she had told Theo on her deathbed. "A Theo always seeks her Meg," her friend had assured her. And a Meg her Theo.

A strange, unexpected sense of peace was gradually replacing Meg's seemingly bottomless anguish. As she stared at herself in the window, she thought she saw, for the briefest second, Theo's face rather than her own. *I will be with you always, even until the end of the world.* She winked back at the reflection. "Be with me always, *compañera*" she prayed.

At last Meg turned from the window, reached down under her seat, and pulled out her duffle bag, her only piece of luggage. She rummaged around and eventually found her worn leather notebook. Opening it, she slid the purple embroidered badge of the three musketeers out of the pocket and held it tightly in her hand. Who would have guessed what would happen to each of them, and that now one of them was dead. She smiled down at the photo, then put it back in the notebook pocket.

She took out a sheet of paper, lit another cigarette, and began to write:

Dear Madre Rosa,

Theo died last week.

I'm taking the body back to be buried on our Motherhouse grounds in Ohio. This is our community's first martyr, and her death has deeply shocked the Sisters.

Ask Molly about Theo—the three of us were classmates and were very close during the Novitiate.

I loved Theo so! Perhaps too much, perhaps more than A. I can't imagine life without her.

I am going to stay in the States awhile, Rosa. I need time to do some thinking and praying. I promised you I'd come back to La Bandera after El Salvador. But I find I have no strength to accompany anyone right now. Maybe one day, when I'm not so confused, I'll join you again.

I plan to spend some time with an aunt in New York. I think she might help me find some answers.

As Meg re-read the last paragraph, she felt her mouth relax into a crooked grin. She hadn't known she was going to stay with Kay until this minute. But now she knew that was what she most wanted.

Kay would be just the kind of retreat master she needed.

Even her nudes, the massages, and doing yoga in the buff might in some screwy way help her find her way again. Most of all, she just wanted to talk to her aunt. To tell her the inside story of what had happened to her niece in these years as a missionary in Latin America. In the telling, maybe she would also understand it for the first time.

The seat belt sign went on and the pilot announced that they were on their final approach to Kennedy International Airport. She hurried to finish her letter.

> *I'm almost 40 now, yet I am painfully aware that I am only a neophyte in the spiritual life. I thought sanctity would come automatically if I cast my lot with the poor. I don't know what I've done wrong. I'm not sure I know God any better than before I started out for Latin America. Or perhaps I've met God and have not recognized Him because I'm missing the eyes to see.*
>
> *I ask your prayers. And the prayers of everyone in La Bandera. You will never be far from my thoughts.*
>
> *All my love,*
>
> *Meg*

The plane taxied down the runway and stopped in front of an out-of-the-way hangar some distance from the main terminal. From her window, Meg could see that there was a good-sized crowd just inside the gate, waving placards.

Good Lord, she thought, *are all those people here to meet the plane?*

The door swung open and Meg suddenly gasped as she saw a fat, round woman in an orange pantsuit nimbly climbing up the scaffolding.

"Aunt Kay!" she shouted, running down the aisle to meet her.

Kay met her halfway down the aisle and caught her niece in her arms. Although Meg was more than a head taller than her aunt, she found herself buried in the folds of the shorter woman's ample bosom, laughing and crying at the same time.

"There, there, Missie. We'll have time for soothing soon, I promise," Kay said as she rested her cheek against Meg's. "But now, well, just look out there at all those people who have come to welcome your friend home, to protest her death."

"They know about Theo and the Sumpul massacre?" Meg asked, raising her eyebrows in disbelief.

"Yes, but not because of any briefings from our own government," Kay said dryly. "But word travels, especially through the solidarity networks that are springing up all over."

"But who are they?"

"Have a closer look and you'll see for yourself. Many of them are from your own community. Look, there's your superior, Mother Ursula. I had a chance to talk with her. A remarkable woman. Most of the rest are religious people of one stripe or another: Catholic nuns and priests, a Lutheran pastor or two. Quakers, Mennonites. A few old-line Communist Party types, a smattering of feminists, gays, and lesbians, lots of peace activists…"

"Theo would be embarrassed over such fuss," Meg said as she allowed Kay to guide her toward the plane's door.

Strains of the crowd's protest song reached them as Meg and Kay descended the stairs.

We shall not be moved.
Like a tree, planted near the water,
We shall not be moved.

"Embarrassed, but at least a little pleased," she added as she held onto Kay's arm. Together they went to meet the crowd.

Afterword

I was in the crowd that cold January day in 1979 when the plane bringing Theo and Meg home taxied to a halt at Kennedy airport. Theo, home to the hilltop cemetery overlooking our Motherhouse chapel. Meg, home to begin the long process of healing.

The whole community had been badly shaken by Theo's death. First, disbelief, then anger and outrage engulfed us as the story of the Sumpul massacre came to light: the heroic role Theo and Meg played in accompanying the villagers on their *guinda*, how Theo had neglected her own wound to nurse others worse off than herself, and, in the end, died of gangrene poisoning.

Most of the Sisters were engaged in their own apostolic works of teaching, nursing, and social work here in the United States, and although they followed events in Latin America more closely now that we had community members serving there, they had no idea of the rawness of life in a Salvadoran village in the 1970s. Therefore, most were too numb to realize that the Sisters of Charity had its first martyr in Sister Theodora Katz. That would only come with hindsight. When Archbishop Romero was assassinated a year later and then four other American religious women were raped and murdered by military henchmen shortly after him, we knew our Theo was the forerunner to a new and growing martyrology.

But what of Meg? I admit I felt a sharp pain of jealousy and guilt when I realized that it was not Mother Ursula or me but rather her famous Aunt Kay who dashed up the steps to meet Meg as soon as the plane came to a halt. Jealousy because she and I were once best friends, guilt because I suspected it was my fault the friendship had stagnated during our years together in Chile.

Those feelings quickly dissipated once Meg emerged. Who had she become, this gaunt woman in the flimsy, too-big-for-her gray suit who clung so tightly to her aunt's arm? As she paused for a moment on the platform trying to take in the crowd below—their songs, the surging applause, the chants—she reminded me of a lost vestal virgin trapped in the wrong timeframe. Once below on the tarmac, I could see it was Meg, still beautiful despite her cracked lips, her sunburned nose, the deep rings under her eyes, the gray in her blond hair.

I was second in line to hug her. She was having trouble focusing. "Meggie, it's Molly. I came as soon as I could get a plane out of Chile. Madre Rosa and all the community in La Bandera are with you in spirit."

"Molly … oh, Molly," Meg whispered, finally recognizing me. And then, "Theo's dead, Molly. She's dead…"

"I know, I know." And it was I who began crying, while Meg

tried to comfort me.

Meg held up quite bravely during Theo's funeral, which received nationwide coverage and attracted an impressive array of church dignitaries and human rights advocates. Aunt Kay and I were her constant companions, because we could both see that Meggie was in deep shock.

Now, with hindsight, we realize that many of our members serving the poor in Latin America have been deeply traumatized—either by what they have experienced directly or by witnessing their friends and neighbors being tortured and abused. Today there are excellent rehabilitation centers for them to work through their trauma and to heal, but in 1979, we didn't know how to treat a traumatized member of our community. Mother Ursula wanted Meg to go through a period of psychological counseling before taking on any new assignment. But Meg's Japanese aunt was insistent: her niece must return with her to New York, where she would work with Meg "in the oriental way of healing." We could see that Meg wanted this as well, so even though it was rather unusual, Mother Ursula said she felt a deep kinship with Kay and believed that if anyone could help Meg deal with all her devils, it would be this aunt of hers.

Kay and Meg faced those devils together, and they were many: the gang rape, sexual orientation, fidelity to religious life, and guilt at not having been the martyr, merely the friend/lover of the martyr. Then of course, there were deeper questions about vocation, God, the meaning of life, and one's purpose in life. Yes, much to ponder. Sometimes I think Meggie lived enough during her ten years in Latin America to spend the rest of her life as a contemplative, trying to fathom the depths of it all.

But that didn't happen. What did happen was that, with

Kay's help, Meg healed. It took a long time. Meg would often say that healing is lifelong, and no one is ever completely healed, just healing. And in that process, Meg herself became a healer.

Throughout the eighties, Meg lived with Kay in New York. For the first year, she simply hibernated, or as Kay would say, she just "let go." Gradually, however, Meggie emerged from her solitude and became active in the Central American and Chilean solidarity movements headquartered in New York City. Ever the teacher, she became a prominent lecturer on human rights in Latin America. She traveled the country giving talks, staging "teach-ins," rallying, protesting, and marching, and she always captivated the crowd with stories of Madre Rosa, Alfredo, José, the people in La Bandera, of Tere, Raul, Paulina, Santos, Don Lucho, and the community of Dulce Nombre de Maria, of Padre Rutilio Grande and the Jesuit seminarians, of Archbishop Romero. Of Theo. And because she brought her friends to life, they believed her when she described the atrocities, the rampant injustices taking place in those countries—and they mobilized.

But by the end of the decade, there was no guerrilla victory in El Salvador. Things ended in a stalemate, in a "peace process" that left everyone dissatisfied. But the war was officially over. In Chile, Pinochet called plebiscite to confirm the aging general as the legitimate head of state. A bad gamble, because he lost, and after seventeen years of military dictatorship, Chile returned to civilian rule.

After Theo's death, the Sisters of Charity sent no more Sisters to El Salvador. The Chile mission blossomed, however. We received new Sisters from both the States and from Chile and eventually became a lively bicultural and bilingual community.

I remained in Chile. After the military coup, I was sent to

work at the Catholic Church's human rights office, known as the Vicariate of Solidarity. I spent ten years there, witnessing firsthand all the sorrow and pain that the dictatorship leveled on the most vulnerable of the Chilean people—and I reported it. I was one of the documentalists at the Vicariate and, if I do say so myself, kept accurate accounts of the torture, the disappearances, and the executions that took place during those years. My job was to interview the victims (or if they had been killed, their family members).

Looking back, I can see now that all that pain was too much to place on the shoulders of a young American nun from Ohio. I became detective, lawyer, political analyst, social worker, and confessor for folks from every walk of life who lined up at our doors every morning. Their stories burrowed their way into my soul and made me old before my time.

In 1986, I was elected regional superior, responsible for the twelve Sisters working in Chile. The community also began a formation program for novices here in Chile, and I coordinated that as well. By the end of the decade, I was suddenly the Chilean version of Queen Mum, God bless her soul!

This is Meg's story, not mine. But as the last of the three Musketeers, it is I who tells our tale.

I would like to think that it was I who coaxed Meg back to Chile, but I suspect that my letters detailing events there were only a part of the ingredients that went into the mix, which brought her back to us in the spring of 1990.

She arrived in time to say goodbye to Madre Rosa, who had a stroke the year before and was waiting patiently for this daughter of hers to return before she left us for good. Meg stayed with Rosa in La Bandera, and I know the two of them made their peace together, even though *La Madre* could no longer speak.

Rosa died just before Christmas that year, and although no one could take her place—icon that she had been for more than thirty years in La Bandera—Meg stayed on. She started a home for battered women called the *Casa del Nuevo Amanecer*. Chilean women had been in the forefront of the resistance movement against the dictatorship for almost twenty years, and they had lots of grief and frustration to deal with. But those scars were only the most obvious; underneath lay layers of hidden suffering they were ashamed to acknowledge—beatings by a drunken husband or father, sexual abuse by an uncle, a grandfather, a father. So Meg set out to heal them, or, as she would say, help them discover how to heal themselves.

Yes, Meg returned to La Bandera as a healer. Her spiritual practice included yoga and tai chi and she gladly taught the women both. She was a Reiki master and also skilled in acupressure and a variety of oriental massage techniques. She'd become a vegetarian and promoted her own combination of herbal remedies, mostly Chinese.

The people in La Bandera loved their newly returned *hermana*. (The old-fashioned term of "Madre" for religious women was used only for the revered Rosa). They flocked to her *casa*—and not just the women. Very soon, Meg's pied-piper ways with the young surfaced, and they too were lining up to discuss their problems with her, most of which I gathered were about their sexual difficulties, fears, and longings.

Meg fascinated our novices. Of course, her story had preceded her and everyone wanted to have this amazing Sister of Charity as their friend and mentor. If this had happened a decade earlier, I would have been jealous of Meg's astounding ability to captivate people, to have them fall in love with her on the spot, but I too had grown in wisdom over the years and could recognize her gift for enchanting us all with a magic none of us quite understood.

My relationship with Meg took a new turn. No, I never became another Theo to her. Yet in the years following her return, we became real companions, comfortable in each other's presence. Meg had changed, you see. She never talked much anymore and was so accepting of everything. It seemed to me that she had traded her humor and her love of adventure for a Buddhist-like enlightenment where all is in all. This took some adjusting on my part, because I was in the thick of things as usual, now battling a Catholic hierarchy that seemed to have returned to the Dark Ages, subverting the vision of Pope John and the Second Vatican Council. During the 1980s, I had completed graduate work in psychology and theology, which turned me into a non-conformist feminist theologian by the 1990s. And when I raged at Meg about the aberrations I was discovering in the Catholic church as I viewed its history through the lens of patriarchy, she just chuckled and led me to her massage table, where she calmed me down with a Reiki session.

In early 1994, Meg was diagnosed with breast cancer, an extremely aggressive type, and by the time she discovered it, it had already spread to her lymph glands.

"It has already metastasized, Molly, so just let me handle this my own way," she insisted. So there was no mastectomy, no chemotherapy, no radiation treatment. Meg simply receded into her deep meditation practice of yoga and subsisted on her herbal concoctions until she was more spirit than flesh.

"Oh healer, heal thyself," I pleaded with her over and over again. "We still have so much to do on this side of the grave, you and I. Please, Meggie, don't you go too!"

She'd just grin up at me from the lotus position on her threadbare rug that had become the centerpiece of her tiny La Bandera house. "Not to worry," she'd say, laughing with that stubborn twinkle in her eye I'd come to recognize so well. "After all, we are but mere earthen vessels fashioned by the Great Potter herself." Then she'd invite me for a cup of green tea.

Meg orchestrated her dying with an odd combination of detachment and zest. She held her own visiting hours for as long as she could from her "magic carpet" and then from her small cot. Only during the last few days would she let me move in with her so I could "midwife her over."

I wish I could report that we had the long conversations we both had postponed since her return to Chile. But we didn't. We never once mentioned Alfredo—that great elephant in the living room between us. But as I kept vigil and held her hand, she shared with me a great love and peace and tried, I think, to communicate the song she'd always heard in her heart. Finally she whispered, "I've been living between worlds for a long time now. Let me go, Molly girl. It's time."

And I did.

Meg died a week before Christmas at the age of fifty-five. Her life was celebrated as only Chilean *pobladores* know how to lay to rest one of their own. The community of La Bandera pleaded with me to allow her body to be buried in the chapel crypt alongside Alfredo and Madre Rosa, but I told them it was the custom for our Sisters to be buried at the Motherhouse. This was a bit of a fib, but I wanted Meg next to Theo—and eventually next to me—overlooking the familiar Ohio farmlands.

As I flew back to the Motherhouse with Meg's body, I found

myself musing long and hard about the way each one of us three musketeers had become our own unique Reed of God. One of our favorite poems by Caryll Houslander came back to me:

I am your reed, sweet shepherd
breathe out your joy in me
and make bright song
fill me with the soft moan of your love.

The moan of God's love—be she shepherd, potter, or weaver—is anything but soft. It is harsh, harsher than I ever dreamed. A crushing alleluia.

Meg's funeral was not the event Theo's was, nor should it have been, but I think Meg would have been pleased by the testimonies and by the folks she brought together. A delegation came from El Salvador—including Tere and Paulina! Tere had gone on to become a teacher, and she now teaches teachers how to teach. Her brother Raul is now deeply involved in the political wing of the *Frente*, which has come in from the cold. Tere says she suspects he longs for the days when he was a *muchacho* in the hills.

Paulina showed me her how her artificial arm works. She still squeezes orange juice for her cronies back in Dulce Nombre de María. She has high hopes of expanding her business to a group of local ecologists who are setting up an organic bee farm for honey production.

Aunt Kay was there as well. At eighty, she looked like the Buddha incarnate. It was she who became Meg's psychopomp, leading her into the depths of her own soul. She showed Meg the face of Kannon, the Japanese goddess of compassion. Kannon has many eyes and many hands, and all are expressions of mercy. Kannon's way teaches that *everything must be accepted*, because all that happens to us is part of a larger whole that we cannot see or understand, except through the eyes and arms of compassion.

"Meg was broken down, broken wide open, and after many nights in the bowels in the earth, she emerged ready to walk with me into the light," Kay told me that day of the funeral. "She embraced her path, Molly; she became another Kannon. And that's who you met when she returned to you to spend her last days in La Bandera. She became the eyes and arms of compassion." Then this tiny, round woman with the piercing black eyes bowed to me.

See, I will not forget you. I have carved you in the palm of my hand. The quote from Isaiah that Meggie loved so much. Yes, I gave the eulogy. I composed the necrology. I wonder who will write mine when the time comes.

So the second musketeer has been laid down, leaving only me to grieve over our lost certainties and our disintegrating gods.

On January 15, 1995, I was elected the community's new general superior, a five-year appointment that I will begin on March 19, the feast of St. Joseph.

Heaven help us all.

***

When I was going through Meg's meager belongings, I found her treasured leather notebook with the breastplate of St. Patrick on the cover. Inside was the faded, purple-trimmed badge with the photos of the three of us from our Novitiate days. It also contained her jottings to Theo. A note was attached: "Molly, when you find these, I give you permission to read them. I was going to burn them, but then I thought you should know of my deep love for Theo. I offer them as a tribute to her memory, which I know you honor. Meg."

New York, October 1982

To my Theo

Ah, love, the chasm is deep and wide when you are silent. And yet, I don't feel abandoned, although God knows you went so quickly. I sense you there on the dark side of the moon. What do you do now that you are on the other side? How do you pass your days? I realize that your time is not like ours. But I need to know: do you dance, do you sing, is your spirit able to swoop up and down the Sumpul river valley free and fast as an eagle? Can you make love with the ancestors? Do you get your pick of the saints? Personally, I'd go for St. Francis—he was always more earthy than the others with his love for the birds and the daffodils, with his Sister Moon this, and his Brother Wolf that. Oh love, I hope you are not just some piece of pure spirit now, not just some filament of memory. That would be dreadful indeed. Please, dear heart, whisper something softly in my ear, and I will catch it in the wind. Print a message in the sunset, and I will read it through the darkening sky. Dance for me tonight from behind the full moon, shimmer and shake across the heavens to let me know that you are well and happy. That you have not become just another archetype, but still exist in some other world, body and soul intact—waiting patiently for me, for us all. And then it really will be "heaven," won't it?

—Meg.

New York, May 1986

Theo, dearest,

    There are Sin Eaters in every spiritual tradition. Because they love us, these gods and goddesses eat our shame, swallow our shit, and bear our guilt. In our own Christian tradition, of course, we have Christ, who took upon himself the sins of the world so we might be redeemed. The Hindi have Kali, the dark goddess who strips us of false images of ourselves, of our façade of niceness. She reflects back to us, like a mirror, anything we have been afraid of in ourselves or rejected. She is the great archetype of our shadow. The Mexicans have the Aztec goddess Coatlicue, the creatrix who gives life in return for suffering and struggle. She is both the source of disease and death and the goddess of healing. Then there is Chamunda, the emaciated, macabre crone goddess from Nepal. Ornamented with severed heads she holds a skull cup filled with blood, which she offers as a Tantric offering of retribution to the gods.
    I think you were my own personal Sin Eater, Theo.

—Meg

Upon returning to Chile, September, 1990

Theo, dear.

Back in Chile. Back in La Bandera. So much has

changed—not the least is that I have missed a whole generation of folks growing up, getting old, moving on. It seems to me that people are different now—much less willing to ride the wind. But I will do my best to offer the healing I have learned. Your spirit is with me always

—Meg

Santiago, January 1991

Dear Theo,

So Madre Rosa has just joined you there on the other side. You two will have much to share. I have been deeply touched by her choosing me to be by her side during her last days. I found myself pouring out my soul to this adopted mother of mine who in the end could only speak with her eyes and her one good hand. But much was settled: without uttering a single word, she let me put to rest my love for Alfredo. She understood how sorry I am that I had misread his love for me. I could confess to her of how I managed to convince myself that he loved me so much that he would have been willing to leave the priesthood. I could even acknowledge that he loved Molly as well—and she him. Rosa forgave me for my youth, my longings, my deep need for someone as prominent as Alfredo to pay attention to me. And I forgave her for shielding the truth from me: that the body we buried was not Alfredo's; that Molly had hidden him in a safe house, then smuggled him out of the country. That the burial was a bluff to stop the military from looking for Alfredo so he could return to Chile and work underground. But Alfredo is still dead. He was gunned down in a shootout with the police in southern Chile in 1982. But this time, a campesino named Feliciano was branded "just another stupid revolutionary" and thrown into a mass grave with the rest of his guerrilla column. It must be hard to die twice.

—Meg

Chile, September 1993

Dear Theo,

A raucous spring day in Santiago. Clouds billowing across a sky bright with expectation. Expectation that all things will rise again—the grass, the plants, the trees, the calico cat, Christ, you, me. Yes, I smell resurrection in the wind as it whistles through my open window. An open window can metaphor the soul and with luck we can suspect its many layers. Layers and layers of reincarnations. Who were we, once upon a time, you and I? Was I once a piece of the moon or a starfish floating on the waves? Old souls, we surely are, my dear. Lifetimes of love and tragedy have been the grist for our mills and have made us strong. Strong and brave and ready to face this once-upon-a-time. This day. This spring. This lifetime. Here's to another round, my love.

—Meg

The Motherhouse, February 1995

Molly's posthumous letter to Meg

So you knew, Meg.

When did you discover that I too loved him? Why could we never talk about this, even as you lay dying? Did you dread having to admit that we had competed for the admiration and love of this great priest—and that much to your dismay, he loved me best?

Oh Meg, I can guess that in your healing process with your Aunt Kay you moved far beyond your passion for Alfredo and liberated yourself and his memory once and for all. You and he now belong to the ages. And I, who loved you both, am left behind to honor your memories. How am I to do that, Meggie? After all these years, we are who we have become: each of us has become a healer in her own way, each has looked into the future and experienced the red heat of God's love.

We didn't choose this time in history. We didn't choose to be members of the same pack, the same tribe. But that has been our lot. No regrets?

For me, no regrets, but, yes, a terrible sorrow because I never told you that it doesn't matter any more. I don't want to deceive you: for a long time I resented the fact that you were the one who could openly mourn Alfredo and boast to the world of how much he loved you. I couldn't believe you were so blind that you didn't notice the attraction between us, discrete though it was. I confess that I was livid with anger at your obtuse, narcissistic behavior that made you the victim, the grieving bride. It was only after Alfredo died so ignominiously in a failed attempt to rally an armed resistance movement that I saw him for the hopeless romantic he was. And it was only when I saw you get off the plane at Kennedy when you brought Theo back that I realized how broken you were. It was then I knew I could forgive you. It was El Salvador and Theo that molded you into the Sister you became—not Chile or Alfredo or me.

So, yes, I forgive you for loving him, and I forgive Alfredo for loving you—and for loving me. What I can't forgive is the chasm we unwittingly built between us all these years. I am sorry for all our lost days, our lost friendship. And so it is I who must now ask your forgiveness, Meg Carney.

In my mind's eye, I go down to my long neglected tomato patch behind the apple orchard at the Motherhouse. I sit down on the earth and let the damp, rich soil seep into my skin. I wait for the sunset. I remember how we Musketeers watched the sky redden that lifetime ago before we set out to conquer the world. I soon see Theo appear on the horizon. Then you appear as well. I can't make out your faces, but I imagine you are smiling.

—Molly

LaVergne, TN USA
17 August 2010
193578LV00001B/2/P